A NOVEL

THE
CROSSINGS

CRAIG
ALEXANDER

Distributed by Bublish, Inc.

ISBN: 978-1-6470444-97 (paperback)
ISBN: 978-1-6470445-03 (eBook)

This book is dedicated to my brother Paul who has spent many years of his life working with the Hispanic youth community on the east side of Los Angeles, California. His faith and courage has been a great example and a gift to all of us.

Contents

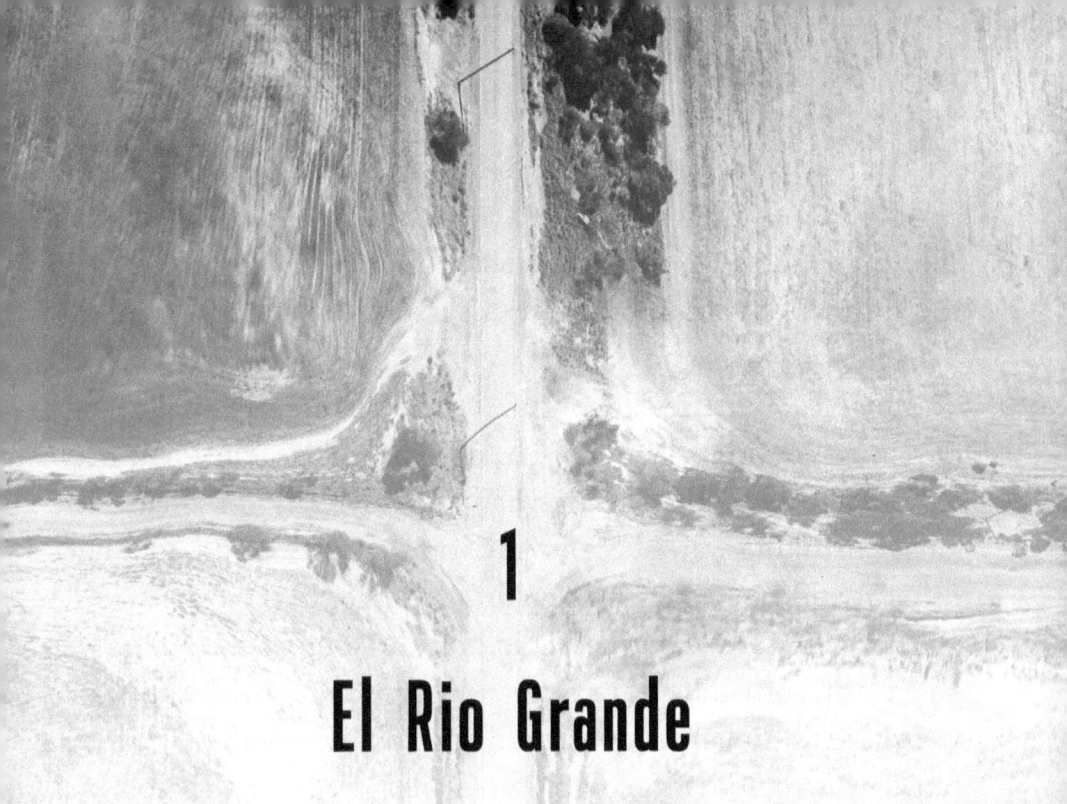

1

El Rio Grande

I t was a bad day to cross. Everyone knew it was a bad day to cross the river. The rain had been falling hard for three days. Just as the sun was coming out, a streak of white shot across the dark Texas sky. For some reason, this made it rain harder.

Elena Velasquez was nine and knew nothing about the place her mom and dad were taking her to on that cold morning in 1992. She remembered it was very cold and the water in the river looked swollen and angry.

"Where are we going?" she asked her mother.

Her mother was in too much of a hurry to give her an answer.

Emielio Estrada, also nine, along with his brother Roberto who was only a year older, knew where they were going. He knew it was a place called "The Americas." That was all he knew.

For many days, they had traveled on the main roads with the larger groups. They ate and drank only small amounts of what they carried. At night they rested and prayed alone, away from the others. Most importantly, they stayed clear of the places where the coyotes and bandits were hanging out.

It had been many days of travel on foot from the small village of Santa Domingo, Mexico. Back at the village, they had been close neighbors. Then things had turned badly for them. The village drinking water became so dirty that they could no longer drink it and the two fathers could no longer find work.

The weather had turned cold and the long walk to the river had worn both the adults and children down. Food and water were hard to find unless you could buy your way with the coyotes, but it was these bad people they feared the most. The coyotes from the cartels were all along the way to the river. *La Migra* was the name for the US border agents who could send them back. There were many bad things that could happen to them.

Still, they had to go north. North was the only hope for them. To cross the border and to find work in America was their only hope.

None of them could swim, so the fathers had made a deal for a small boat to be hidden along a less traveled path close to the river. Holding the dented boat over their heads, they were now running on the last part of the journey. The mothers instructed the kids to follow closely and keep up the pace.

So they did.

The end had finally come. All of them were soaked and cold when they arrived at the edge of the levee overlooking the river. The other side looked like any other piece of land to Elena, but it was America.

Shaken by the sight of the powerful water, they all stood frozen. The crashing of the thunder that followed the light in the sky startled Elena. She looked up to her mother who was shivering from the cold and seemed just a little frightened.

Turning back was not possible. Behind them were only more desperate border crossers. They could hear them coming. The men had been seen carrying the boat and now it wouldn't be long before they could be overrun by frantic migrants.

On the other side of the river stood Father Pedro Moreno, a Catholic priest, author, speaker, and advocate for the many migrants who crossed the border every day. He was from the east side of Los Angeles and was the point man for an underground organization known as *SOMOS*.

The word *SOMOS* was used by the Mexicans to express "WE ARE" in English. *SOMOS HUMANOS* which translated to "WE ARE HUMAN, "were the words they wrote on their signs and what they yelled out when they walked the streets of downtown Los Angeles. Most of the time the people just called them SOMOS.

Fr. Pedro, now fifty, had been in the public eye for more than a decade. He may have been as much of a mystery to a young person today as he was to Fathers Tomas and Santino in the early days. They belonged to the Catholic order of priests known as the Jesuits.

He had been in trouble with the Archbishop of Los Angeles and his Provincial who was the head of the Jesuit order. Because he never directly told them what he was doing, they would turn their heads. *SOMOS* was very popular among the people living in east LA. The newspapers and the community leaders all supported and stood up for them when they were in trouble.

Although Fr. Pedro's public work and life were well-known, there remained deep truths that he told bluntly and that he saw only because he stepped into the darkness that surrounded the angst and agony of the Latino immigrant.

Today, Fr. Pedro was not concerned about the authorities or what his superiors thought about his work. He was perched on a levee road peering out of his ten seater school bus. His eyes were locked on the river.

He stepped out of the bus. Pulling his glasses off, he raised his binoculars. Following closely beside him were Father Tomas and Father Santino.

"Don't do it," Fr. Pedro said shaking his head.

"There are two families. They have little ones," Tomas added.

"We have to get down there to stop this craziness. That river will kill all of them," Santino said.

But it was already too late. The three children were in the rocking boat. Waves of cold river water slammed over the bow and onto all of them. The chill from the rain and the splashes of the colder river water made Elena shiver as her mother struggled to board. Once inside, she pulled Elena tight against her body. Soon, all but the men were in the boat.

The old boat was now taking on water and the two men agreed to just hold on the sides, but as they began to push off, a scream came from the levee just above them in English.

"Stop!"

It was a man running and pulling along a young boy.

"Take us with you or we will be killed. Me and my boy Hector!" he said.

Before they could answer, he again asked,

"Let the boy into the boat and I will help you push off."

"No. I can swim or I will stay here." Hector yelled back.

The man swung swiftly around, striking Hector on the cheek with his open hand. He then picked him up and threw him into the boat where Hector slammed heads with Emielio. The two exchanged a short but angry look at one another. Bracing themselves on each side of the rocking boat, the fathers worked to balance their weight. Hector's father hung to the rear as they pushed off into the swift current.

The cold of the water soon wore the three men down. Roberto could see that his father was losing his grip on the boat edge. He was choking and coughing up water. Roberto reached out to him, but the more his papa tried to pull himself up, the more the boat dipped down to the surface of the waves taking on more water.

"Papi?" Roberto yelled, again trying to reach out to him. His mother then wailed out to the river,

"No, Papi!"

The father then let go as the boat rolled along the crest of the fast moving waves. Roberto and Emilio could only watch as their papa's face faded into the lather of the white water.

On the other side of the boat, Elena's mother was struggling to hold on to her father with both hands. Elena saw her mother's arms shaking as she moved closer to the boat's edge. Emielio reached out to stop Elena from falling onto her mother. Both Elena's parents looked at one another realizing that the only way to save the children was for them to leave the boat. Elena's mother looked back to her baby daughter as if to say, *I must do this.*

"I love you, *Mija*" she lipped as her hands broke free from her husband.

She then turned and followed him into the water.

5

The boat reacted to the release of Elena's mother by rebounding into a steep pitch, tossing Emilio and Roberto's mother into a free fall. Unable to recover her balance, she too went head first into the water.

Fr. Pedro had now reached the shoreline with the other priests. The three watched helplessly as the tragedy continued to unfold.

"I've seen enough; they're all going to drown. Tomas, do you have the rope?" Fr. Pedro asked.

"Yes, it is in the bus."

"Can you tie something to the end of it like a piece of wood or something that will float? They're coming this way. We could try to land them somewhere around here."

He pointed to a small beachhead.

The boat continued to rock wildly as it breached the middle of the river. Hector's father was still holding to the outside at the rear of the boat. Like the others, his hands were slowly weakening and sliding to the edge. It was clear to all that he would soon be the next to be taken by the river. He looked to his son, but Hector remained seated only starring back at him.

It was Roberto who made the move to help the man. At first, he was able to hold him, but the cold soon filled his arms making his grip weaken. The longer Roberto held, the more the man dragged him toward the water. Finally, it was the man who gave way by releasing Roberto's hand and falling back into the water. His eyes locked onto Hector and like the others that was the last of him.

All on the boat were shaken by the sudden loss of those they had counted on to bring them through. They were now on their own and if they were to make it, they would have to save themselves. Emielio braced Elena and himself against the hull of the boat. They feared that it would only be a short time until they too would be gone.

Most of the boat was now sinking below the surface of the river as they drifted toward the shore on the US side. Roberto could now hear voices from the side of the river calling out to them. He turned to see Fr. Pedro and the others running along the shore keeping pace with the boat as it slowed slightly.

"*Tengo una soga*, a rope! Fr. Pedro shouted out in Spanish.

"Si," Roberto shouted back.

The water had almost filled the boat, when a rope with a float vest tied to the end flew through the air, landing just close enough for Roberto to reach it. Roberto guided the end of the rope line down to Emilio who wrapped it around his chest. He then dropped the vest into Elena's arms. Roberto then looked to Hector, offering him a part of the rope, but Hector only stood and looked briefly at Roberto. He turned away and dove into the water, swimming toward the US shore.

Emielio and Elena slid out of the boat together into the current. Roberto wrapped his wrists and followed them. They were all now free of the sinking boat, but at the mercy of the current and the strength of the three men working the rope line.

The closer the three drifted to the shoreline, the more the current slowed until they were close enough to be pulled onto the sandy beach. They finally reached the safety of the shore. Fr. Pedro laid on the beach, just out of the water trying to catch his breath. In each of his arms were Emielio and Elena. Roberto sat alone next to them with his head tucked into his knees. Slowly he began to sob. Just downstream lying on the beach was Hector. He was too exhausted to move, but he had made it to the shore alive.

Slowly Elena released herself from Fr. Pedro. She stood, but could barely walk. She dropped to her knees, then to her side. Folding her legs, she held them tight like a child in the womb. She then began to wail. Emielio followed her and then laying down beside her, he wrapped his arms around her and held to her tightly.

All were shocked by the events that had taken place. The adrenalin still rushed through Fr. Pedro's body.

"We need to carry all of them up to the bus, where we can heat the inside and warm them. Go now or they will become ill from the cold!" Fr. Pedro said to Tomas.

Each of the children were carried up the levee and laid down in the bus. Even Hector was too weak and cold to fight off Santino who brought him up the levee. They were dried and covered with blankets which had been stored in the bus. The heaters were turned up and the doors closed. Soon all of the survivors were fast asleep.

Once settled, Tomas leaned over to Fr. Pedro and asked, "What do we do now boss?"

"We'll have to find a way to get them out of here," he answered.

"But where will we take them?"

"We can't leave them here. Maybe the parents, maybe they survived?" Santino said.

"It's not likely. You saw what I saw. The water is crazy mad," Tomas replied.

"Then we may have to take them back to the Mission until we can sort this out. Look at them, they're in shock," Fr Pedro said.

Tomas suddenly called out to Fr. Pedro, pointing down the levee road. Moving toward them was a Border Patrol unit with a single officer driving.

"La Migra!" Santino shouted.

Fr. Pedro watched closely as the officer stopped. After putting on his rain slicker and hat, he stepped out and walked slowly toward them.

"What will he want?" Tomas asked.

"I don't know. Make sure everyone stays where they are. No one runs."

Fr. Pedro then began to walk toward the officer by himself.

"Stay where you are!" the officer yelled as he placed his hand onto his sidearm.

He then continued toward Fr. Pedro but did not speak. Instead he slowly walked past him and around the bus. Father Pedro could see that he was a young agent who looked Hispanic.

Looking inside he saw all of the children. He continued his walk looking around at the ropes and floats scattered around the scene. He then sized up Tomas and Santino who sat by the bus still and quiet. Finally, he walked back to Fr. Pedro.

"You are all wet from the river more than from the rain?" he asked.

"Yes. The children," he pointed to the bus. "They were alone in a sinking boat. We did what we could."

"The four children are okay?"

"Yes, they seem to be, but they should be checked over by medical."

"Do you have some sort of ID you can show me?"

None of the priests were wearing their religious clothing. They rarely did when working for *SOMOS*. He pulled out his wallet and handed him a wet California driver's license.

"From California?"

"Yes. Los Angeles, I am Father Pedro Moreno."

"You are *SOMOS*? You are the leader of those crazies from California?"

"Yes," he answered.

"I have heard of you. What are you doing in Texas?"

"We travel along the border. Most of the time we are in California, but today we had business in Brownsville. We were heading back along the highway, and we stopped to check this stretch of the Rio when this happened."

"You should know that we just fished out five." He held up five fingers. "A mile or so up river."

"Five?"

"All adult Hispanic, three men, two women. No IDs."

Fr. Pedro hesitated to ask, "Dead?"

"All of them. Drowned."

The officer then looked over to the bus which held the four children.

"The minors, they're now orphans?" the officer asked.

Shrugging his shoulders, Fr. Pedro replied, "I don't know. I have seen no one around to claim them."

The officer reached up to adjust his hat, which was now saturated and dripping with rain water.

"Can I speak to you in private over here, padre?"

When they were far enough away from the others, the officer looked directly into Fr. Pedro's eyes and said,

"I'm going to have to take the children to a processing center in McAllen."

"I know of that place. It's no good, no good for the kids," Fr. Pedro said as he took off his glasses. "What will happen then?" he asked.

"They will be assigned a US caseworker. Most likely they will end up back in Mexico within forty-eight hours. The Mexican authorities will drop them off at an orphanage." The officer pointed across the river to Mexico.

"That is worse than being on the streets in Mexico. They will probably escape and be out on the streets in a week or so."

Both men took a worried pause. The officer then added, "Unless. . ."

The officer paused again.

"Unless you tell me that they are with you. Then, of course I will take your word. If you say they are. After all, you are a padre, right?"

"Then they are with me," Fr. Pedro replied.

The officer studied Fr. Pedro again and then with a grin said, "I will need to go to confession after this one."

"I think you are confessing this very moment and I absolve you of your sins. As I am certain that the Lord absolves you. I know He is happy that you show such compassion for these little ones."

"You know huh? Did He already tell you that?" he said with a smile.

"They have suffered such a loss and at such a young age," Fr. Pedro said.

"Watch my patrol unit when I leave. Follow my route along this same road. I will leave the gate open for you. You will not be seen. Be sure to lock the gate once you pass."

The officer then turned and walked toward his patrol unit.

"Officer!" Fr. Pedro called out.

The officer turned back.

"Gracias."

The officer offered nothing back but a wink.

Once Fr. Pedro was back to the bus, Santino was sitting in the driver's seat. He slowly rolled down the window and asked, "Where are we taking them?"

"To the Mission. But we need to stop at the clinic first."

"They all seem to be okay. They have scrapes and bruises but. . ." Fr. Pedro cut in,

"I am more worried about their little minds. They have seen too much today."

"Si," Santino answered.

"There can only be one thing at work here today and it isn't us," Fr. Pedro said.

"It can only be God."

As Fr. Pedro opened the door to the bus, he paused to say a small prayer. He was thankful to the Lord for saving the children and for the kindness of the border agent.

He made the sign of the cross and then turned to look one more time down to the angry river. The water continued to run fast and high. The rain still fell. It was cold. Slowly shaking his head, again he said to himself,

"It was a bad day to cross the river."

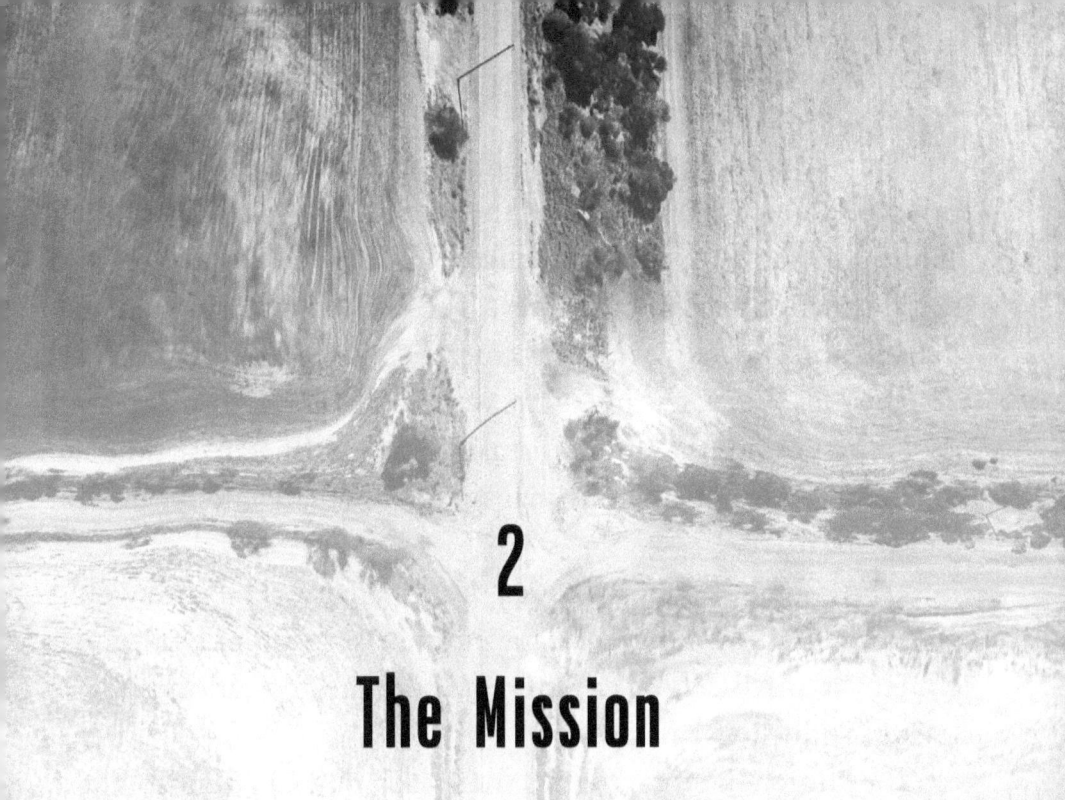

2

The Mission

TWO YEARS LATER. . .

After those days at the river, the four children who had been saved were taken to a place called the Mission in East Los Angeles. The Mission was in a hood called the "Heights." Fr. Pedro was the boss there.

The Mission was named after some saint. The four didn't know which saint but the people who lived in the Heights just called it the "Mission," and just like the "Heights," everyone knew where it was and what they were talking about.

At one time, the Archbishop told everyone he was going to tear it down before it was condemned by the city, but Fr. Pedro somehow stepped in and talked him out of it.

The Archbishop then offered him a chance to raise money and bring the buildings up to meet the earthquake code. Everything at the Mission was old. It smelled old, like old wood that had been polished too many times. The old church smelled like incense and the paint on the statues were peeling.

The roof, windows, and doors were all still good, so he replaced a lot of the things that might break and fall during an earthquake or fire. The city finally said that it was now safe enough to live and work there.

"The church is opposed to the death penalty," Fr. Pedro would say to the Archbishop. So he stayed the execution of a rundown church, a small school, a kitchen, and the recreation hall, at least for now.

The church had two Masses there each day. On Sunday, there were four masses and all were crowded. The hall had a dormitory at the back which had once housed priests. But now, only a few nuns and some of the people who worked at the Mission stayed there.

Fr. Pedro had offered each of the four children their own room. Roberto and Emilio chose to stay together in one room and Elena stayed across the hall from them. Hector insisted on being as far away as possible from the others. Fr. Pedro gave him a room at the far end of the dorm. The thing Hector didn't realize at the time, was that Fr. Pedro's room was near that part of the dorm as well.

Sister Rita lived at the Mission and helped to teach and take care of all the children. She washed their clothes and most of the time, she cooked food for them and would help them to bed. She also enforced the curfew which was eight o'clock on weeknights and with special permission, ten o'clock on the weekends.

Sister Rita also handed out the weekly list of chores. Most of the time the sisters were nice, but there were times when no one would think of crossing them. Sr. Rita was the most feared because she was a big woman and had a loud voice. You could hear her coming because of her voice. She wore her religious clothing most of the time and just looked like someone you wouldn't want to mess with. When they weren't off on a trip somewhere, Fr. Tomas and Fr. Santino also stayed at the Mission.

It was Fr. Pedro who was like their very own family and they called him *Tio* when they talked to him. *Tio* was the Spanish word for uncle. Even though they didn't know much about where he came from, they figured he was Mexican like them.

Sometimes his friends would call Tio a "Mexican Hippie." He had long, wavy gray hair that he sometimes pulled back into a pony tail. His beard was thin stubble and he always wore a pair of glasses with rounded lenses. He only wore his religious clothing when he was doing Mass or when people from the state or the Archbishop's office came around.

Even though Elena, Emielio and Roberto called Fr. Pedro Tio, he wasn't related by blood. That was just the way their world was, all messed up when it came to what they were and where they came from, or whether they were American or Mexican or both.

Tio spoke to them loud and had a nervous habit of taking off his glasses. He would wave them at whomever he was talking and then put them back on again. He was loud, but his voice didn't sound like screaming. Like Sister Rita, you knew when he was around by the sound of his voice. He also had to be bossy because he was in charge. He would say things like, "You boys, if you want to go out and play, stay off the streets and out of the dirt."

You could tell if he was pissed off by whether or not he had his glasses on. If they were off, then something was up and everyone knew it was the wrong time to mess with him. Roberto and Emilio talked about how he had probably been on the streets at one time. He knew too much about the streets.

The people in the Heights would say that when he was young, he was a really good boxer. In fact, he coached Roberto at the Mission. Later, they had even won some titles.

Whatever Tio had done when he was young in the Heights, the people respected it. To them he was a bad-ass and they had crazy-mad respect for him. Roberto, Elena, and Emilio all felt the same way. It was hard to tell how Hector felt.

Tio always spoke to them in English and he made sure they could write in both English and Spanish. When they spoke to one another, they were mostly using English. In fact, they were beginning to understand English better than Spanish. If they spoke to anyone important, or to a stranger, or to Tio, it was always in English. Except for Hector, who spoke Spanish mixed with nasty stuff just to piss Tio off. The others never really understood why Hector did that. But, there were a lot of things the others didn't understand about Hector.

Tio called Emilio by his real name, but everyone else called him "Mielo." He didn't know why people called him that name. However, Roberto was always calling everyone by crazy names. Sometimes the name made sense like when he called Hector the "*Culebro*." Hector did seem like a snake, a sneaky snake.

A lot of times Mielo thought they were just dumb ass names. He did like being called Mielo though. Hector seemed to like being called *Culebro*, but sometimes if you called him that, it would set him off. It was Tio who finally learned from Hector that his last name was Alvarez.

But like *Culebro*, no one ever said his last name to him, except for his teachers during school. It just made him mad to hear those names. No one could really understood why, not even Tio.

Even though Hector had been with the other three, he didn't consider himself to be one of them. He didn't want to be one of them and he was always letting them know. Tio called him a "work in progress." But deep down inside, he was really scared for him. It seemed to Tio that each day, Hector's behavior was becoming more aggressive and more dangerous.

There were times when Hector would do things that made all of them think he was crazy-bad. *"Mui Malo"* is what Sister Rita would say in Spanish. Tio would tell them that they needed to be good to him and include him in things. They tried to do that, but it was hard. Actually, Roberto thought Hector was possessed by some bad demons, so he never really tried to be good to him.

Tio was the boss of the small school at the Mission. The tuition was used to pay the costs and to keep the Mission looking and working good. The Heights was a poor Hispanic neighborhood and Tio would help many of the parents with their tuition. It was the type of tuition assistance that came from fund raising.

It seemed there was never enough money, so the fund raising was always going on at the Mission. When it seemed the funds were almost gone, somehow Tio would always come up with the money. He would say that he got the money from people who called themselves "Friends of the Mission."

After school, most of the kids went home. They had families so they slept in a bed at their own home. For Elena and Mielo who were in the sixth grade and Roberto and Hector who were in seventh, there was no home. They stayed after school. They did their homework with the sisters, ate dinner, and went to bed in the dorms. Even though it seemed like they had lived at the Mission forever, memories of their village in Mexico and of the day they lost their parents in the river still haunted them. Back there, they belonged to someone. Now they didn't belong to anyone.

At the Mission, at least they were all still together. They were tight and did everything together. At times, Tio even persuaded Hector to do things with them. He spent many days with all four of them. Everyone at the Mission knew their story. They knew they still needed to grieve about what had happened to them. Tio had the doctors who worked with him help them to understand why the bad things happened that day at the river.

Roberto was pretty sure Tio wasn't allowed to have the four of them live at the Mission. Whenever the people from the state came around to inspect the school, he would take his glasses off and get really nervous.

He had taken steps to get all of them something called a "temporary visa" based upon what had happened to them. This took a long time so they just remained illegal. Everyone at the Mission knew they could be taken away and be deported at any time. Even the four of them knew it.

Tio tried to keep them out of the sight of authorities while he and his *SOMOS* friends continued working to get them legal status. Tio would always say to his staff, "It's a crazy business, but we have to work with it. We have no choice."

Even after two years, Tio still met with them as a group to talk about that day at the river. Each month he would check their needs and struggles. He and his staff agreed that they were getting better, except for Hector. As hard as Tio tried, he seemed to always miss with him.

Each time in group, Tio would tell the story about what happened to all of them that day at the river. He would tell it just slightly different each time. This morning it was Elena who seemed to be having a hard time.

"Elena, why the long face? What's the crying for?" Tio asked.

"In this place, sometimes I feel small," Elena said.

"You are small," Roberto said, making the group laugh.

But Elena remained still and silent.

"I mean, I feel lonely."

"How so?" Tio asked.

"I still think of mi mama and mi papa."

"Why do you keep telling us that shitty ass story? It makes people cry and shit," Hector asked.

"Crying is our way we let our hurt out," Tio said.

Roberto interrupted, "It's just that everything comes and goes for us, Tio. First we have a family, then we don't. Then we live here, but not really because we're not from here."

"Your real home is in heaven. And you have each other. That has not changed. We are all family," Tio said placing his hand on Elena's shoulder.

"Some people are together by blood and some by things that happen to them. We are a family because of what happened to us and where we have come from."

"That's bullshit," Hector said.

They were all used to Hector disrupting, and they usually ignored him, but Tio was beginning to feel like he was losing Hector. He could see that he was being influenced by things outside the Mission. His stuff was becoming darker and darker each time they met. He felt the need to keep him involved, so he asked him,

"Why? Why is this bullshit to you Hector?"

"Because it is. The truth is we don't belong to no one and you are trying to poison all of us with these fairy tales."

Hector continued to answer while he rocked back on his chair.

"We are not *familia* and I am not part of your fucking family. We are a bunch of Mexican wetbacks without anyone or anything."

"I think of you as *mi familia*. You are my son. I think of you as a son and like the Lord, I am proud to be your Papa," Tio said directly to Hector.

For just a moment, you could see those words sinking into Hector. It was like he was ready to believe, but then something evil took over. He then belted out to Elena,

"And, I don't give a fuck about your papa or your mama. So stop your fucking baby-crying, you little *puta*."

In Mexico, the word *puta* was reserved for a woman who sold herself. It was that nasty word that started it. Both Roberto and Mielo stood up in Elena's defense. Roberto reached Hector first and landed his fist onto Hector's face. Hector fell back in his chair and onto the floor.

Tio quickly stepped in, grabbing Roberto and then Mielo both by the back of their hair. Both squirmed, but Tio had a strong grip on both of them. Hector was in a rage. He had been embarrassed by Roberto and in front of Elena. He rose from the floor and wiping the blood from his swollen lip, charged toward Roberto. This time, Tio reached out with his leg and landed his foot onto Hector's chest, knocking him back again to the floor.

Tio then dropped Roberto and Mielo back into their chairs. They both were now done with it and followed Tio's order to sit back down in their chairs.

Hector again stood up, his eyes spitting out rage.

"Hector, back to your chair or I will put you there."

Hector, like the others, had come to respect Tio's street skills and slowly retreated back to his chair. Elena was now standing with her back against the wall.

"Elena, sweet girl. You should leave now," Tio said.

Her eyes were streaming as she closed the old wooden door behind her.

"We need to talk about this anger," Tio said.

"Fuck you and your anger. Here is my anger!" Hector said as he raised his middle finger to Roberto and then to Mielo.

Tio talked about anger and violence and to be honest, much of what he said rang true to Mielo and Roberto.

Tio soon realized the rage inside of Hector was too much and too fresh. His words were no longer getting through. So he ended it with a prayer and said they should,

"Surrender all of this rage to God."

"Can I add to the end of your prayer?" Hector asked.

Tio paused and thought carefully before answering. He knew Hector was ill tempered and that a yes answer would most likely lead to another wrong by Hector. But, the need to include Hector in the group was of a higher value to him. Good or bad, Hector needed to know that he was one of them. So Tio allowed him to add to the prayer.

"And may we all, especially Roberto and Mielo, rot in the fucking fires of hell forever. Amen," he said, smiling at all of them. Hector's smile was not normal. It was scary. It was evil.

Tio ended the prayer by adding,

"And forgive us our sins, oh Lord, for sometimes we know not what we do."

The thing that Tio didn't surrender to God that day, was his way of punishing bad things with hard work. He made Mielo and Roberto serve the altar at early morning mass for two straight weeks. They were each given a full day's work. Because they still had to attend school and do homework, this meant that the extra work could only be done on the weekend.

Of course, Hector would fight against doing any work, but even he would learn that sitting in his room without anything to do was a worse punishment.

Roberto wanted to talk to his brother and Elena about what happened with Hector that day.

"I know a place where we can go. No one knows about it."

His work assignment had been to help the school fix-it man repair the church roof. The man had given him the key to the ceiling hatch leading to the bell tower and had forgotten to ask for it back. Since he still had the key, Roberto told them to meet him at the tower after dinner.

The next evening, after doing the dinner dishes, all three of them drifted out of kitchen and over to the ladder leading to the roof hatch in the bell tower.

"Follow me," Roberto whispered.

Roberto watched to make sure they hadn't been seen by any-one. He led them up a long wooden ladder. The ladder swayed and squealed as Roberto climbed. Once to the top, he unlocked and lifted the squeaking hatch. Elena was behind him at the ladder. She looked up at him and seemed unsure about stepping on the first rung. Roberto looked down and said,

"Elena, it's not bad. I am bigger than you and the ladder holds me. Mielo is behind you and he will catch you if you fall."

Elena took her first step and then did not stop until she reached Roberto. Mielo followed. The tower smelled of old feathers and the waste that lay on the floor. The barn pigeons were startled by the sudden entrance of the strangers. They darted clumsily across, flapping their wings loudly as they flew out of the tower.

The largest hoot owl Mielo had ever seen glared down upon them from his perch.

"This way," Roberto said.

He led them through a rickety old door and onto a rusty scaffold. You could tell it had been built many years ago. It was made to provide a resting place for the men who built the roof over the church. Although it looked crude and old, the bones were made of large iron pipes and it was still sturdy. From here, they had a clear view of the downtown skyline in the city of LA.

They all climbed to the highest platform and sat down beside one other. Their feet dangled far above the Mission grounds. It soon became clear to all of them why the workers had chosen that spot.

For the first few minutes Mielo sat, overwhelmed. You could hear Elena breath in deeply, holding her breath. Everything was all around.

"You can see everything," Mielo said.

You could see the Mission, the blacktop, the school, the hall, and most of the Heights.

"Roberto, I have never seen anything like this. So big! I feel like I am a bird," Elena said.

The sun was falling in the west. Far off stood the tall shadows of the downtown buildings. They had seen them before but only on the TV.

"I've seen those big buildings. Those are the ones that you see behind the guy on the news that Tio watches. I forget his name," Roberto said.

"Downtown is where the rich people live," Mielo said.

They could see and hear the freeways: what the people in the Heights called, "The two ten," "The five," or the "San Gabriel." They could see it all, even the smoke from the barbeques and their friends playing basketball outside at the Boys and Girls club.

Even Roberto, who had been up there for most of the last two days, was caught up in what they were seeing. The city lights were beginning to flicker. Sirens could be heard far off in the background.

"This view is crazy. I see so many things," Elena said again.

"When we need a place to go. When something is wrong. We can come here," Roberto said.

"We can never tell anyone about this place, especially Tio. "

No one answered as they continued to look at the view.

"Can anyone see us?" Mielo asked.

"That's what makes it *primo*. We can see everywhere, but it's hard for Tio and the sisters to see up here."

Roberto sat back in the evening shadow of the church steeple. He had found an old paint bucket to sit on. Elena and Mielo stayed on the scaffold platform. Their eyes lingered on the setting sun. The marine breeze coming in from the ocean was beginning to cool the air down. Everything was good.

"What about the *Culebro*?" Roberto finally said.

"I was ready to take him on again," Mielo replied.

"We can't trust him. Not anymore, Elena," Roberto said.

"It makes me sad to be around him. I see him alone all of the time. But Tio is right. We need to give him a chance," Elena said.

"Forget that shit. This is our family. The three of us and I say we can't trust the *Culebro*," Roberto said.

"Like Tio said, the closest people in your life may not be blood, but they can still be family. The people who pick you up when you fall. The people like Tio who take you in," Mielo said.

"We need to say right here, right now that we are family. No one and nothing can break us up. We will always be family," Roberto said holding up his fist.

He then put his fist on top of Mielo's. Elena placed her hands open and over both of fists. She then said,

"The same small village where we came from is still in all of us. All I know is you both have been there to pick me up when I fell. And we have to keep helping each other."

"I don't know how long this will last. But whatever happens to us, I promise to be there for both of you," Roberto said.

"Maybe the worst is over. Maybe Tio will make us real Americans. Then we are a family forever. Tio says we are family and I believe that with all my heart. I too promise to always be there for both of you," Mielo said. They dropped their hands and huddled together like a family would do.

Below, in his office and out of sight of those in the bell tower, Tio was greeting his own sort of family. It was another secret meeting of *SOMOS*, one of many that took place in the evening and sometimes late into the night. The Mission was the unofficial home for *SOMOS*. It was held loosely together by a band of Catholic priests, nuns, and just ordinary people working out of Tio's office.

Although they did many things to help the migrants, they were best known for their work helping the migrants who crossed the border into the US. It was common to call people who led crossers "coyotes," but Fr. Pedro would not let the people of *SOMOS* use that name. He said, "*SOMOS* was NOT made up of coyotes."

They were "shepherds finding the lost sheep and bringing them to the Promised Land."

The word coyote was closely connected to the Mexican cartels and gangs. Everyone knew what the cartels were about. They were nothing but bad. They would kill you if you got in their way. He didn't want anyone to look to the cartels for the way to do things. *SOMOS* had its own ways of doing things and its own connections. Most of the time, *SOMOS* tried to stay under the radar of the authorities and most of the time they succeeded.

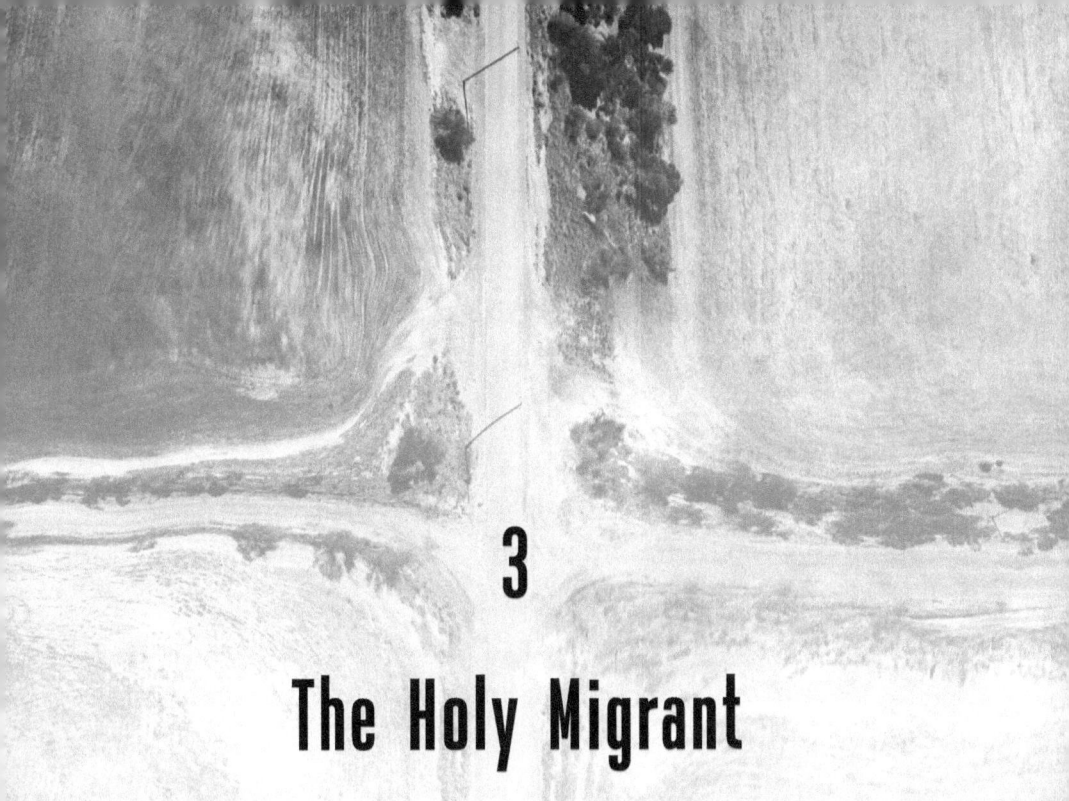

3

The Holy Migrant

It was Saturday morning and inside the Mission, things were mostly quiet. Tio was in his drafty office taking advantage of the lull in the action. He wore one of his over-sized hoodies. The hoodie was ragged and faded red with the word "HARVARD" on it in white peeling letters. On his desk was his usual warmed-up cup of coffee. He pulled his reading glasses out of his desk and put them on slowly. Then he raised the morning newspaper and began to read to himself. Soon came a voice from behind his paper and it seemed to be coming from the open doorway.

"Father?"

Tio was used to being interrupted. His small office was in a long corridor of the grade school and he always kept it open so that it was easy for the children to get to him.

"They are my work and the most important part of my work," he would say to the sisters when they asked him if the children were bothering him.

"Father Mario is here," Sister Rita announced.

Fr. Mario represented the Jesuit Provincial. He was the second highest in the order behind Fr. David who was the Provincial. Fr. Mario was also a very good personal friend to Tio. He was sympathetic and a supporter of Tio's work with *SOMOS*, but him stopping by the Mission unannounced was a sign that something wasn't sitting right with the bosses.

Tio folded his newspaper and threw it on his desk.

"*Jesus, Marie, Jose,*" Sr. Rita added while making the sign of the cross.

"It's Father Dante from the Archbishop's office. They are both here together," she said watching through his office window.

Father Dante was second only to the Archbishop of the Diocese of Los Angeles. He was also a "pain in the *culo*" as Tio would often put it.

The two visiting at the same time could only be bad. Tio took his glasses off and then put them on again.

"Mario, it's good to see you," Tio said holding his hand out. Fr. Mario embraced him.

"Always good to see you too, my friend."

Tio moved the stacks of books and newspapers off his office chairs.

"And Fr. Dante, this must be an important visit. Please both of you, please have a seat," he said as Sr. Rita stepped into the room.

"This a surprise. Can I offer to get you some coffee? Water?"

"Yes, I'll have some coffee, black," Fr. Mario answered.

"Just some water. Thank you, Sister," Fr. Dante followed.

"I hear some young voices. Do you have Saturday classes?" Fr. Dante asked.

Tio paused to answer, looking over at Fr. Mario who remained silent. Mario's silence was a sign to Tio that he was there reluctantly. Fr. David had sent him out of respect for the Archbishop's request.

"Yes," Tio answered smiling back. "Just a few who need a little extra help."

Sr. Rita brought Fr. Mario his coffee.

"Thank you, Sister."

"Excuse me, Sister, could you please close the door behind you?" Fr. Dante asked.

"Of course Father, we'll be right outside should you need anything."

"Wow, a closed door session. This is serious?" Tio asked.

"It always seems to be serious when it comes to the activities here at the Mission," Fr. Dante answered.

"Our visit today is not official, but as you can see, I have been asked to come here by the Archbishop and," turning his head toward Fr. Mario, "your Provincial Fr. David has asked to be represented here today by Fr. Mario."

Tio pulled his glasses off. His face color was rapidly changing to a darker brown as he spoke,

"Father Dante, let's stop with the authority bullshit. Who's pissed off and why? I know you two wouldn't be here unless your bosses were feeling nervous about something. So here I am. Tell me what's up?"

Irritated with Tio's tone, Fr. Dante glanced over to Fr. Mario who remained silent drinking his coffee. He then continued,

"The Archbishop and your own Provincial, Fr. David, have received serious inquiries about your activities here at the Mission."

"These inquiries are obviously from wealthy or influential connections to the church? Otherwise, I know the Archbishop in the past has been supportive of what we do here at the Mission."

"The Archbishop has very little if any knowledge."

"Pedro," said Father Mario as he quickly took over the conversation. He did so to avoid what he saw coming from Fr. Dante. Accusations that would surely set off his good friend. He knew both priests well and wanted to avoid that conflict.

"Over the last year, the Mission and not necessarily SOMOS, has taken on new responsibilities and in particular, four new responsibilities."

Tio removed his glasses and glared at Fr. Dante. Fr. Mario continued.

"Those four new responsibilities have leaked out to the public and in doing so, have caused some of the Archbishop's advisors to be very nervous."

"And you, Father Dante, are one of the advisors?" Father Pedro asked.

"Thank you for your clear statement of the issue, Father Mario. In fact, his Excellency has been taking calls from the county Sheriff, the city Police Chief and now most recently the Mayor, who has caught wind of your organization. In the past he has been able to turn his head," Fr. Dante said.

"Pedro my friend. . ." Fr. Mario cut in again.

"In the past we have understood that what you were doing was good and it is supported by many of those who live and work in this community.

"But as you know, times have changed and the church is under tremendous pressure because of the crisis with the children." Fr. Mario was now looking down and into his coffee cup, but continued,

"In particular the leaders of the church are under great scrutiny. That's why we are here."

Fr. Dante added,

"It is one thing for the Archbishop and your Provincial to ignore a few violations of the law in order to save lives. It is another for us to ignore reports that undocumented children are being hidden on church property. Some for maybe up to two years? These are very sensitive allegations. It opens up a whole new set of dangerous circumstances and puts all of us in a very vulnerable position."

Tio sat stunned and silent, shaking his head as he looked down at his desk.

"This is the devil getting his way."

He then put his glasses back on.

"Satan thought this one out well, didn't he? He draws a few bad priests in. Get the press involved and bingo, then he brings down all the good priests as well."

"Pedro, we are not here to judge anyone," Fr. Dante said.

Tio continued talking over Fr. Dante. . .

"He could then get all the people to believe that all the priests are bunch of sick fucks!"

It wasn't rare that Tio used swear words, but it was rare for him to do it in front of his fellow clergy. In the past, he had scolded the children for using those words. For Tio, they were usually reserved for times when he was out of control with anger.

So he paused briefly to regain his composure. He then apologized to both the priests. Slowly he began again.

"Look at all that has become of the crisis in the church. No one trusts us, and in this case, it is because we are priests. The church has messed up big. And it is good for us to see it for what it is. We should all be talking about it. And there should be a price for such behavior.

"It will do all of us good to be humbled. But we cannot let all the good fall because of this evil. We can't let Satin win this one."

"Fr. Pedro, I know, and everyone who has anything to do with this Mission knows, that there is nothing inappropriate going on here. But this is unfortunately how the politics line up," Fr. Dante said, now sitting tall in his chair.

"Not only do you need to take action to stop holding on to the four children, but the Archbishop is also requesting you cooperate with the immigration laws and stop the crossings."

"In response to your first issue of removing the children from the Mission, I have one simple question: where will they to go? If they cannot stay here under my protection, I guarantee you they will be out on the streets.

"They have no mothers or fathers and they have no home or country for that matter. They will be arrested and hauled away like a dog caught by animal control," replied Fr. Pedro.

There was no answer offered, only silence.

"Has the organization attempted to get them adopted and legal?" asked Fr. Dante.

"Yes, and we are almost there. I do believe that if I can keep them for another two months, they will be legal," Fr. Pedro answered.

"And in response to the second issue regarding the work of SOMOS, I will stop the activity at the Mission. I will continue to oversee the Mission, serve the masses, serve the community, and run the school. But I tell you this, *SOMOS* has a life of its own. It is a community all its own. I do not control it."

"Then perhaps you can preach against the illegal entry into this country. Perhaps you can influence the illegals to stay in Mexico or to return to their original country?"

Fr. Mario knew that question was the wrong one to ask Father, considering he had spent most of his priesthood helping them to cross over to the US and most importantly, to a better life. He sat a little lower in his chair as Tio fired off his response.

"You know Fr. Dante, I've done this work for many years and over those years, I have noticed something very troubling to me. I've noticed that those people who are most opposed to other people coming into a country are always the people who are already there.

"So here is my message to my Archbishop and to my Provincial. I will do as you tell me to do. While I can control what happens on this property, I cannot control the will and actions of those who are called *SOMOS*. They are a part of my heart and soul which will always be open to them."

"Well, that will have to do for now. I'm sure his Excellency appreciates your cooperation. And I hope you know of the great respect he has for what your organization has done for the immigrant church.

"One final point, Father Pedro. In order that his Excellency has a plausible position of denial, I will not speak of this meeting with him and if asked, I will deny that we ever spoke in this way."

"I also have one final thought. Maybe you can consider it my advice for all of us at the top of church food chain. Maybe it's time for everyone to stop thinking so much about how things look from the outside in, and think more about how things look from the inside out."

All three men sat in a pensive silence.

"Well, now that this is resolved, I look forward to seeing your facility here. Both the Archbishop and I are amazed at the work you have put into saving this place."

"Also," Tio continued, "and I mean this with great respect. Maybe it's worth reminding his Excellency that Jesus himself was a migrant."

Another awkward silence fell in the room. It was abruptly broken by the sound of a high-pitched voice coming from down the long corridor of the school.

Both Fr. Dante and Mario were struck by the natural beauty of the tender voice. Together they listened.

"That's the Ave? Are you also harboring angels?"

Tio smiled and opened the door to hear it better.

"Seriously, that's an amazing voice. Who is that?" Fr. Dante asked.

It was Elena, or as many of the people around the Mission called her, *El Rossinyol,* which is Spanish for the Nightingale.

The three Fathers followed the voice to the music classroom door. Inside was Sr. Rita seated at the piano with Elena. Together, they were working on the Ave Maria. . .

When the priest entered the classroom, Elena cut it off mid-verse. A vigorous applause by the three of them followed.

"All you need is a couple more like you to have a choir of angels!" Fr. Dante said.

"That is Elena, one of the four from the river that day," Fr. Pedro said.

"She is exceptional. The voice is rare," Fr. Dante added.

"To all of us at the Mission, she is *El Rossinyol.*"

"Which means Nightingale," Fr. Dante quipped.

Besides her singing, all anyone could say about Elena was that she was really nice to be around. Everyone, especially the boys at the Mission school and around the Heights, wanted to be with her. Roberto and Mielo looked out for her like family, but secretly they both thought of her as their girlfriend. Both wanted to marry her when they were older. They just hadn't shared that dream with one another or with her yet.

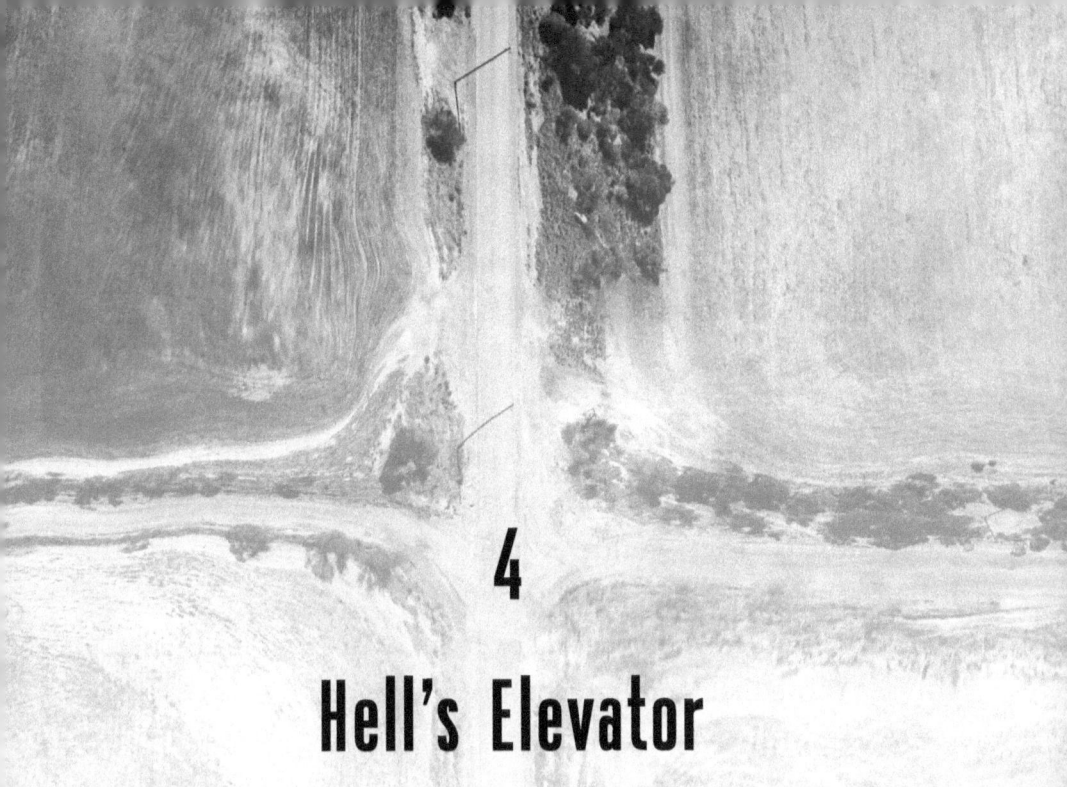

4

Hell's Elevator

O ver the next few days, Tio was a little more nervous than usual. He had assumed the visit from Fr. Dante had more of a message than simply the wishes of the Archbishop and a warning about SOMOS. The children were at higher risk now that the word was out. He had to be careful to keep them busy and to have an eye on them at all times. The people at *SOMOS* continued to work hard each day to push forward on an agreement which would allow them a temporary visa. But with each day, there continued to be delay after delay.

In late March, the Catholic season of Lent started at the Mission. This was the time of the year where the school would teach the students about the sacraments. Many of the children would have their first exposure to the sacrament of confession, where each one would tell their sins to a priest in a confessional.

The younger students were the ones who always fell for the "hell's elevator" story. So today, Elena was the person they chose for the set-up. Because Mielo sat directly behind Elena, it fell to him to set her up.

Elena and the rest of her class sat there all morning watching the older students go in and out of the squeaky doors of the dark confessionals. They wondered what things went on inside those little rooms with the red lights above.

After a while, Mielo leaned over and whispered to Elena, "Do you see those little red lights above the doors?"

"I see them. What are they for?"

"You see, when the person goes in, there is a secret elevator and when they step into the elevator, the red light comes on from the outside, watch." Mielo pointed to the small red light above the door that turned on just after the student went in and closed the door.

"Yes, I see it," Elena said.

"After the light goes on, you kneel inside there and then the father talks to you and if you did something very bad," Mielo used his fingers like flipping a light switch. "Then boom! The priest will flip the switch and the red light will go off and the elevator will go straight down to hell. It's really, really fast. Then you will never see that person again."

Mielo continued, "I am really scared. I know some stuff I did was bad."

"What stuff did you do?" Elena asked.

"I don't know, I can't tell you in church. But it's bad. You know I will probably be okay. Most people go in and the light goes on and then it goes off and then they come out. But if the light goes off and I don't come out," he said now shaking his head, "Then I want you to know that it's okay for you to marry Roberto since I am gone. And then someday if you pray hard enough, the elevator may take me back from hell and I will come back as an angel to help all of you. Okay?"

"Mielo, don't go in there if you will not come out," she said with her eyes fixed on the red light.

Mielo pretended to be afraid but still brave as he made his way to the confessional door. He slowly opened the door and looked up at the red light above. He then looked back to Elena, slowly he stepped into the confessional, and then closed the door. After only a few seconds, he knelt down and the red light outside the door came on.

Inside the confessional, Tio slid the small window open and even though he could not be seen, Mielo could tell Tio knew it was him by the way Mielo said his beginning prayer. Mielo finished the prayer and then didn't say anything for a while. Tio waited patiently for Mielo to start, but he was just frozen in his angst. He didn't like going to confession. He thought it was crazy to tell somebody all your bad stuff, but it meant a lot to Tio that Mielo and the other three had their sacraments. So he tried really hard to do what Tio liked, but an uncomfortable silence had fallen between the Father and his young confessor. After some time passed, Tio finally prompted Mielo along, "It is time for you to tell me your sins."

It made Mielo feel pressured so he looked down at the little book Sister Rita had given him. The front cover of the book read, *Confessing Your Sins to Jesus.* Tio was not Jesus. He was just a regular old guy. A priest yes, but still just a regular person. He quickly looked through the pages of the book but was too nervous to read any of it. It was just had a bunch of hard-to-say words that were supposed to be sins. Mielo just didn't get any of it.

"Okay, so I did some bad stuff." Mielo always seemed to use the word "okay" when he was reading or talking to someone important.

"Okay, what?" Tio said.

"Okay, so I took the watermelon from your garden last summer and so Roberto and me, we ate it while you were not around."

"I know that one. I already gave you a penance. Remember when the both of you pulled weeds and fertilized my garden that whole week? But Emilio, what have I told you about this sacrament? The sacrament of confession. Didn't I tell you that you have to prepare and examine your conscience before you come in here? Did Sister give you a small book to see what sins you may have done?"

"Tio, my little book says I gotta say this to Jesus. I looked around but I don't see Jesus," Mielo answered.

"Emielio, I have told you before, you are to call me Father Pedro when I am working. Listen closely to me: you tell your sins to God, like a prayer. I listen. Then the Holy Spirit works through me to help you to be forgiven by God, and then you promise to try harder to not do it again," Tio continued, "And in the end, God is the one who forgives you, not me. But it's all like a prayer. A prayer that I have to listen to with God. Come on, Emielio, this is not the first time we have talked about this."

Tio was beginning to sound mad and it was making Mielo feel even more nervous. So Mielo looked down and opened the little book again, but he still did not understand any of it. He had to say something so he quickly picked a sin. Then he picked another one, and then another straight off the list in Sister's little book.

"Yes. There are some things in this book that I did."

"Okay then, let's start over."

Tio seemed calmer now.

"So tell me your sins."

Now Mielo read straight from the book, picking a couple of words that he thought looked important. Then as if he was ordering off a menu, he said,

"Okay, so I did the ADULT-ERY and the FORTIFICATION. Both of them I did twenty-five times and that's it, and that's all I can remember, Tio."

Even though he could not see him through the little window, Mielo could hear him sit back in his chair. Whatever he had said to Tio must have been not so bad. But Tio got quiet and stayed quiet for a while. Then he started to speak again.

"Emilio, you don't have any idea about the sins you just confessed, do you?"

"It's something that's not that bad, isn't it? Or you would be mad."

Tio had other young confessors waiting outside to come in, so he decided to end Mielo's confession.

"Go now, I forgive you all of your sins in the name of the Father, and the Son, and of the Holy Spirit. For your penance, you will come to see me tomorrow morning and we will talk more about this confession. Now go and send in the next student."

The ending of the confession reminded Mielo of the scam they had going with Elena. He stood up fast and the light went off. He knew he couldn't step out of the door for a few minutes or he would blow the whole scam.

"But, Tio, I need to wait a minute."

"Why? Have you come up with more words in your little book?"

"No, I just need to wait for a minute."

Tio had been around enough to know about the hell's elevator scam and when he heard the sound of laughter coming from outside the confessional, he knew something was up.

"Emilio, what have you done? The elevator joke?" he asked.

"Yes," Mielo quickly confessed.

Tio then came out from behind the small window barrier and took his glasses off. He then pointed them directly at Mielo.

"On who? Who did you boys do this to?"

Mielo was really scared now. "Elena," he said.

"The little nightingale?" His voice had now changed to a little louder, another sure sign that he was mad. Suddenly, Tio had a firm grip on Mielo's shoulder pulling him out of the dark confessional. When Mielo's eyes adjusted to the light outside, he looked around. He could see that many had gathered around Elena and that she was upset. The Sisters and some of her friends were trying to calm her. Then at the other end of the church were the rest of the boys who were in on the joke. They were all laughing and hurrying to get out of the church before Tio could catch up with them. Mielo started to laugh too. Then he saw Elena's face. She was looking directly at him. She looked at him in a way that made him sad. To her, the joke wasn't funny. Mielo stopped laughing immediately while all the others continued. All the others except for Roberto.

That day ended up being one of the worst days Mielo had ever had at the Mission. He got into a lot of trouble. Tio and the Sisters made him do extra chores for all of two straight months.

But worse than that, Mielo had now given Elena a reason to no longer trust him and a reason for her to like Roberto better. Instead of laughing at her, Roberto helped her and in the end, she now trusted Roberto more. It took a long time for Elena to forgive Mielo. He had to ask Tio for help, and after several days, she finally forgave Mielo and even laughed about the joke a little. But things were never the same.

Tio never forgot the incident. In the end, he used the scam as an example of the kind of sin that should be confessed. Not only did he use the example to preach to Mielo, but he used it to teach all the kids in the whole school. As far as anyone could tell, the hell's elevator scam never happened again at the Mission.

So Mielo learned that day how things that he thought are funny can sometimes hurt other people. He learned that sometimes he did things without thinking them through and they just end up being stupid. Mielo told himself that he didn't care that Roberto was now Elena's favorite over him. But he did.

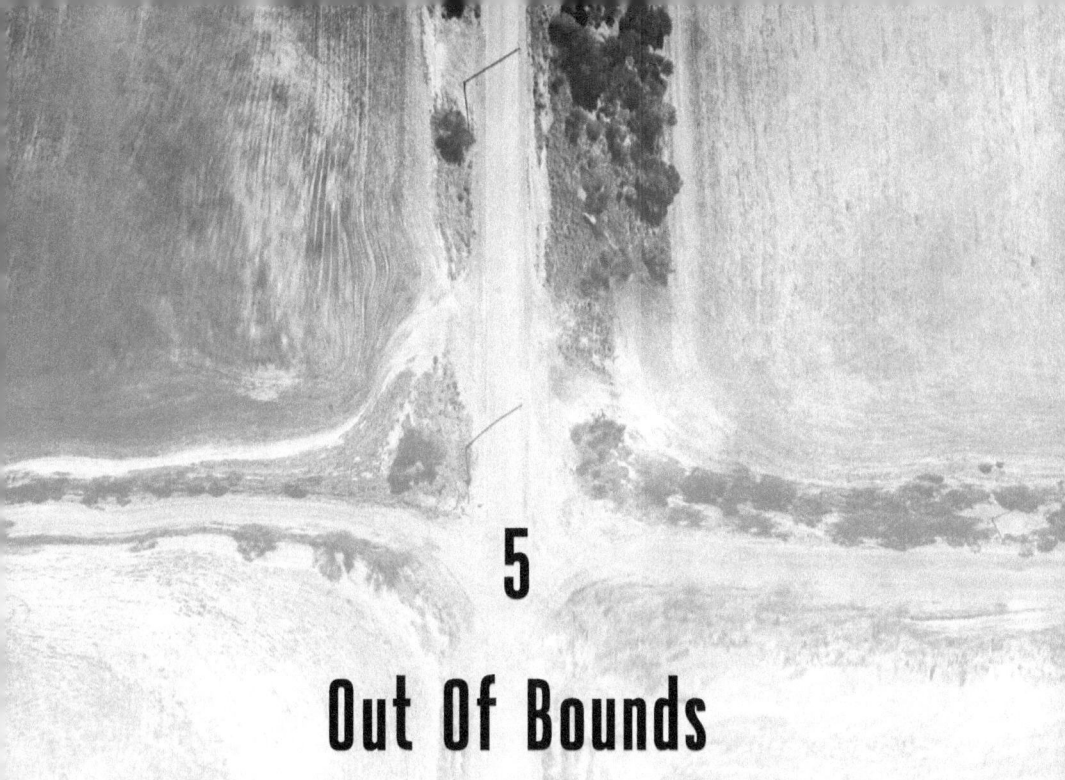

5

Out Of Bounds

"**O**nly yesterday, the school inspectors were here asking to see documents," came the warning from Sister Rita. Yesterday's visit had been different from other visits by the state. They usually just focused on the school, but this time, they wanted to know more about the adoptive parents and their citizenship of the four children. They had obviously been tipped off and were following through on their suspicions.

Putting his glasses back on, Tio stroked his beard again like he always did when he was worried. Then he leaned forward in his worn leather chair to look out of his rain-streaked window. What was all that noise coming from the playground outside?

Hector was cheating. That's just what he did. Roberto and Mielo were always getting into fights with him. Today was no different. The two brothers were trying to play a game against two others and one of them was Hector. The playground area was always covered with loose gravel and today the potholes were full of rain water from an earlier downpour.

Practically nothing, not even a hard rain, could stop the Estrada brothers from playing futbol. These games were all they had to keep themselves busy outside, and they had to make the best of it or have nothing at all.

"Hector, you're out of bounds. The ball is out and the shot is no good. No *bueno*!" Mielo shouted.

Hector swiped the ball out of the hands of Roberto.

"There is no out, Homeclub!" Hector shouted back.

Homeclub was a name Hector had made up to bother Mielo ever since he got his new shoes. At least to him they were new. Home Club was the name of the thrift store where Tio had bought them. Mielo was thinking maybe someone had worn them first before him.

"Even new shoes are worn already." Tio would say, "People try them on their feet all day and they put them back into the box. Then they sell them like they are brand new." To Mielo, Tio made perfect sense because he really liked those shoes. Hector talked shit about them all the time and they just thought he was jealous. Mielo really didn't care what Hector said. To him, the shoes were cool and he wore them every day.

Hector moved in and put his face real close to Mielo's. They were both locked in a classic Mad-dog stare down. The rain was falling hard now and was dripping off Hector's long, black hair.

"I said the shot was good and I don't need your little *pinche* ass face to tell me how to play the game!" Hector said.

Roberto stepped in between them and jerked the ball back from Hector. Mielo pushed Roberto back out of the way. Even though Hector was older and bigger and even though Mielo thought he was going to get his ass kicked, he could not back down.

Roberto had just started to box in the city leagues and Tio coached him. Mielo remembered right then what Roberto had told him about fighting.

"Even if you are afraid, to let the other man know you are afraid is when you lose the fight," so he couldn't back down.

After brushing him back, Mielo yelled at Roberto, "I don't need you to help me!"

It was then that Hector fired off his first punch. It was a cheap shot that landed on Roberto's left cheek while he was distracted listening to Mielo. Roberto dropped the ball to the ground and returned his own blow which landed square onto Hector's nose. Hector fell to the ground as Mielo rushed to scoop up the loose ball.

And just like that, the tables had turned on Hector. Even his own teammates and the others who had been watching were now starting to walk away. He was alone standing up against Mielo and Roberto. Blood was streaming from his nose. He reached up to try to stop the bleeding, but it just kept coming. When he finally squared back off against Roberto, he was dizzy and his eyes were watering like he had been crying. The rain had mixed with the blood and his shirt had quickly turned to a pink, bloody tinge. Then slowly, a grin started in the corner of Hector's mouth. It was a grin that Roberto and Mielo knew well. When Hector grinned like that, it was his way of letting people know he was going to do something bad. As the grin grew, he pulled out a street blade from his boot.

"I'm gonna cut you!" he said.

Roberto jumped back as Hector lunged at him fully extended. The blade missed his chest, but only by inches.

"Hector! Drop that shit!" Mielo shouted, "you're going to get us all in trouble."

Mielo's words only seemed to make him more angry as he swiped wildly again with his blade. Mielo turned to block the swing using the ball. Air whistled from the ball as it spun out of Mielo's hands to the wet ground. There it lay flat and sliced half open.

Then, for some reason, the rain just stopped and all three boys stopped too. It was like someone had blown a whistle. All of them just stood there out of breath, dripping wet, staring at the messed up ball. Soon they looked back to one another like they were not sure what the next move would be or who would make it. Maybe they all wanted to stop, but maybe things had just gone too far.

Just as Mielo and Hector were starting to square off again, Tio showed up and he didn't have his glasses on. He grabbed Hector by the arm and slammed the wrist which held the blade, against the corner of the goal stand. Both the knife and Hector flew over the cross bar and onto the ground. Roberto and Mielo stood still. They were frozen in place because they had seen what Tio could do when he was angry. Even though he was kind of old, Tio understood street fighting and could easily handle himself. Even Hector knew that and didn't call him out.

"This is not how real men conduct themselves! Estrada boys, go to the wall!" Tio shouted, starring back at Hector who was still on the ground.

The wall was where they were sent to chill out. It was a sort of a "time out," which was what they called it when they were still small kids. Both Roberto and Mielo did not hesitate to head to the wall quickly. Tio picked up the blade and began to preach like they had not heard in a long time.

"Hector! Holding a blade does not make you a man," Tio said. "It makes you a fool. To carry such a thing will take you to places I promise you do not want to go. Look at you, all covered in blood!"

Tio held the blade up high as he continued, but this time his words were for all the kids present. "I swear to all of you, it is only a fool who lives by the sword, and only a fool who will die by the sword. *Tonto, Loco!* Those are my words for anyone who carries this nasty piece."

When Tio spoke that way, it was always good. Most of what he told them held true and would help them when they got older. However, Hector wasn't ashamed, and he didn't care about Tio's words. He just cared about where his blade was and where Tio was going to put it. The blade had been given to him by the leader of a local street gang called the *Los Lobos*. It meant a lot to him and he would probably be jumped if he lost it. To him, that blade was way more important than a bunch of holy words.

It was at that very moment, as soon as Tio finished those words about fools and knives, that Roberto, Mielo, Elena, and Hector would all learn an even bigger truth about their messed up world.

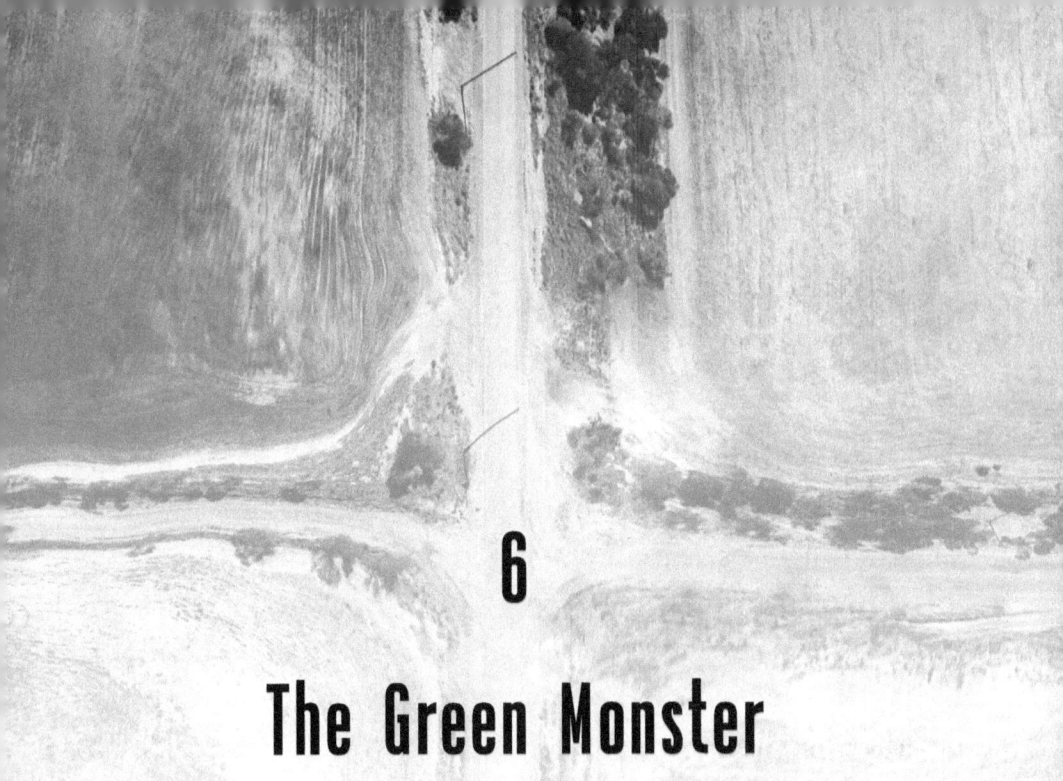

6

The Green Monster

t first, it began with a heavy rumble in the ground. Then with a loud pounding sound, Mielo looked up to see a large bar being slammed into the lock which held the gate to the mission playground closed. The gates soon crashed wide open and busting through came a large green truck. Mielo could never forget that truck. It was like a green monster. The doors on the truck had big silver badges and though he had never seen them before, he had heard many times about them. This was what everyone called *La Migra*. The green monster came to a sudden stop in the middle of the playground and out of the back came a bunch of men who looked like army *Vatos*. Only they were in green uniforms with big yellow letters on the outside of their jackets.

The first two men came directly at Mielo and Roberto. They were both holding a piece of paper out in front of them. They moved quickly first, looking down and studying the paper and then straight back at them. Other men were going after Hector and others went to the school doors where Tio was trying to block their way.

Mielo had seen stuff go down before, but never anything like this. The first few minutes were like the riots when the Eighth Street Lobos went crazy mad on each other. This was big, green-hooded cops going off on a bunch of kids. It was a good thing too that most of the kids scrambled into the school office. Everyone, even Tio, knew it was the safest place for anyone to be. They had learned long ago not to mess with the sisters. They could tear you up without laying a hand on you.

"Sit down on the ground, children!" Sister Rita instructed.

Then looking back at the officers she began to scold them boldly, "Good God on earth! What is this all about? You do realize that these are defenseless children?"

She was now walking straight toward them. Sister Rita was a good-sized woman and the officers soon backed down as she squared off on them.

Outside, things were not so controlled.

"Come here, you little shithead!" came the cry from the redheaded officer as he reached at Mielo trying to catch his arm. His fingers caught a piece of Mielo's old T-shirt. The shirt ripped in the front from the neck down to his lower chest. Mielo pulled out of the officer's reach and ran full speed to the Bell Tower. He had remembered Roberto saying that the Bell Tower balcony was the place to go when trouble was going down. Today, trouble was going down like Mielo had never seen before. When he finally climbed the ladder and got onto the balcony, he felt good because Roberto was already there. He was low on his knees, watching everything down on the playground. Waving his arm in a downward motion, he whispered forcefully to Mielo, "Get down."

Hector was fighting off two of the green men. They had him by the arms and were trying to cuff his hands. Hector was yelling, *"Chinga la Migra, Pinche Putos!"* These were all bad Spanish words that they were not supposed to say.

"Hold him down. He is stronger than he looks," said the one who seemed to be in charge. The others called him, "Lieutenant Baca."

Tio left the trouble over by the office and ran to the officers holding onto Hector.

"You are the one in charge?" he said to Baca.

"Yes, I am Lieutenant Joseph Baca."

"Joseph, which was the name of the Lord's father, a good man. What is this all about? All of these children are legal. They have been here for two years at this school."

"Not this time, Father. The papers you gave the school inspectors checked out bad, false, illegal. I have warrants for all four. These kids aren't supposed to be here. But of course, you already know that, don't you?"

Tio was too smart and he knew better than to answer that question directly.

"Come on, you need to show some mercy. These are your people, and you know that, don't you?" Tio pleaded.

"Padre, you know what this is all about probably better than I do. I don't make the rules, but they do exist and for a reason. If you choose to ignore them, you take your chances."

"We know nothing about chances. This is all part of a church program. How can you march in here and tear these kids away from us?" Tio again pleaded.

"Don't play the church or poor migrant card, at least not here with me. But you and your Archbishop will need it later when we get into the thicker details of what's going on here. So again, you know how that game is played already, Padre."

Baca then turned back to help the other man when suddenly he was hit in the face by a shot of Hector's spit. Hector was immediately slammed with a kick. It came hard and fast in the stomach by the redheaded officer. It was a man-sized kick, and Hector started coughing and working to get his breath. When it looked like another blow to Hector's face was coming, Tio stepped in again waving his arms high. He yelled to the officers, "No! He is just a boy!"

"Stop!" Baca ordered.

Lt. Baca wiped the spit off his face with the sleeve of his coat. Then another officer took Hector by the collar and paused to look at Officer Baca as if to get his permission while he cocked his fist back.

"We have him in custody. That's enough for now."

The officer dropped his fist.

"Thank you," Tio replied.

Still watching from above, Roberto grabbed Mielo by the shoulder, "I've got to go get Elena or they will take her away."

"What should I do, Roberto?"

"Run," he said, firmly holding both Mielo's shoulders and looking into his eyes. "Now is the time to run, Mielo!"

Mielo watched as Roberto left the Bell Tower and ran straight across the playground toward the school. He turned back to look up at Mielo, then he shouted again, "Go. Now Mielo. *Vamanos!*" he yelled.

"Go where?" Mielo yelled back.

Roberto didn't answer. Mielo had always listened to Roberto when he was scared or in trouble. Roberto always said the right thing. So that's what he did, just what Roberto had said. He took off running from the Bell Tower. He ran as fast as he could, past the officers, out the Mission gate and all the way down to Sixth Street. He had turned and ran half way up Olivas Street when he finally stopped to look back. He could see the crowds gathering. He could still hear sirens and the other vehicles racing to the Mission.

He was all alone. He had outrun everyone and it didn't feel right. What about his brother Roberto? And what about Elena? Did they get out? He didn't want to be alone and especially without Roberto and Elena. So he ran back just as fast. As he got closer, everything came back into view. There were more trucks and cops with flashing lights. There were many people who lived in the Heights who were watching and they were yelling at *La Migra* in English and in Spanish. It looked like a riot was about to begin. Bottles and rocks started to fly with some landing on police cars. Los Lobos gangsters were beginning to gather.

A lady who was friends with Tio recognized Mielo and grabbed onto him. She bent down and whispered to him, "Mielo, go hide, go now, you can't stay here." She told one of her older kids, "Take him! Take him and hide him!"

Mielo could not remember the older boy's name, but he knew him from the neighborhood. The boy took him by the arm and led him away to a bakery truck sitting across the street from the Mission. He helped him to the top of the truck.

"Get down on your belly. From here you can watch and see it all," he said.

He was right. Mielo could see it all. He saw Baca who had Hector and was putting him in the green monster. He saw the other men, too, and Tio was following them and pleading them to talk to him.

He saw Roberto, who had Elena's hand. They were trying to break away and to jump on a slow truck that was passing by the Mission gate. Elena was not fast enough to keep up with Roberto and he would not leave her. The truck stopped and the next thing he saw was Roberto and Elena being dragged off to the green monster. Mielo wanted badly to get up and help them. When Roberto finally spotted him on top of the truck, Mielo could tell by the shaking of his head that he did not want him to help. Mielo thought that if Tio couldn't help them, what could he do? So he stayed put, watching Roberto and Elena being taken away, listening to the officers and trying to stay calm.

"We have three of the four in custody. Did you find the one that ran off?" Lt. Baca asked the redheaded officer.

"No. The little shit got away. He was fast like Speedy Gonzalez," he said.

"Let him go. We'll see him again later. We gotta get out of this place. It's going to hell fast."

"What about the priest and the nuns?" asked another officer.

"No. Leave them be. I've had trouble with that Padre before. He's connected with the church and this community. We would just be filling out extra paperwork. Trying to get a Fed judge to lock up a Padre and some nuns? Not going to happen. Prosecutors will laugh in my face. I'll give him the talk, but he's been around for a while."

Mielo could hear someone crying. He thought it was Sister Rita or maybe others on the playground who were scared, but he didn't know for sure. Then after Roberto and Elena were put into the green monster, they slammed the doors. All Mielo could now see were their faces looking out of the two little windows on the back doors. They were the faces of the last of his family and his only real friend. The truck started up and began to drive away. As the truck passed by him, rocks and stuff were hitting the truck from all over. Still, Mielo could make out the face of his brother Roberto for what he thought might be the last time. In the next window he saw Elena. She too was looking out a small plastic window. Mielo now realized that it had been Elena all along, who had been crying.

7

The Gathering Fields

The thing that Mielo noticed most about being twenty-one, was that time didn't pass so slowly and when you live in LA, a lot can happen in a short time. That's how it was for him living in the Heights and close to the Mission for the last ten years. Within a month after the raid by *La Migra* at the Mission, Tio and his *SOMOS* lawyer friends were able to get Mielo a temporary sponsor family who lived close to the Mission. Mielo had now become legal in the US.

"One month! All the time I needed to get all of you legal, only one more," Tio would say over and over again.

It was like he had let them all down and Mielo could see it in Tio's face and hear it in his voice. But Mielo didn't blame him.

It was true Tio had always come through for the four of them when things went bad. Mielo was starting to see that Tio was just a normal *Vato* like everyone else. Mielo realized that sooner or later the kids Tio worked so hard to help would have to stand on their own to make their way.

Sure, it felt like death. Losing his brother and Elena that day made Mielo feel like they were all suddenly dead. Tio was right. He always had a way of saying things, like when someone died. He would say "death is a punk." *I think he may be right,* thought Mielo.

All of the good people who worked at the Mission were shocked and messed up by the event too. Definitely, Tio was the worse. Everyone knew that things would never be the same for him and there was nothing anyone could do about it. At least not for now.

It had been over ten years and Tio had worked hard to find the three taken that day. Because of his close ties with *SOMOS*, he was able to learn that Roberto and Elena were living in Mexico and they were doing okay.

It had always been his plan to send his Shepherds into Mexico one day to bring them back. However, so much time had passed and when *SOMOS* finally made contact with them, things were different.

First, Roberto and Elena had married and they had three children. Two of them were boys and one a girl. So now, to cross the border with the small children was much more complicated.

The children were too small to make such a hard journey on foot and a family of five would easily be seen and be a target for both the cartels and *La Migra*. Now it was a matter of waiting it out.

Then there was the other problem. The problem of Hector. He could not be located by *SOMOS*.

Then one day word came back to Tio that Hector had joined a Mexican cartel known as *Los Zetas* and went underground. No one could back this information up, so Tio did not believe it.

He opened the wall safe in his office. There sat the knife that Tio had taken from Hector that day at the Mission right before the raid by *La Migra*. He pulled it out and looked closely at it. On the side was the carving that said "*Culebro.*" That's the name Roberto had long ago hung on him and now it was the name Hector used as a Zeta. That was his gang name.

Tio put the knife back in and closed the safe door. After that day, Tio never talked much about Hector, and Mielo tried to not bring him up anymore. It was hard because everyone still had a lot of questions about him.

Since he was now legal, Mielo had found a job which allowed him to move out on his own and pay for his stuff. Since Mielo lived so close to the Mission, he stayed in close contact with Tio and still thought of him as his closest *familia*.

Even though he saw Tio every week, things were different now. That day back on the Mission blacktop was a movie that played over and over in Mielo's head. Tio thought about it a lot too. He would always remind Mielo about the way he was able to out run *La Migra*. Tio would bring it up as if he was proud of him like a son.

Tio also talked about Roberto and Elena all the time. He would tell Mielo what he had heard from his friends in the south. The "south" was what Tio and his friends said when they talked about being south of the US border down in Mexico. Tio knew that Mielo was interested in Elena as more than a friend, so he held back for a while on telling him that she had married Roberto.

Then one day, Tio told him that his brother had married Elena and they had three kids. The first was a boy named Roberto, but they called him "Junior" so they wouldn't mix him up with his father. Then they had another boy named Rafael, and then another baby but this time it was a little girl named Serena. Two boys and a baby girl and Mielo was happy that he had two nephews and a niece. He was happy because for a long time Mielo had never had any family besides Roberto. It was a funny feeling to have a family and be happy about it, but also be sad because he wasn't with them and it made him feel more alone.

Still, life continued to change at the Mission. Back when Mielo turned sixteen, he got bored a lot. He started getting into trouble outside of the Mission. He was with a lot of different girls. He stopped cutting his hair and he started to buy smokes. He didn't do anything bad or criminal, but these things made him come up on Tio's radar more than he wanted.

Tio soon found ways to slow him down. Mielo had been hanging around and learning about cars from some of the old black men at the gas station on Fifth Street close to the Mission. Tio was connected to almost everyone in the Heights and soon he got the old men to let Mielo do some work.

Mielo took well to working on the cars. He got so good at fixing them that soon he only had enough time to go to school and fix cars. When Mielo looked back on that time, he realized that Tio had again made things happen in his life. With all the people Tio knew, they were all able to keep a close eye on Mielo all the time. Mielo was now so busy, he no longer had the time to hang out on the streets and that was a good thing.

With all of the cars and motorcycles Mielo worked on, people started paying him under the table and asking him to stop by their homes instead of bringing their cars to the station.

Getting his own money started new problems for him and for Tio. It wasn't such a good thing because Mielo could now get beer, smokes, and cool clothes. Then Tio really got upset when Mielo showed up at the Mission with a Harley Davidson motorcycle. Mielo had paid for it and rebuilt it all on his own. It was slicked-out with black and silver flames on the tank and blades on the wheel rims.

But again, Tio was a smart man especially when it came to the streets and kids. Every time Mielo did something troublesome like straying into the gangs or playing with drugs or alcohol, Tio would be on top of it. He just turned up the heat by providing a job and other challenges for Mielo to become busier each time.

When Mielo got closer to eighteen and graduated from high school, things got more serious. Tio started to let him know more and more about *SOMOS* and the work they did outside of the Mission. A lot of it, Mielo never knew.

It didn't take long before it all started to come together for Mielo. He began to understand why Tio was always working late into the night and why so many outsiders were always coming and going from his office.

He now understood why all the people from down south would show up at any hour of the night and why Tio would take them in at the Mission and allow them stay for only a day or maybe two.

It was all about this thing called *SOMOS*. To Mielo, Tio was like a leader of a gang. It wasn't a gang like the Eighth Street *Lobos*, but a bunch of older people who all worked together to help the poor people in the Heights and those who were just lost after crossing over the border. It was like a club, a secret club that tried to do good stuff.

Then one night out of nowhere, Tio asked him to take a ride with him to a meeting. So for the first time Mielo rode in Tio's old pickup out to what was called a "gathering field." These were hidden places where *SOMOS* would meet up to talk and plan out crossings.

Sometimes they called a gathering field, a "G" field for short. A G-field was usually on private property and offered by SOMOS sympathizers or where SOMOS would have to ask or sometimes beg for the space. They could be in a different place almost every time and hardly ever did they meet at the same G-field twice in one day or night.

They were places that were checked out as safe and where they could all come together to meet. They had look-outs who stood to watch for anyone who shouldn't be around or looked out-of-place. The G-fields were the places where they took in the crossers from the south and where the Shepherds could meet up with other Shepherds. Shepherds would lead the flocks across the border to the north. Because danger was always just around the corner, a flock was usually no bigger than five crossers and was usually two, or in some cases, only one.

Each flock had a lead Shepherd and sometimes a second Shepherd depending on size of the group and where they were going. They tried to avoid children if possible because they needed to be able to move or hide quickly. The rule was one child for each adult to carry if they had to run. But it was Tio who would say,

"It's more of a guideline."

Tio was more quiet than usual as they rode out. He didn't even look at Mielo for most of the time heading out of the city. Mielo thought maybe Tio was just trying make sure he knew this was a serious and important trip. Then as time went on, Mielo could tell he was upset about something. Mielo decided not to talk much either and it seemed to take forever to get away from the city and all the LA lights.

Finally, they reached the end of the paved road and passed through an unlocked gate. They turned up a long dirt road with a lot of muddy holes and bumps.

The further along the road they went, the more the side of the road was littered with plastic bottles, empty cans, wrappers, and torn-up backpacks. Further off, Mielo could see small groups of people with campfires. As they slowly passed, he realized that some of them looked like whole families.

It was getting dark but the headlights of the truck brought many of them out of the darkness. To Mielo, some looked like wandering ghosts. He couldn't see their faces very well, but could tell they were from the south and probably fresh from a border crossing. Mielo saw Tio looking at the people too.

"They are from all over the south," he said. "Some from Mexico, but many from Honduras, Guatemala, El Salvador. All in South America."

Some walked slowly as if they were sick and almost all of them carried plastic bags or water jugs. One of them stood out to Mielo because he had on a dark T-shirt with bright yellow words that read, "The Grateful Dead."

Tio stepped on the gas and as they began to climb up a steep hill, Mielo heard the pickup engine rumble and knock.

"Tio, you need to stop putting cheap ass gas in this truck. The knocking when you step on the pedal is because you are a tight Padre who puts crappy gas in his engines."

At first Mielo said that just to tease him. But soon he realized he had started something with those words. It was like the time Hector pulled the knife or when *La Migra* came into the Mission. Tio was so serious and didn't want to mess around with this stuff. Then he took off his glasses and that's when Mielo knew what he had said had started something more than a tease. He got ready for what Tio was about to say to him.

"That's what you think I brought you here for? You are my mechanic? My Harley rider who drinks beer? Chases the *Viejas*? And smokes? And who knows what you smoke?"

So now Mielo knew for sure that Tio was pissed at him, but he didn't know why and that made him a little pissed off too.

"Tio, I don't do no *pinche* weed."

There it was. Mielo had now said at least two swear words for sure. But he didn't care. He felt he was now old enough to talk the way he wanted to Tio.

"It's all over the Heights, but I don't roll with it. It makes me sleepy and the *Viejas?* What do you mean? I don't go out with old ladies."

"I know you are with the ladies twice your age," Tio said.

The neighbors come to me and say the older ladies all love you and want to adopt you. But I know what that means and what really happens when you go to their houses late into the night. I know who those ladies are and some are married."

There was not much Mielo could say. He wouldn't lie to Tio. He had learned long ago not to do that. Anyway, Tio was right. Mielo had been with a lot of the ladies around the Heights and some of them were married. So he knew that was wrong and he had no story to give back to Tio.

It was quiet again, for a long time.

It made Mielo nervous and even more pissed off. They finally finished the slow drive to the top of the hill. Once again, Tio made Mielo think about his own words.

Another long pause took place.

"Emilio, I say to you again, you have learned what is right and wrong. It is now in your heart and gut to know this. That is the most important point here. Do you know where the difference between bad and evil lies?"

"They are the same, no?"

"No. Bad is what we all sometimes do, even me. We do things we are not supposed to do. But what separates the bad from the evil is when we do bad stuff and we know they are bad in our heart, and we say we are sorry.

"Evil is when we do bad stuff, but don't see it as bad and can't stop doing it. Or when we lie to ourselves so we don't have to say sorry and then things only get worse from there."

"Like Hector?" Mielo asked, only to remember after he had said it that he was not supposed to bring him up.

Tio slowly replied looking out his side window,

"Hector? Yes, but it is our job to pray for that boy. The Lord says pray for your enemies, Emielio.

"But let me tell you some more about the bad. Remember the time you dropped the orange juice in the Mission kitchen? When it slipped from your hands and spilled all over the floor?"

"Yes, Sister Rita yelled at me."

"Yes, but did Sister Rita forgive you?"

"Yes," Mielo replied slowly.

"That's because she knew you were sorry and she loved you."

Mielo looked at him, trying to get what he was saying.

"But there was still orange juice on the floor, right?" Tio asked.

"Ya," Mielo nodded his head.

"Then Sister handed you a towel and a mop and you still had to clean it up?

"Ya."

"It's that way, Emilio. When we do something bad, we are forgiven and confession is where we as Catholics go to make good with God. But we all still need to clean up our mess. Everything we do is this world, good or bad in the end, we will have to answer for."

"When you put it that way, Tio, I probably have a lot of stuff to clean up. A lot of juice on the floor," Mielo said.

"We will all have to clean up our messes," Tio said as he glanced over to Mielo.

"So when you die, you can still go to Heaven despite the bad things that you say you have done. Because you have said you are sorry and have been forgiven. But first, along the way to heaven, Sister Rita will probably hand you a mop."

Even though the last part of what Tio said was a little funny, Mielo really wasn't happy. Tio had again made it all sound right and for some strange reason, Mielo didn't like it as much as he did when he was younger.

This time, Tio being right just pissed him off. Mielo was just getting used to the idea that he would never go back to confession or even to Sunday mass. He had decided confession was silly and he was pretty sure he could talk to God anywhere and anytime he wanted.

Mielo knew he shouldn't bring that one up because Tio probably had another crazy answer for it. So he just kept thinking his way through stuff and asking questions only when he was really worried about something. After all, the old man was right. Mielo was growing up and he would be making a lot of decisions by himself. Decisions about what was right and what was wrong.

Mielo thought they would never reach the G-field. Tio finally stopped close to a tree near the top of a hill. He set the brake while Mielo stepped out to light up a smoke. Tio was soon by his side.

"Have you ever seen anything like this?" Tio asked.

The dark of the night had fallen. At the bottom of the ravine were clusters of people with fires sheltered inside a grove of oak trees. A dark set of clouds were settling gently behind the hillside. The moon had a cover of light fog that seemed to touch the top of the hill.

Out of the dark emerged a boy who looked to be in his early teen years. He was young, Mielo thought to himself. He slowly passed looking at every move Tio and Mielo made. His clothes were dark and his shoes looked wet and muddy. He wore a light ball cap and a day-pack. He said nothing, but he didn't need to. It was all in his eyes. They said, "I am lost, I am afraid, and I am alone."

"All these people are SOMOS?" Mielo asked.

"No, these people are part of nothing. SOMOS is merely a small bit of help for them. They just want to find a job, work hard, buy a home, and raise their kids in peace.

"But for some reason they were not lucky enough to be born in a place where they have the freedoms to do that."

Tio was throwing his arms up now as he continued to preach.

"They are turned away and told, sorry we are CLOSED and to go back to where they came from!"

"Where do they come from? I mean, what's it like where they come from? I don't remember much about it anymore," Mielo asked.

"They come from places where water is like the gold. Where their floors turn to mud with sewage if it rains. Dogs in the US live a better life than they do.

"Worst of all, they get shaken down by sick gangsters and the corrupt Popo. They've learned to trust almost no one. If and even when they get here, they are like lost sheep."

Mielo continued to ask questions that Tio was more than happy to answer. "What happens after that?"

"Most are ignored by the Americans. They just want them to be taken away. *La Migra* takes them back to their holes. But we are *SOMOS* and we become like the Shepherds looking for the lost sheep. Just as in the scriptures, Christ too sought out the lost sheep."

Mielo had never seen Tio say so many words at one time. He thought Tio was crazy mad now like the preachers in the circus tents.

"We are *Somos Hermano's* brothers! And *Somos Hermana's* sisters! And most important *Somos humanos;* we are most of all, human!" Tio yelled as though others were listening.

He was on fire and was raising his fist in the air. Mielo had never seen him act this way. It was the first time he had ever seen Tio look like he was crying.

"This too is where I came from? I am one of them too, Tio?"

Tio looked down at the ground as though he was trying to gather his thoughts.

"I brought all of you to the Mission and things worked for a while. We were happy for a while."

Mielo wanted to know everything, so he pushed Tio for more.

"Tio, are you an outlaw? Does Popo chase you?"

Tio thought about Mielo's question for a few seconds while he slowly stroked his graying beard. Then he took off his glasses to answer.

"Emilio, some of the things SOMOS does are outside of the laws of this country. I am not going to tell you that it is right. Like I told you in the truck, you can now make those decisions for yourself."

Mielo waited but Tio paused for a second as though he was dreaming about the old days when he was a protester in LA. He must have been thrown in the *pinta* once or twice, thought Mielo.

"I will say that there are not always honest players in this game. People cut the cards to fit their own needs. And sometimes God's laws and man's laws do not always work in harmony. There are times when you will have to choose the greater good and what that means to you."

"I want to help. I want to be SOMOS. I feel like I already belong here, Tio."

It was true in his heart that Mielo somehow knew all along he would someday be someone who would help people. It was like he finally felt he belonged to something. He had finally found his gang to belong to. He now had a history and more importantly, a family. An answer for when he was asked, where is your *familia?*

He thought back to his village of San Domingo and the memory of his parents' deaths that day trying to cross that river. His parents had died helping others to cross the border. He knew that he was one of them. In honor of his parents, Mielo stood there in that gathering field beside Tio. He was now certain that he wanted to be part of something the same as Tio. He wanted to be *SOMOS.*

Tio teased, "Are you sure Emilio? You know what I have told you about being in a gang?"

"I am for sure, Tio. This is where I belong, helping you and the others to make things good. I will do this in honor of my parents and for my brother Roberto, and for Elena."

"Emielio, I knew from when you stood up to Hector on the blacktop that morning at the Mission and from when you outsmarted *La Migra* on the same day, that you had been blessed with the courage to be a leader. A Shepherd who could lead his people."

For the second time, it looked to Mielo like Tio was ready to cry.

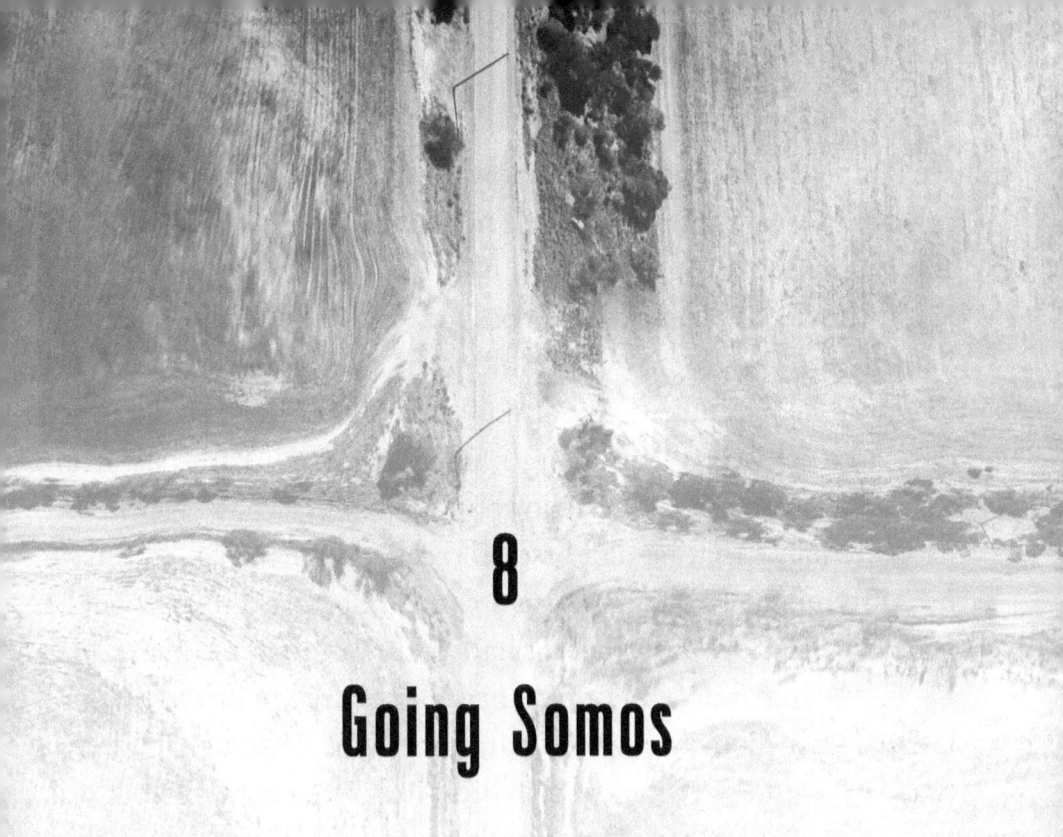

8

Going Somos

After that night, Mielo had no more time to chase the ladies or any other stuff. Tio introduced him to experienced Shepherds who worked with *SOMOS*. He primarily worked with Fathers Tomas and Santino and a new Shepherd named Enos Rivera when he went on crossings. *SOMOS* quickly took over his days.

He learned much and he learned very fast. He learned of all the gathering fields and the shortcuts. He studied the ways to avoid *La Migra* and the cartel. He learned how to smell out danger and how to defend himself. It all came at him hard and fast. Tio wanted to keep him busy and that's what he did.

By the time Mielo had reached the age of twenty-five, Tio was letting him cross over the southern border to Mexico alone. There he would meet flocks of two or three and lead them back.

He had learned much, but what was most important to him was to learn the ways of the cartel. Understanding how they thought and worked was most useful to him.

He learned things he could only learn from seeing and doing. So he spent most of his time thinking about what he had seen and to whom he had talked. What was strange for him was that every once in a while Hector's gang name, *"Culebro,"* came up from someone on the streets. Mielo found it strange that Hector had used the name that he had first been called by Roberto whom he hated so much. To Mielo, it was a name that caused respect out of fear. For the most part, Hector had a reputation as a bad ass, *mui malo*, but that was something that Mielo already knew. He had learned that from Sister Ana Rita long ago. Although he knew that Tio would never agree with him, in Mielo's eyes, Hector was forever broken. He was bad to where he could never be fixed.

In the south, crossers were called *"pollos"* by the cartel. The coyotes would round them up and ship them on busses to small towns like Altar or Juarez. Once there, they were stashed in flop houses. Arrangements were then made for more coyotes to cross them through the desert in vans or if there was no wheels available, they would cross by foot.

Some would pay from two to five hundred dollars to their coyotes who would usually then vanish into the night. These coyotes were at the top of the food chain and closely connected to one of the main cartels.

SOMOS was different. They were all about doing things underground and took no money from the crossers. They were all about protecting and saving as many border crossers as they could. In particular, they wanted to save children from the brutal abuses of the cartels and their smuggling business.

Near the end of his training, Fr. Tomas told Mielo about the tunnel that *SOMOS* had worked on for years. They had run out of time and money. Now the cartel had found it and were trying to finish it and take control of it. The last time he had seen it, the cartel was building a compound over the top of the entrance. Tomas didn't tell him where it was, but Mielo was quick to figure out these things. He knew all of the secret places to hide, and where to find rest, water, and shade. There was a code between the *SOMOS* Shepherds and that they kept it all within their own world. It was like a secret club.

Once Tio let Mielo out on his own, he found that he liked working for *SOMOS*. The crossings were never easy and each one had its own challenges. He was good at it and getting better every time. Another reason he liked going south was that sometimes he would run into his brother Roberto and Roberto's oldest boy Junior who was twelve. It was Junior who gave Mielo some of his best information on where the cartels were doing their shit.

It was Junior who was the first to tell Mielo about how the Zeta and the *MS13 Pachucos* were stealing kids and selling them to rich men. They would also use them to cross into the US disguised as a family. All of them knew that families were treated better by *La Migra*.

Junior was very smart and Mielo became fast friends with his nephew, often warning him and his father Roberto about the dangers Junior was putting himself into by spying on the cartels. But Junior didn't care. He hated the cartels and all the *Pachucos* who were like them.

Mielo didn't see Elena, Rafael, and Serena because it was too much of a danger for him to go in and out of the slum alone. It also took a lot of time when he was usually in a hurry anyway.

He thought maybe that was okay. He figured it wasn't a good thing for him to see Elena. He was pretty sure he still had strong feelings for her, but now she was with Roberto forever. He didn't want to go through any more pain. It would just make him confused to see her.

Over the next three years, Mielo focused on nothing else except being the best *SOMOS* Shepherd he could be. It made him happy to see Roberto when he could, even if it wasn't very much or for very long.

Over the next year, things started to change again. It got even worse for the people down south and for Roberto, Elena, and the little ones. Mexico was having one of those bad drought years again and the water was full of bad stuff that would make people sick. The government had not planned well and good water was becoming hard to get.

The cartels were taking advantage of this by controlling the supply. They were selling the good water at a high price. Most of the wells had price tags for anyone who needed to fill their bottle of water. Then government eventually stepped in and set up trucks to bring water to the people. Things were only better for a short time. Soon even the water truckers sold out to the cartels who would get the water first. It was clear that the government was being bribed and it just turned its head away from the cartels.

Things were getting more dangerous for *SOMOS* too. They were running into the bad guys more and more. On the last two crossings, Mielo had close brushes with *La Migra*. They too were beginning to hear more about the name *SOMOS*. They had stopped Mielo and talked to him. They made a copy of his passport and driver's license. Tio was worried that they were on to him.

"We're gonna slow down. Take a vacation. The *La Migra* heat is on right now. We're gonna take a few months to get off the radar and just let things settle down. It's too dangerous right now," he said.

With things getting so bad, it was time for *SOMOS* to retreat and regroup. They needed to figure out ways to be more careful about their work and how to handle new threats. Mielo went back to the Heights where he hung out for the most of the summer.

9

Solo Crossing

I t didn't take long before *SOMOS* went back into action. In the early fall, the number of crossers needing help was building to where Tio could no longer say no to requests for help. Reports were that many were trying to cross on their own without help. Many were also dying. They were dying from the weather, by drowning, or just being killed or swindled by coyotes who were connected to organized cartels. Tio was very upset about the growing numbers and finally he asked Mielo to start leading flocks out again.

This time Mielo would be given a special mission, one where Tio himself was emotionally involved. Mielo would be going in to find and rescue a small boy. His grandparents were close friends with Tio. Tio had baptized him and he had been a student at the Mission school.

Mielo would have to meet up with Fr. Santino and Enos just outside the small city called Leon in the Mexican state of Guanajuato. There he would learn more about the mission and how to find the boy. For now, all he knew was that the boy had been taken in the area of Acapulco. It had taken almost two weeks for *SOMOS* to locate him. He was now in a stronghold camp of the Zeta cartel on the outskirts of Leon. Not only would Mielo be working alone, but he would have to disguise himself and somehow breach the insides the *Zeta* cartel.

Guanajuato was a state in Mexico where the cartel were well established and Tio warned Mielo that he would have to negotiate with them to get the boy out. All of the Shepherds agreed that because Mielo was so young, he was least likely to be made out as *SOMOS* by the cartel. He would also have the best chance to enter the camp without being shot on sight.

Hector had reportedly risen to be one of the leaders in the Zeta cartel. He had been spotted only two days earlier in an area between the Mexican city of Saltillo and the Texas border. This was a long distance from where Mielo was heading. Hector would have to travel far in short time to run into Mielo. Still, this was a risk that Mielo and Tio had agreed to take.

To Mielo, this was a chance to show Tio and the rest of *SOMOS* that he was one of them. He could show that he knew his stuff and was good at it. Mielo wasted no time leaving for the south and left Tio to do what he did best, which was to worry. And for an old man, he was pretty good at it.

10

Morning News

I t was only the beginning of fall, but it felt like a hot summer morning at the Mission. Tio sat quietly in his office. This time he had on an old and tattered T-shirt. It was black and had the word PRINCETON on the front in faded gold letters. If you looked closely enough, you could see random old coffee stains on the chest area.

He never had anything like an award or a picture up in the walls of his office except one scribbled up piece of old paper that read, "*A single prayer can last forever.*" It was the only thing that he had taken the time to have framed. Someone important must have written that to him, maybe his father.

The rest of his walls were covered with scribbled letters, things like crayon drawings, and paintings made by small fingers. Most of it was from the little ones who came to see him in his office just about every day when he was there. One day, Fr. Tomas asked him why he never showed off all his college awards and stuff.

"I live for today. What I did yesterday is not as important as what I am doing today," he answered.

Most of the time, the people who worked at the Mission messed with him about the way he was old school about getting his news and information. He was always looking at the *LA Times* and the messed up stuff on TV.

"You can get all that information in seconds online or on your cell," Sr. Ana would say.

Tio was never one to give up on something he relied on for so many years. He had a way of sticking to what worked. He ignored his cell phone and his laptop. Even though he knew how to roll with it, he for some reason never trusted them. It had been two days since Mielo and the others had left to go down south. Tio continued to run the Mission, all the time trying to avoid running into problems with the Archbishop and the law. It was a tight line to walk but it was hard for him to keep his mind off the happenings with his Shepherds.

It had become very hot where Mielo had gone. Not only was central Mexico hot but they also had a water shortage. The papers were reporting stories about the water turning bad. The paper was late that Monday morning so Tio turned on his little TV. He pulled off his glasses and slowly stroked his salt-and-pepper colored beard. The worn cable to his TV was so frayed that he could barely make out what he was watching, but he could see what they were saying and that was all he needed.

The news was coming from a station in San Diego. The lady reporter stood in front of the car crossing at the US and Mexican border. Tio listened very hard to what she was saying.

The heat wave here and beyond this border continues to be a big story. We have this morning learned of another major developing problem for our neighbors to the south.

Prosecutors in Mexico suspect that one of the country's most feared drug cartels have switched their major activities from trafficking drugs to rationing clean water and most disturbingly, trafficking little children across the border.

Over the last three months, the US government has seen a major increase in immigrants fleeing the conditions in the Central Americas. They are from areas as far as Columbia and Guatemala.

The fleeing migrants have learned that if they come seeking asylum and have small children, they can be released within twenty days into the US to await their asylum hearings with a US judge. The migrants who come alone are held longer and face more scrutiny from officials. The cartels have learned quickly to take advantage of both of these situations: first by controlling most of the clean drinking water in the smaller and poorer boroughs, and now by kidnapping and offering the children to those who can pay for an easier time getting into the US.

This in addition to other organized illegal drug activities is building a formidable power structure for the cartels in Mexico. All of these crimes seem to be escalating out of the Mexican government's control.

This information was reported Monday by the Mexican newspaper Excelsior. Reportedly, Mexico's

Attorney General has launched two hundred and twenty-seven preliminary investigations against members of the Los Zetas gang who seem to be the largest and the most prominent cartel involved in these schemes.

Prosecutors also told Excelsior that dog fights and cock fights are taking place in Mexico City and in the states of Veracruz, Tamaulipas, Coahuila, and Tabasco. All of these activities are allegedly tied to illegal gambling. Officials from the Attorney General's office confirmed that the criminal groups breed their own animals for illicit activities like dog fights and cock fights. They also hold fights between humans that include boxing matches or full contact bouts in which participants fight to the death.

These allegations are not altogether surprising, but the reports of the Mexican cartels moving into activities like kidnapping, illegal extortion, and smuggling immigrants across the Mexican Border is a very scary development for which both the US and Mexican governments are reacting strongly.

Tio shook his head and then reached to turn the news off. He too was not surprised by reports that things were getting worse. It was good that the American press was beginning to pay attention to the problem. Maybe now the US government would see what has been going on for so long and get involved. Maybe they would see that part of the world as he did when he was young. It was a world where just staying alive from day-to-day was not only a struggle, but also illegal if one wanted to live in the US. It was where living on the margins means dodging bullets while people think about where their next bite of food was coming from.

He thought back to his father when they lived together on the streets in Durango, Mexico. They lived in an abandoned bread truck they had made into a home.

Tio slept on a wood pallet and his father slept on the floor of the truck. They cooked on a small stove his father had put together out of old metal grates and steel foil they had pulled from garbage piles. They used an open fire to heat their stove.

Sometimes Tio's Papa was lucky enough to find work for them cleaning stores in the plaza. After they worked, the store bosses would give Pedro and his father cans of food and old beer.

One night when it was really hot, Tio's father opened the back doors of the truck to cook. After the stove got warm, he tossed a can of potatoes onto it. Over time, the kids on the streets started to stand around watching like they were very hungry. Pedro quickly protected the food by standing between them and the stove. It was as if Pedro was saying, "Go away, this is mine."

Tio's father just stood over the stove with a hand rolled cigarette hanging from his mouth. Then to Tio's horror, his father started giving out cans of the corn, beans, and hash, one by one until he had given away all their stuff. When it was all done, Tio was mad and turned to his father to ask,

"Papa, why did you give the food away? All of it. We worked for weeks to get all that. Now what are we going to eat, Papa?"

Tio's father said nothing. Instead, he just sat down and opened a bottle of lukewarm beer. Then he pulled an old and worn out rosary from his pocket. He looked again at Tio as if to answer his question, but then looked away and down. He just stared down at the ground.

Tio knew his father had grown up hard, but it took him a lot of years to know what that night was all about and what his father was teaching him. Now those memories were a comfort to him. In some strange way, they were now happy thoughts. He smiled to himself as he wondered how he could have been such a happy kid even when there was so much bad stuff going on around him.

Tio prayed to God for those people who ate his food that night, for his dead father, and the lesson he had learned from him that hot summer evening. He then asked God to protect all his friends in *SOMOS*. He prayed that God would protect Roberto and Elena's family and that they might be able to one day cross back home soon.

His mind, though, was mostly on Mielo. He prayed the most for Mielo and all the stuff he was doing. Then, his mind drifted off again to all of them. All of them down in those boroughs. In the heat of those slums down south.

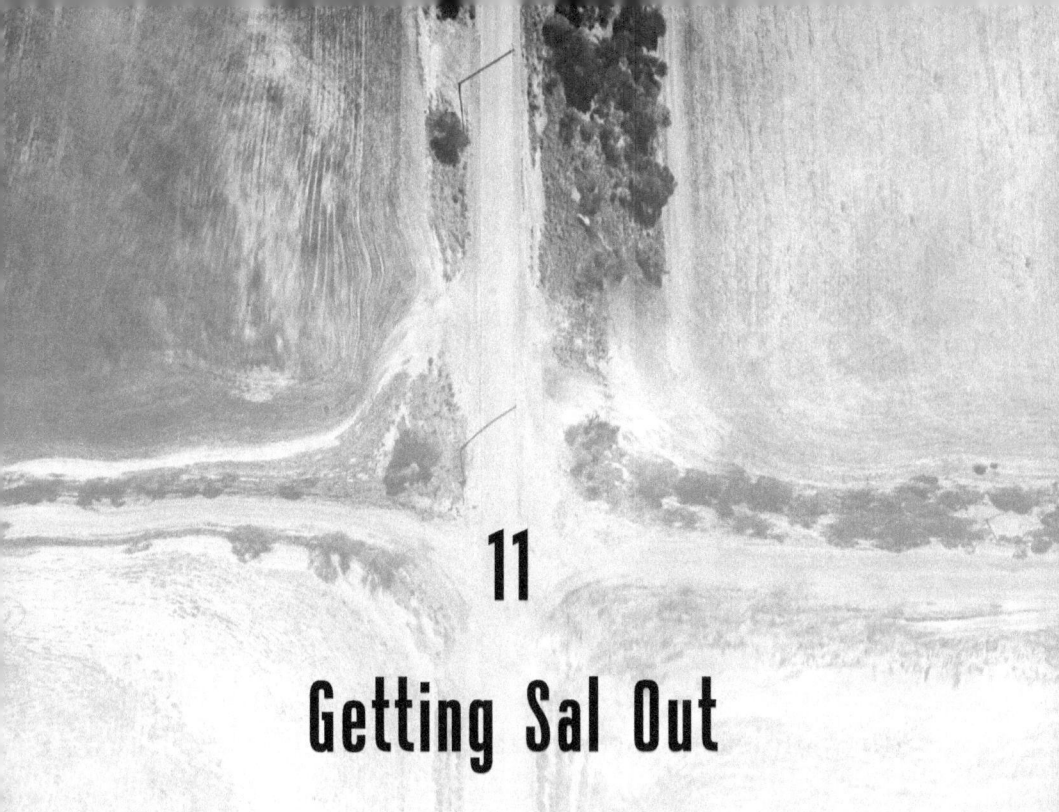

11

Getting Sal Out

Mielo remembered what he had learned about crossing with children. They could be a big problem and were thought to be high risk to a crossing. They slowed everything down and got sick a lot, but mostly they were high risk because they attracted the cartels. Stealing children was a passion among them and they would kill the parents, coyotes, or anyone else for a child.

They were even bigger targets if their ages were around six to twelve years. They would take them and sell them to mostly single men. They paid to make them seem like their kid. When they reached the border, Immigration would have to take them and keep them together as a family. They also sold them to perverts who liked to have sex with little boys. The men who bought young boys were usually very wealthy and connected. They were also willing to pay a much higher price.

Once Mielo had arrived at his G-Field close to the city of Leon, he met with Fr. Santino and Enos Rivera who briefed him on the important mission.

"Mielo, it's a long story, but I need to tell all of it to you. It was a family. The grandparents and a young boy named Salvador. He is nine years old. They got split up near Acapulco. They stopped at a food wagon, when a gang of three broke into their car and pulled the grandparents out. Then they stole the car, driving off with the boy."

Santino put his hand across his heart and continued,

"The grandparents are US citizens and very close to Tio."

"The boy, though, is not US. Tio and the grandparents all agree that if we get him out, we should try to bring him to the US as soon as we can to help him get asylum. If we don't, it could take more time and maybe even years to get him across legally. So for the purposes of this mission, he should be considered illegal," Santino said.

Enos took over the briefing with more.

"He was raised in Mexico by parents who were both killed. The father was a gangbanger who reportedly got on the wrong side of the Z-1, Armando Vega, who as you know, is the Zeta boss.

"At the time the boy was not home, but the mother was killed too. After that, the grandparents came to live with the boy here in Mexico until they could get asylum for him in the US. But the Zetas apparently changed that plan. So my point is that you should also know he is already on the Zeta radar. If he gets out, they will definitely be hunting for him."

"They will also be hunting me," Mielo said.

"The whole thing is going to bring down heat on SOMOS from the Zetas. Vega himself will be interested in this situation. Enos and I swore to Tio and the grandparents that we would go back and bring the boy out as soon as we could. It didn't take us long to find him. He was where we thought he would be, in the hands of the Zeta coyotes at a small camp just outside of Leon. That's about a mile east of here."

Enos started sketching out the camp using a stick on the dusty ground.

"We tried to go in there, but it got hot fast. Too hot and we had to get the hell out fast. It has to be you, Mielo, and you have to go alone. They have seen us and know our faces. You're our best hope to get into the camp, get the boy out, and across the border. Tio insisted that we have you go in," Enos said.

He continued to sketch on the dust showing Mielo the details and location of the Zeta camp. They all agreed that Mielo should consider using the tunnel as an option to cross back to the US, depending on the situation once the boy was out.

The entrance was within a mile and a half south of the small town of Campo, California. The cartel had finished building the compound which now completely covered the entrance. The tunnel had been widened and reinforced. But for most of the way, it was so small that even a child would have to crawl. They had improved it by adding some rest areas large enough to stand and stretch.

Santino reminded Mielo of the layout of the tunnel. He showed that the tunnel was almost a mile long and about ten feet below the surface. The lighting was poor and so was the ventilation.

"They have done some major work since I was last there," Fr. Santino said.

He warned that there are crawl holes where they had blasted through granite. The holes are so narrow that they can only pass by crawling flat upon their stomachs. There are areas that have some type of ventilation coming in through a pipe from above, but still most of the tunnel is hot and muggy.

"Most of it can be very dark if you don't have some kind of personal lighting. There are some battery-powered lights hanging here and there and if you're lucky, they might be working but don't count on it. Both the entrance and exit areas are well dug out and usually have some reliable electrical lighting above, said Santino.

There were lockers that they use to drop and store drugs. This made Santino assume that the Zetas were using the tunnel mostly to smuggle their drugs.

Even though the tunnel seemed all but abandoned at times, Enos warned that it wouldn't take long before word got out and the tunnel could soon become crowded.

"I didn't get to the end, but I can tell you where it was designed to come out. There is a hatch that is hidden on the floor in a large warehouse. The warehouse is in an area called Tarlow, near San Diego. Once you're out, you are in the US and the "five" runs just west, maybe half a mile," Santino said.

"Are the Zeta soldiers at the tunnel now?"

"When they are using it. Which is almost all the time now. So the short answer is, I don't really know," Enos answered.

Other than the tunnel, Mielo was aware of the other routes that he could use. Many of them were secrets shared only between the Shepherds. Only Tio would talk openly about these things and then only with the Shepherds or very close friends of *SOMOS*.

Mielo made a final call to Tio who also agreed that the tunnel could be the safest and fastest way to cross back to the US. Especially if they were on the run.

Now the only unknown was how the boy would react to being inside a tunnel and crawling through the small granite holes in a hurry. If he was being chased, the crawl holes could slow the chasers. This could prove to be an important advantage to Mielo.

The other problem was the heat and dust could make it hard to breathe and to see. All of these hazards along with crawling in a dark space may cause the boy panic and freeze. Mielo thought about making it a game where they pretend they are soldiers escaping. It was all an unknown and a risk Mielo would have to weigh once he had the boy with him.

Everything about this crossing was a roll of the dice, but Mielo could not turn back now. He had to get this boy out. He knew Tio would not have sent him on this mission if he didn't think he could do it. Both Tio and the grandparents were counting on him.

When Mielo got his final briefing from Santino, he learned that the boy's full name was Salvador Chavez, but he answered to the name "Sal." His grandparents were well-off Americans. The father was a childhood friend to Tio and had provided much needed help to *SOMOS* during an important and desperate financial time.

"The boy may no longer answer to Sal," Santino said. It was the cartel way to change a child's look and to train him through intimidation to no longer answer to his given name.

It was clear to Mielo and the others that the boy had been taken to sell to the highest bidder, either for passing the border or for sex if desired. Sal was very valuable especially if he could be trained to come back to Mexico and be recycled by the coyotes. He would then be sold over and over again. Mielo needed to get to him before that happened.

Sources deep within SOMOS had reported that they had recently seen Sal at the Zeta camp along with other children. They were all seen at night sitting in a circle around an open fire. A picture and basic description of how he looked was given to Mielo. The good news was that it appeared Sal was not locked up. They brought them out at night and when they did, they kept them seated in the circle around the fire. The circle was there so that interested buyers could easily see each child as they walked along. The circle was also well guarded.

They all thought that Mielo would need to come off as a wealthy man of importance. He would also need to seem perverted in his taste for young boys. The safest way to get the boy out was for Mielo to pay for him. The exchange would be costly. Even if Mielo was only dealing with one of the cartel coyotes or a soldier who was directly connected to the top, Mielo would need thousands of dollars in cash. Moving around in that area of Mexico with that much cash in his pocket was be a very high risk. The boy's grandparents provided the money in cash.

"Here is a picture of Sal. Tio sent it. He got it from his mother. They may have cut his hair and added a few things," Enos said.

Mielo looked at the picture, but didn't understand what Enos meant when he said "added a few things."

"They sometimes put tattoos or earrings to help disguise the child, and one more thing, Mielo." Enos put his hand on Mielo's shoulder. He pulled a sharp, long knife, holding it out for Mielo to see. On the side it had the name *Culebro* carved on the side.

Mielo recognized that it was the same knife Hector had pulled on him that day at the Mission in the playground.

"That's the knife," Mielo said.

"Yes, the one Tio took from Hector that day. He sent it here along with the money. Apparently, it's the one he tried to kill you and your brother with and the one he said he would kill Tio for if he didn't return it to him. I think Hector is now pretty messed up and big in the cartel. I don't know how big, but he is high up," Enos said.

"So, does Tio want me to give it back to Hector?" Mielo asked.

"No, he wants you to use it if you need it. Bargain for your life or for the boys. All the cartel will know of Hector which makes it very valuable. If along with some money, it may save a life rather than take it."

Mielo accepted the knife, looking at it closely before he slipped it into his coat pocket.

"Also,"

Enos handed the envelope with the money to Mielo.

"There is twenty thousand in cash. Remember don't let yourself be too much of a fool. The kid should go for no more than ten thousand. Hide the other half somewhere outside the camp before you go in. The rest is for your safe passage back to the north."

"I will be heading out to the camp tonight," Mielo said.

"And Santino and I will be praying for your safety. We will all be praying for your safety," Enos said.

It didn't take long for Mielo to get close to the camp. He soon found a tall tree near the camp. After watching for most of the evening, he spotted what seemed to be a group of boys being brought out to sit in a circle around a fire. He wasn't confident that he could pick out Sal from that distance, so he moved to another tree that was closer to the fire and pulled his binoculars out.

On his first scan, he spotted a close resemblance to the description of what he had been wearing in the camp. Mielo covered his head with a small towel. Then he shined a small light on the picture from Tio and studied it closely. The darkness and the distance made it so Mielo was not completely certain, but it was close enough for him to make his move.

Entering the camp, the cartel soldiers held up their rifles and aimed them straight at Mielo. The entire camp fell silent as he slowly walked toward the man who appeared to be the leader of the group. Mielo did not slow. He was dressed in expensive clothes and spoke English so that he would come across as a wealthy American. The leader was a Zeta soldier they called Chingo. He walked directly toward him and stood face-to-face,

"You speak English? How much for a boy?" Mielo asked.

Chingo squared his shoulders up with Mielo. They were now in a straight on stare-down.

"You like little boys? American? I do not know about you. Who just walks into my camp? You should be dead already."

Mielo knew that if he showed no fear, they might make him out to be the law or maybe SOMOS. He smiled timidly as though he was very nervous when he answered.

"Yes, I like to have my way with them. I want one of them," he pointed to the group of boys sitting near the fire. Chingo smiled wide and slowly began to laugh at Mielo aloud.

"You want your way? First tell me who sent you here? What's is your connection?" He asked.

"I know Alvarez, Hector Alvarez."

Chingo's laugh abruptly stopped. His smile left him and his eyes turned to stone as they locked down on Mielo. Chingo then leaned his head to one side as though he was looking at Mielo sideways.

"Again, what's your connection?"

"The *Culebro*," Mielo said.

Mielo had taken a chance that Chingo would recognize Hector's gang name.

Chingo challenged him further.

"Who the fuck is the *Culebro*?"

"Alvarez, Hector Alvarez."

"I brought this to show you. So you would know what it means."

Mielo held out Hector's knife. Chingo slowly smiled again only this time his face was more relaxed. He took the knife, turned and held it up to read the carved out name on the side.

"The *Culebro* has talked about this knife. It will be nice to get it back to him. What is your *pinche* name?"

Mielo gave a false name. "Ricardo Juarez, I was with him as a boy. He called me Cardo. We both were at a place we hated. I stole the knife back for him and was always trying to find him to give it back. I am returning it now. To show trust. I tell you now, I am his friend from when he was with me at the *Eighth Street Lobos* back at the Heights in LA."

"*Si*, the Mission. He hates the Mission in California."

He then put his hand out and pointed to the boys all sitting on a log near the fire. Mielo then pulled out ten one hundred dollar bills.

"More. A lot more," Chingo said.

Mielo gave him another five thousand.

"Since you are *familia* to *Culebro,* I will let you off cheap. Which one?" Chingo asked.

Mielo walked slowly along the row of boys as he looked close at each face for a match to his memory of the photo he had studied. Soon he came upon a face that matched. It was a young boy. It was Salvador. Like Enos had said, his hair had been shaved off and his neck wore a large tattoo.

"I will take this one," Mielo answered as he pointed.

Chingo signaled to one of the guards to release Salvador. Mielo slowly reached his hand out to Sal. Sal looked at Chingo who signaled for him to go. Sal then met with Mielo's hand.

As he walked out, Mielo handed another thousand to Chingo.

"I will leave the camp with the boy, and when I am done, I will then send the boy back to you and with more money. So let the others know."

Chingo looked at Mielo as if he was amazed that he knew how things worked inside the cartel. Mielo had been warned by Enos and Santino that if the other soldiers knew he still carried money, he would be followed and jumped.

Chingo took the money.

"Go," he said.

For the next two days Mielo and Sal traveled by foot across the desert. *SOMOS* had stashed plenty of supplies along the trail that he had chosen. He often saw larger bands of migrants being led out by cartel whose coyotes passed him off as just a young man traveling with his son. Mielo tried to talk to Sal but he was mostly quiet. When he did talk, it was about the frequent nightmares he had each night.

"The monster, get the man, kill the monster!" he would shout while he slept.

Mielo would calm him and try to help, but the boy still wouldn't talk to him. Mielo was pretty sure that he had been molested and attacked by other men or maybe other boys.

When they reached the small town of Castillo, they stopped to use the toilets and wash their faces. For the first time, Mielo left Sal alone giving him some privacy to use a toilet. He had stepped out in front for only a few minutes when a husky Mexican man walked in and spotted Sal's feet dangling in the stall. The man walked over to Sal's door and looked over.

"Where is your father?"

Sal had seen the man who had said those words before, at one of the camps where those men had made him stay in a small room. For a long time he had been in a room. He did not know where the room was but it was near the camp. He had heard that same voice in that room.

"Are you alone, little Vato?"

The man pushed the door open and grabbed ahold of Sal's arm as Sal tried to pull up his pants with his other. Then he slammed the toilet stall door back closed.

"You will come with me. But before we leave this room, you will do something for me."

The man then pointed to his zipper.

"My zipper is stuck. Can you pull down on it?"

Sal was frozen. He looked up at the man, then looked away.

"Here," the man grabbed the back of Sal's head.

"Get down on your knees."

Suddenly, the force of the stall door opening pushed the man's face up against the divider. Mielo yelled at Sal,

"Go Sal. Leave now!"

Sal stood frozen in fear. Mielo grabbed and pushed Sal out of the stall. He continued to hold the man jammed up against the stall divider with the door.

Now giving the man his full attention, he backed the door off and grabbed the hair on the back of his bloody head and then slammed all of his face into the pool of stagnant toilet water. He held the man under while he rolled a fistful of old toilet paper out into his hand. Then, pulling the man's head back again by the wet hair he shoved the wad of paper into the man's mouth and then inch-by-inch, he forced it down his throat.

The man's eyes began to spasm while he violently coughed. Mielo slammed him down to the floor and put his knee and the full weight of his body on the man's head. The man was now gasping to breathe through his bloody nostrils. He was pale and fighting for air. Then as he was near to passing out, Mielo pulled him up by the hair and again dropped his face to the floor. His head bounced hard on the dirty tile.

The man slowly turned to look up at Mielo. Mielo stared back down on him. Then with a final kick to the face, one of Sal's monsters had been vanquished.

Once outside of the town, Mielo set up a camp where he could safely light a fire and they could both eat and rest. Soon he and Sal were resting beside the fire. Mielo could see that Sal had not been hurt, but the fight and the blood on Mielo's boot and hands had shaken him.

Mielo knew that he would have to get Sal talking if he stood any chance of getting his trust. Sal had to understand that Mielo was trying to help him and not to hurt him. It was something Sal was still confused about. Mielo squatted down to where he was face-to-face with him.

"Sal, you speak English, don't you?"

Sal shook his head yes.

"My name is Raul, no Sal, just Raul," he said.

"No Sal. Do you know who I am?"

Sal looked into Mielo's face which reflected the flames of the fire.

"You are fucking *La Migra*!"

"No. I am from the US. Your grandmother and grandfather sent me to find you. Juarez is your real name, Salvador Juarez. I am Mielo. I am here to help you. To help you get back to your grandparents. I am taking you to them."

The boy then looked upon Mielo again, only this time with the look of relief. Salvador could now remember some of what the cartels had tried to erase from his head. His eyes began to fill with tears. Then, Mielo reached out his hands and felt the trembling of a boy who leaned slowly into his arms.

12

Slum Heat

R oberto and Elena lived in a borough of Mexico City. The locals considered it a slum and called it the slum. Roberto was gone and so was Elena's oldest son, Roberto Junior. Even though his name was Roberto like his father, they all just called him "Junior.". Roberto had left to find work four days earlier and Junior had left the flat this morning to get water. That left Elena alone with her two youngest, Rafael who was age six and Serena who was a year younger.

Walking slowly out of her flat, Elena could see that the mid-day sun was directly over her. She looked down her long street where most of the people crossed to get to the downtown marketplace. It was very hot and except for a few neighbors out doing their afternoon chores, there was no activity on the main street.

Roberto, Elena, and their three children were friendly with almost all of the people in the slum. This was the only thing that reminded Elena of how things were back when she was a child growing up in the village. Back then, things suddenly turned badly for her parents and now she felt the same was about to happen in her life. She was afraid that her young children would have to go through what she had experienced at such a young age.

Things were turning badly and moving in on her and Roberto quickly. Roberto had been driven away, not only to find work, but to talk to others who might know the best way for their family to survive these bad times. Roberto had turned desperate trying to find a way to survive.

No matter how bad things were, Elena made people feel good about themselves and like back at the Mission, people just wanted to be around her. Sometimes she was so beautiful and so friendly that it was misunderstood, especially by men. A lot of times, if she was standing around by herself, men would try to mess with her and say they would give her money if she left with them. She would always refuse. If Roberto heard about it, he would jump them. Elena would try to call him off, but he had a bad temper when it came to his wife.

Roberto remembered all that Tio had taught him back at the Mission. By the time he left the Mission, he had become a very good street boxer and everyone around the Mission knew it and nobody messed with him.

Elena still held a great love for music and at night in the center of the plaza, she would sing songs that she had learned at the Mission and some that the older people in the borough had taught her. Junior would tell her that her voice was magic because when she sang, the hat he put down in front of her would fill with food and money. For many nights, the sweet nightingale would pierce the streets with her tender voice.

But now, no one came to the plaza and if they did, seeing Elena so badly off just reminded them of how bad their own lives had turned. The Americans were no longer coming because they could not get clean water to drink in the hotels. Without them, there was no work around anymore and there was nothing that anyone could give to help Elena and her family.

Her thick, black strands of hair matted by sweat stuck to the back of her neck and around her forehead. She struggled to keep her shoulders covered from the worst of the sun's rays. If someone did come along, they were probably lost and not interested in helping her.

Elena saw a man walking towards her. As soon as he saw her, he crossed the road and stepped up his walk to move away quickly. She remained on the street anyway.

Staying close to her flat, she began to sing a Mexican folk song. In the plaza, she had others who would play the guitar or the mandolin, but today she sang alone. The sweet nightingale was at her best and her voice cut through the street noise, touching almost all that passed. But today, there was no one to hear the songs.

When Elena looked down along the dusty main street leading to the plaza, she spotted a lady who looked American walking towards her. As the lady got closer, Elena stopped singing.

"Senora, my name is Elena Estrada," she said in English and with a polite smile.

"Can you help me? I have three young children and we have nowhere to get water. Is there somewhere you can tell me? Somewhere I can find water to drink?"

She would be no help or even pause to listen. The lady did not even cast an eye toward Elena. Elena knew she had to try as much as possible to get help. She had prayed to the Virgin before she came out. She had prayed with her two young children before she laid them down to rest. They had prayed that someone would pass who could help them and get them something to drink and maybe food.

The city had barely recovered from an earthquake two years earlier when the problem with the water began. Of all the boroughs near Mexico City, it seemed that theirs had been hit the hardest. The government had struggled to repair the main water lines, but it seemed to Roberto and Elena that the problem with the dirty water would never end. Many people in the borough were sick from washing in it or drinking the dirty water.

Down at the Marketplace, they had clean water. The wealthier boroughs like *Las Lomas* had water and the people there had hoses that had running water and they could wash their cars. It was like the drought had not come to that part of the city.

Then for a while, the trucks were bringing clean water, but now they no longer came. The cartels had taken over many of the places where there was clean water and they wanted money to give it out. That's where Elena's oldest son, Junior, had gone today. He would have to walk to the well at the main part of the city to get drinking water. Even though the cartel was at this well, they could not force the people to pay because the city *Policia* could not be bribed. Junior would wait in line at the city well and sometimes it took all day and part of the night. If it got too late, Elena would be afraid Junior was in trouble or worse yet, that he may be hurt.

Elena had good reason to worry. One time Junior wandered into *Las Lomos* and filled his bottle from a running hose. There were private guards who worked for the people that lived there and when they caught him, they beat him badly. Young Junior was only eleven years old, but it was clear to Elena that he was learning about things that he was too young to know and he was learning very fast.

Junior had left earlier that morning. He wanted to get clean water for his mother and brothers from the well at the market place and be back before dark. But first he had to find a bottle or can to carry the water. The water bottles and cans had become hard to find now because they were the only way to hold water and all his neighbors needed them too. His last bottle had been stolen from the flat and so now he would probably have to steal to get another one.

Elena could no longer bear the heat. It had made her thirst worse and it was quickly wearing her down. For a little while, she was thinking about leaving to find Junior or maybe to find her own water. Then she thought better and her hazy mind cleared, reminding her that to leave the two children alone any longer, might cause them to panic and go out looking for her. If that happened, all of them could die from being so long in the heat and without water.

Turning back, Elena surrendered to the heat and went back inside her flat. Stepping into the shade of her flat, she was soon cooling down. Holding back her tears, she thought about how slow it took for the cooler evenings to settle in. Her two children were still laying quietly on the bare floor. The younger Serena was still asleep while Rafael turned, struggling to find comfort. Insects were on the crawl and a small flock of mosquitos swirled overhead. Rafael looked up and, reaching for his mother, quietly complained,

"Mama, I am thirsty please."

Elena had tried to teach her children both Spanish and English like Tio had taught her. Shaking her head slowly, she looked to the child and pulled him close to her.

"No, my baby boy, our water is no more. Brother Junior has gone to the well to get a drink for all of us. It is too hard for us to go out and too far. We must wait for brother. He will come. Rest now, it is time to rest, just rest. He will come."

"I am afraid that I will not be able to be alive if I do not have a drink now," Rafael said.

"My baby boy, you must be brave like your father. Your Papa says that it is our love for each other that will keep us going. Now don't think about anything. Just rest."

Elena slowly stroked his moist forehead while peering down at her other hand that held rosary beads tightly. She then began to sing and her voice slowly calmed him. Rafael dozed off while Serena occasionally opened and closed her eyes. Elena's mind drifted off to thoughts of Roberto and then to her son Junior. She wondered if they were safe and what they were doing right now.

13

Large Man

Junior had spent all of his day and most of the night traveling to the city and waiting in line to fill his bottles with drinking water. It was nearly sunrise when Junior finally made it to the well at the plaza. His dirty hand held out one of the two small, plastic drinking bottles he had found earlier in a trash pile. He put it under the small trickle of water coming from the rusty faucet. Behind him even at such an early hour, was a long line of others who were waiting their turn.

Slowly, the first small bottle filled to the top and with his other hand, he capped it. Then, as soon as he placed his second bottle under the trickle, a large hand slapped his cheek. Then another hand just as large sent the second bottle flying out from under the faucet. The empty bottle tumbled across the dusty road and bounced off the adjacent adobe wall. Some of the people in line chased after the valuable container.

Junior watched the bottle come to a stop and tried to hide that he was shaken by the sudden blow to his face.

"Only one!" Came a deep and loud voice.

Junior touched his cheek with his hand then looked to see blood on his fingers. He slowly looked up to see what he thought was the largest man in the world. He knew the large man had to be cartel because he looked so angry, and all the cartel gangsters looked that way. He had big eyes, dark and long messy hair, and a big mustache.

He held in his large hand a plastic jug almost full to the top with the water. The man took a deep swallow from it, recapped it and then set it down beside himself on the shaded bench. Junior was still holding his one full bottle when he looked across at the empty bottle and then back at the large man. The man then yelled again and this time loud enough for those in the long line to hear,

"Uno! Only one!" This time he held up one finger.

Junior did not know of the one bottle rule. It must have been made up that day by cartel. When he looked around to see the hands of those behind him, for the first time he noticed they all had only one bottle, but they were much larger bottles and some were very large plastic jugs. It was all starting to make sense why he was waiting so long in the line. They were only allowed one bottle, so they were getting as big a bottle as they could. This was just some kind of new cartel bullshit for sure, he thought.

Junior looked down at his one full bottle and then up again to the man.

"Mine is small," he said in English.

Like his mother, Junior had become good at speaking English and Spanish. He spoke in English to try and trick the large man into thinking he was smart and important.

The man repeated himself, but to Junior's surprise, he too spoke English,

"I said only one, you little asshole."

It was then that Junior walked respectfully straight toward the big man. Looking up at him, Junior squinted as he blocked the high sun out of his eyes with his left hand and holding his single full bottle up with his right hand. He said to him,

"Then I will give this one to you, sir," as he set his small bottle down beside the man's large one.

The large man stepped back slightly, puzzled that Junior did not seem intimidated by his size. Junior could now see the man was surprised and confused. This reaction gave him the chance to make his move.

"And I will take this one!" Junior said.

He then reached down and grabbed the larger water jug. The large man took a swipe at Junior, trying to grab whatever he could to grab hold. Just as fast, Junior picked his smaller bottle up and threw it straight into the face of the large man.

The full bottle smashed into side of the man's nose and mouth. A nostril immediately erupted and blood was now streaming over his mustache and down his chin. Junior then turned and sprinted down the road lugging the heavy jug tightly with both hands.

Some of the people in line were too startled to do anything. Most seemed to be cheering Junior on and some were laughing loud enough for Junior to hear. The large man and a posse of two nearby cartel soldiers gave chase on foot. Junior soon had a good lead and once he jumped the concrete fence line, they lost sight of him.

"Find that little *Essa* and kill him!" said the large man.

The two soldiers then took off on foot in opposite directions along the fence, each carrying an automatic rifle in their arm.

14

Junior's Problem

Mielo had set out a plan to cross with Sal early in the morning. As they were passed through the city, Mielo was startled by the sight of a kid in the distance running. As the runner got closer, he saw that the kid looked like he was carrying something heavy. There was a lot of yelling and kicking up dust. Then he saw that the kid was being chased by two men carrying rifles. The running boy was fast and as he got even closer, he looked at Mielo who could see that he resembled his brother's oldest son, Junior.

"Mielo!" he yelled as he continued to run.

"Help me, Mielo! They want to kill me!"

To Mielo, it looked like Junior was moving faster than the two chasers and would soon be getting away. At first, he just stood frozen and watched as the two men turned the corner racing after him. They were heading toward the central marketplace and Mielo could not risk the chance of being spotted there with the Sal. If Hector had figured out by now that his men had been tricked and that the boy had been taken by SOMOS, then there might be a cartel bounty on his head. It was a chance he wasn't willing to take.

As Mielo thought better about it, he realized it was Junior and that he was in big trouble. Junior would be getting tired running with that large jug. So Mielo knew he would need to help him and soon. After all, he was his brother's son.

"Sal, we need to help this boy. Can you run?"

Sal nodded yes.

"Then run fast with me and follow what I tell you to do!"

This time, Sal trusted Mielo and he stayed close running behind him.

Mielo decided to take a chance and cut into the old Slaughter yard which took up almost the whole block. He was hoping that Junior would be thinking the same. Junior could easily go around the front of the yard and come back towards him on the other side. The slaughter yard would be the perfect cover since it was surrounded by a high adobe wall that was built to block the public from the sight of the slaughters.

"Stay here Sal, against the wall. Stay down right here!"

Mielo ran to the other end of the stockyard where he was able to unlock and open the iron double gate. He stepped out into the road and saw Junior heading directly toward him with his chasers closing in from behind. Mielo's instincts about Junior had been right. He had decided to come back around.

"Junior! This way!" he yelled, waving his hands out and high.

The chasers began to take wild shots from their rifles. All of the shots missed, randomly hitting parked cars and breaking windows. Mielo ducked and took cover behind the cars as broken glass flew. When Junior got closer, Mielo ran to him and steered him into the stockyard where they quickly closed the heavy gate. Mielo then slide the sturdy ledger into place locking it closed. He grabbed Junior and pulled him away and down. Rifle bullets could be heard peppering the gate.

"Stay down. Sal, stay down." whispered Mielo.

Then he waved Sal to follow. The three of them slowly crawled onto the cattle decks and down into the slaughter house floor. Once back on their feet, Junior seemed to know his way around.

"Follow me Tio Mielo. I have been here many times. Follow me!"

Mielo followed as they raced up an empty loft and across a rusty roof top until they slide down a trough into an empty corral. The corral was surrounded by concrete walls with more locked gates at each end. It looked and felt like a safe place to hide while they rested.

All three sat against the wall for a few moments trying to catch their breath. Mielo noticed Junior still had the water jug with him and it was still full to the top.

"That's heavy," he said, looking down and pointing to it.

"*Si*, I have to carry it to my mother and my brothers."

"Now I get why you didn't drop it."

"Mielo, we have no water at home and we are thirsty and hot."

"Where is Roberto? Where is your father?" Mielo asked.

"We are bad. No work. It's hard to get food and now the water is so bad no one can drink or wash with it."

"And what about your father?" Mielo asked again.

At first Junior hesitated to answer, but as Mielo glared back at him a little longer, he dropped his head down and answered,

"He is with Hector."

"What? Hector Alvarez? Roberto would never do anything with him. He hates him!" Mielo said.

"It's a fight at *El Rancho Pollo,*" Junior replied still looking down.

"Who is fighting?" Mielo asked.

"My father."

"Your father is fighting Hector?" Mielo asked as he placed both hands on Junior's shoulders. He looked closely into his eyes.

"I don't know. I don't know if he fights Hector or someone else. All I know is he gets five hundred to fight. He told me it would give us food and water and a place to live for a while. That's all I know."

Thinking back, Mielo could remember how Tio had coached Roberto and Hector in the city leagues. Hector was kicked out of the league for fighting too wild. His temper would always flare up and he could not finish a fight.

Roberto was good boxer with what Tio used to say was "a good head." He had won some big bouts, but it had been at least ten years since he had worn the gloves. To Mielo, this was all about Hector trying to get back at Roberto for the younger years when they had stood up to him and punked him.

Hector was still no good. Mielo knew from stories that came back to him, that he had become worse than bad. He was maybe evil, he thought to himself. The whole set up smelled. The fight was a set up and Roberto would look like a fool. If Mielo could figure that out, then Roberto would for sure know that too. *Things must be really bad for him to take a bullshit fight like this one,* thought Mielo.

"Does your mother know about this?" Mielo asked.

"She knows he went off to do a job. But Papa did not tell her of the fight. He told me not tell her anything."

"Junior, we can't let this happen. I can get him and all of you out of here. Back north to America. There is a way. When does Roberto fight?"

Junior shrugged his shoulders and pulled a small folded poster out of his pocket. Mielo unfolded it. It was in Spanish and read,

"Saturday as the sun goes down at *El Rancho Pollo.*" This was three and a half days away. Mielo had just enough time to finish his mission with Sal and return to try to stop the fight.

"Do you want me to go with you, Tio Mielo? I can fight."

"No, I know where it is and I will find it, Junior. It is more important for you to go home to your mother with the water. You go and do not stop. I will handle this."

"Wait," Junior said.

"It is a long way for me to carry this water and all those *Pachucos* will be out looking for us. And you need to get back fast too. So I think we should take that."

He pointed to an old dump truck full of rotting dead cattle.

"They will not look or try to stop that. It smells too bad and they know what is in it," he said.

It took him only a few minutes to check for gas and to start the truck without a key. Then, what was crazy to Mielo was to see Junior handle the driving. He put two wood blocks on the driver's seat so he could see high enough and to reach the steering wheel. Then he rolled up old newspapers he had found and tied them around his foot to reach the pedals.

Mielo went out first to scout the gate and the street. It was clear. For now, they had lost the bad men who were chasing them. So Mielo lifted Sal into the truck cab and then jumped in himself. Junior put on an old cap and sun glasses and drove slowly through the gate and down the street like he had driven that truck for many years. Mielo thought to himself that maybe he had.

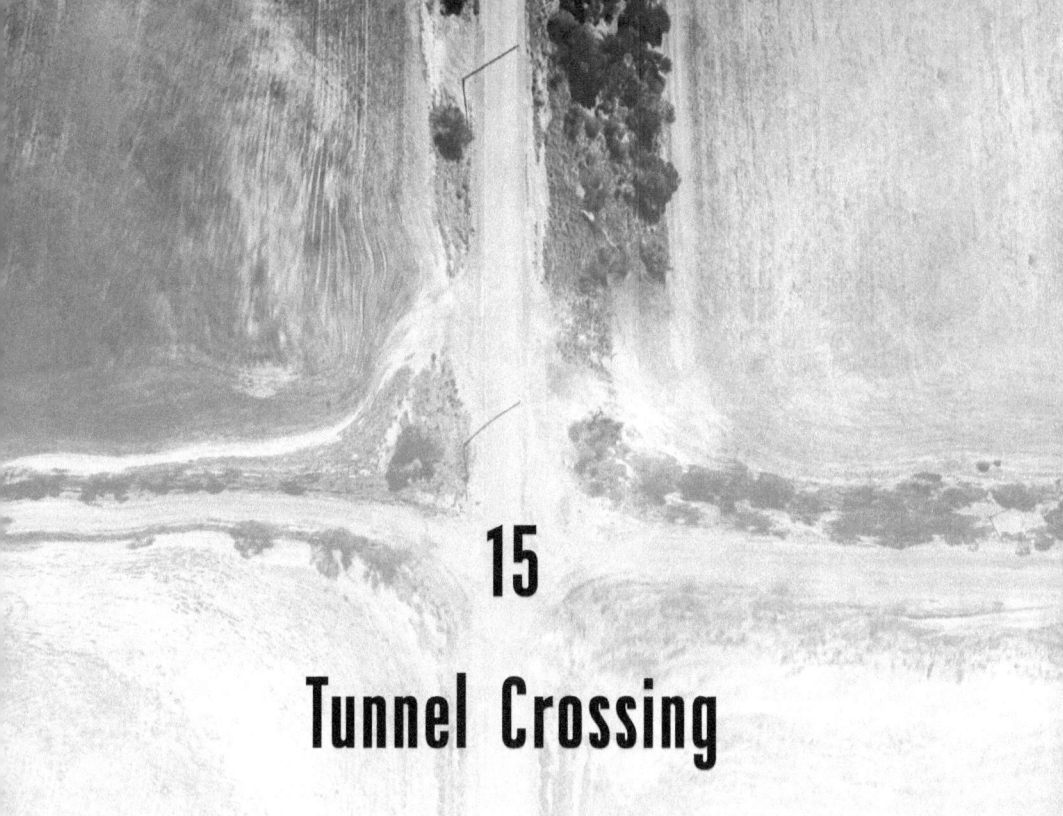

15

Tunnel Crossing

Junior had left the truck when they reached the dirt roads leading to the slum. Mielo was amazed at Junior's courage and his street skills at such a young age. He was right about the smelly old cattle truck. Not only did it cut down their travel time, but not once did the *Policia* or cartel look at them.

Even though Sal's grandparents were US citizens, there was little they could do to help him get back to the US through regular customs without a long and complicated process which included going to a US court.

By late evening, Mielo had reached to within a mile of the tunnel. He ditched the truck and made camp. Even though Sal had slept some while riding in the truck, Mielo knew it would be too hard for Sal to make it through the tunnel crossing without some good sleep. So both he and Sal laid down by the fire for a few hours.

When daylight broke, Mielo woke Sal and after they had eaten, he set out a plan to enter the tunnel and cross. The episode with Junior had helped Sal to see that Mielo was good to kids and this had helped to build the trust Mielo needed from Sal. In a strange way, Mielo was grateful for the interruption that Junior had provided for them.

"We are only a short way from where we cross. Listen to me, little Sal. We will be in a tunnel. Do you understand? Tunnel? It will be dark. You will have to carry this."

Mielo held up a small flashlight for Sal to take.

"You will be in back of me because at some times in the tunnel there is only room enough for one at a time to crawl. Let's make it like a game. We win if we make it all the way through. You will follow me everywhere I go. Okay?

"So stay close to me and watch or listen for me to tell you what to do and we will make it out to the other side. That's where your grandma and grandpa are waiting for you. You have to trust me Sal. Okay?"

"Okay." Sal answered.

"And little Sal, there may be bad guys around."

Sal stood still thinking about what Mielo was telling him.

"But don't worry, little one, I will be with you this time. I will help you to get around them. Just watch, listen, and follow everything I tell you. Yes? This is very important."

Sal shook his head yes.

Just before he entered into the tunnel, Mielo checked to make sure his pistol was loaded. Mielo had never been forced to use the weapon, but he had learned to use it during his training.

Self-defense would be the only reason to carry and use it. Mielo knew how to handle it and felt more secure with it in his holster on his belt. Quietly and to himself, he prayed that it would stay there.

The first part of the underground trek took three hours to cover just about a quarter mile. Mielo had to stop twice inside the tunnel where it opened up wide and had small lights. The temperature in the tunnel mixed with the high humidity caused both of them to sweat more than Mielo had expected. The dry dust was also a problem causing Sal to have coughing fits from inhaling it.

"I'm sorry. I didn't plan well, little Sal," Mielo said

"I didn't think about this dust and how much water we would need."

Because of the sweating, water had quickly run low, forcing Mielo to ration. This made both of them thirsty all of the time. Sal became confused for he did not understand why he could not drink water. This frustration made him more insecure about Mielo and he started to resist following his instructions.

By the time they arrived at what Mielo thought was the midpoint, he could see that the dust was now causing Sal breathing problems. Sal was now breathing fast and working hard to get his breath. Both of them were tired and dehydrated. Mielo did what he could to help the boy, even offering him water when he himself did not drink. Mielo too was struggling to concentrate on finding his way through the dark and narrow areas of the tunnel. For the first time, he was doubting himself and uneasy about what lay ahead for them.

The only good part of the trip so far was that they had only come upon one man and even Mielo was not sure he was connected to the cartel. It was at one of the wider areas of the tunnel.

It was an older man sitting alone in a chair under a light bulb. To Mielo, he appeared to be unarmed. When he saw them, he just looked at both of them and then looked away saying nothing.

"How far?" Mielo asked in Spanish.

The man did not answer the question. Again he sat in the chair, looking away from Mielo.

"How far to the end?"

The man slowly turned his eyes to Mielo. He pointed to the next crawl hole opening.

"The tunnel stops. It ends when you get there," he said.

Was this strange answer a warning? Mielo thought to himself maybe cartel soldiers lay ahead waiting for anyone to arrive at the next opening. Maybe the old man was just a lookout sending warnings ahead to others so when they arrived there, they would be ambushed and robbed.

"Are you cartel?" Mielo asked.

The man looked at him, but again said nothing. Mielo took it as a sign that he was not an immediate threat, so he carefully walked away. As he and the boy entered into the last part of the tunnel, Mielo realized that they had made it through a lot of it with almost no sight of anyone else. It was a sign to Mielo that word had not gotten out to the other crossers yet.

The tunnel seemed longer than a mile to Mielo. Sal's breathing problems had turned so bad that they had to stop and rest him about every ten minutes. There were times when Mielo was not sure if the boy was going to make it.

When they reached the exit area of the tunnel, Mielo stopped before stepping out. He carefully peeked before stepping out and saw two men. Each with automatic rifles laying on their laps. Looking closer, he realized that each of them appeared to be asleep with a loud fan blowing directly into their face. The warning that the old man had given him was sincere. Who was he and why was he there? It was a mystery but also a gift to him and Sal. Maybe Tio's God was helping the two of them.

Mielo's mind quickly snapped back to planning his way out past the cartel soldiers and out of the tunnel. Mielo could see the way out. It was through a hatch cut out between two beams at the top of the opening. He was hopeful that the hatch was part of the floor to the warehouse that Santino and Enos had described. There was a small ladder leading up to a small deck, then another ladder going up and finally to the hatch. The soldiers were flanking both sides of the first ladder.

Sal had become too weak to walk on his own. His breathing had become labored and noisy. Mielo was thankful for the fans. Without their buzz, the boy's breathing would surely have alerted the soldiers of their presence.

The plan was to carry Sal on his back. With the roar of fans blowing in their faces, Mielo could slowly exit the hole, lift Sal onto his back and pass directly in front of them while they were out. He would then move up the ladders to the exit hatch.

To Mielo's surprise, the plan went off well until the two of them reached the exit hatch. When Mielo quietly sat Sal down on the deck, he saw that the hatch had been padlocked closed.

He now knew that he would have to use his hand gun to blow the padlock open. Timing would be everything. He would have to blow open the padlock with one shot and then push the hatch open. He would then lift Sal through and then climb through himself.

After thinking it through, he realized that it could take long enough for the sleeping guards to react and come after them shooting. It was then that he realized the choice he had ahead of him: he would either have to kill the two men or take a chance where he and the boy would most likely be killed by the automatic rifles resting in their hands.

Mielo said a short prayer and then took his pistol. Jumping off the ladder, he quickly turned and fired off twice, killing both men before they knew what had hit them. They both fell from their chairs, lifeless. Sal had fallen to sleep and before he had a chance to understand what had happened, Mielo blew the hatch with his third shot and then lifted him up and pushed him through to the warehouse floor.

Mielo emerged from the tunnel with Sal on his back. He was now on the US side of a large and busy industrial park called Tarlow. The warehouse was filled with freight, but there were no others to be seen inside or on the outside. Once outside, Mielo made contact and was picked up in a van by SOMOS Shepherds. The two were then driven to East Los Angeles.

It was late evening by the time Mielo was finally able to reunite Sal with his grandparents in the parking lot of the Mission. A boy who had been taken by Mexican gangsters had now been returned to the arms of his grateful grandparents. As Mielo watched, he could not help but remember what had happened to himself on that same blacktop playground only twenty years earlier.

Mielo's mind drifted. What had happened to Sal during that long week he had been held in the Zeta camp? What had been done to break that boy in such a way that he no longer trusted any person?

Although Mielo felt a small bit of pride in knowing he had successfully completed a very tough crossing, he was still deeply bothered by what he had seen and the bad stuff that the cartel had done to Little Sal. Still, in truth, he was even more upset by what Junior had told him about his brother Roberto and his dear friend Elena.

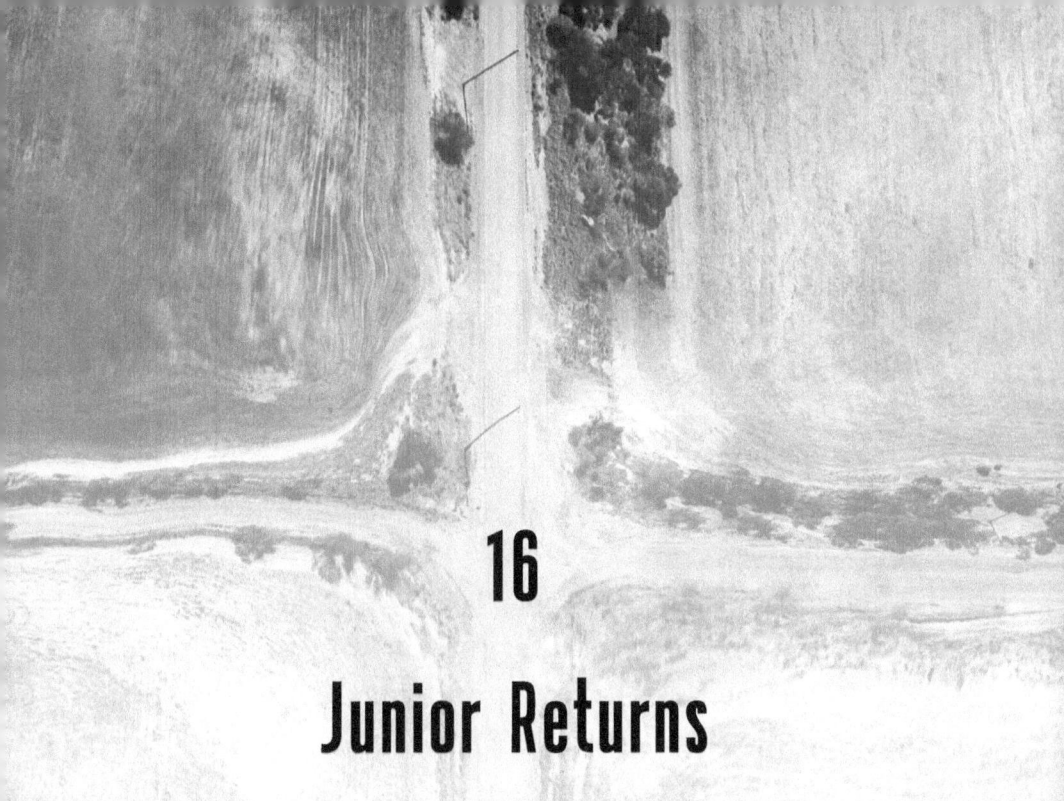

16

Junior Returns

Elena settled her children for the night. Both Rafael and Serena laid on their backs taking in the cool breeze that was passing through the flat. The breeze made the heat bearable but it couldn't stop the formidable insects. There were still enough flies and mosquitos bothering them that sleep came on slowly. As she tried to comfort them with her singing, her mind was filled with many thoughts about the safety of her husband and her oldest son.

By early morning, Junior did finally return from his task. He slowly opened the flap at the entrance. His mother looked up through sleepy eyes and was relieved to see Junior had returned and with him, a plastic jug full of drinkable water.

"You've found us, my baby boy! I was upset that you may have become lost or hurt," Elena said.

"No Mama. I knew what I had to do and where to go."

Elena noticed the bruising and the swelling on his face.

"Why the cheeks?" She touched them with her fingers. "What happened to you?" she asked.

"I fell trying to get the water jug from inside the garbage," he answered.

Elena knew her son well and she knew he was not telling the truth. She let it go because she was so thankful and pleased to see him. She wiped away the dirt on his chin using her spit and kissed him on the forehead.

Junior proudly handed the water to his mother. Looking closely at the water, she held it up and asked, "This is all the way from the well at the marketplace?"

"*Si*, I took it from a large man who was very bad. But it is mine. I mean, it is ours. We need to save the jug when we are done so I can refill it again," he said.

She then realized that he has not taken any of the water for himself. She smiled and the thought of his courage warmed her spirit to tears of pride. The two younger ones were now awake, sitting up and staring from the floor at their mother and the water. They waited patiently for a drink.

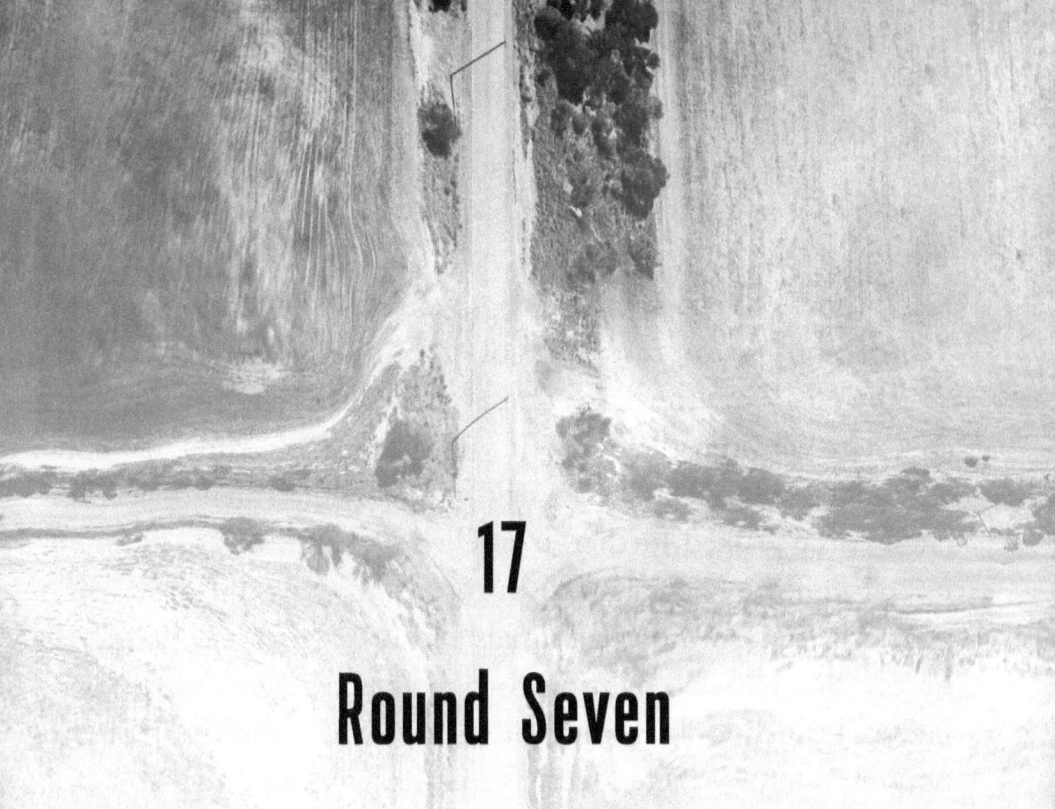

17

Round Seven

El Rancho Pollo was hidden deep into the rolling hills east of the city. Mielo was heading east on foot when he came across an unusual but welcomed sight. Sitting by itself and parked along the outer edge of a large hacienda was a stray motorcycle. It was an older brand, one that he knew well so he was able to hot start it quickly.

It had plenty of fuel and ran well. He felt a little guilty about taking some rich *vato's* bike, but the feeling didn't last long. Besides he thought to himself, it would only be for a day or maybe two and the donation was for a good cause.

When Mielo reached the ranch, he quickly stashed the bike close to the main entrance. He hoped that it would make for a fast getaway if he and Roberto were in trouble and there was a good chance they would be.

He loaded his pistol and put it in his boot. Then he stuffed a couple of grease rags in his back pocket. He was hoping he wouldn't need to use either one, but he just didn't know what he was going to run into. The rags would be good to cover faces. The gun was just in case they got deep into it.

The ranch was the perfect nest for the cartel gangsters and the gamblers who ran the show. It wasn't for Mielo though. As he entered the ranch, he was struck by the strong smell of chicken crap. As he walked further, it smelled like all kinds of crap. He passed fighting cocks locked in cages and pens full of snarling dogs. The noise from the animals and the crowd grew louder as he got closer to the fighting ring. Before he went in the barn, he did a quick look around for other ways in and out. He also needed to know where Hector's soldiers were holding.

Mielo first noticed what looked like a set of doors in the rear of the barn. It was being guarded by two Zeta soldiers who were sharing some weed and beer. They were wearing AK's.

It wasn't uncommon for the cartels to have escape routes for when the *federalies* would raid anything illegal going on, which was almost all the time. So if something like this was going on, the feds had already been paid to ignore it. If he needed a way out in a hurry, those doors would be the way.

He entered through the main doors and worked his way through the noise into the sweaty crowd. It was then that he was made by someone looking out for him. It wasn't Hector or one of Hector's bad guys. It was his own nephew Junior who was well hidden high above him. Junior had an excellent view of the fight. He had the reserved seats up in the dusty rafters of the old barn.

He was hiding behind a large timber truss that was jutting just above the noisy crowd. Yes, he was supposed to be in the city getting water for the family once again. But he wasn't. He just couldn't stay away from Uncle Mielo's action. He had given his mother the excuse that he needed. The truth was that they had enough water for another week and that he just really wanted to help Mielo save his Papa.

Junior was relieved to see Mielo finally show. He worked his head around the beam to watch the end of the sixth round. The crowd noise was so loud that it made him nervous. He had his cell phone and some ear pods on him. Whenever he was nervous or scared bad, he would pop the ear pods on and try to block out whatever bad things were going on with his music. This was bad. So in between rounds, he sat back resting his arms and listening.

He was now just kicking it and watching Mielo. He was waiting for him to make his move. He closely followed every move he made. When and if things broke out, he would jump in and do whatever he could to help his uncle and Papa.

By the time Mielo had reached where he could see the fighting ring, he was too late. Roberto had finished six rounds of the bout. He continued to push his way forward until he was close enough to see and hear Roberto's corner. Roberto wasn't boxing against Hector. He could see Hector seated at ringside and now Hector could see him. He was dressed in a black suit with a silver shirt and black tie.

It looked like Hector was the main boss and all the girls were getting him drinks and all his stuff. Mielo thought that Hector was probably the only one making any money off this fight.

His eyes were mad-dogging Mielo as he looked directly at him while he took long puffs off his cigar. Those were the same eyes Mielo remembered seeing that day at the Mission. That was the day they both went off and threw blows at each other.

Mielo knew the name on the sign posted above the ring. The name of the other fighter was Alberto Sanchez. He knew him as a Zeta. He was a major soldier and Mielo had crossed paths with him once or twice while on SOMOS missions.

Mielo watched Roberto move in the ring. He seemed to be dazed and weak. He had lasted six rounds against what Mielo thought was a bigger and dangerous street fighter.

Tomas had warned Mielo that Sanchez was in with Hector. Mielo had seen many fights before, but this was different. There was a way about Sanchez that was dark. He didn't fight by the rules, like Mielo had learned in the city league fights back at the Mission. Sanchez was all over the place. You could tell he was fighting in a ring for his first time.

Mielo had never known Roberto to fear any fighter or anyone who would come up on him. The Roberto he knew was almost fearless, but he could tell that Sanchez and maybe even Hector was in his head.

"Once the fear enters a boxer's head, it's over." That's what Roberto would always say to Mielo.

So Roberto was in trouble. On top of that, Mielo could tell the referees and judges didn't care. They had probably been paid off by Hector. The fight was bad. It was all bad and Mielo knew it was made to be bad.

Mielo made his way past the coaches to get front and center with Roberto's face. Out of the corner of his eye, Mielo saw Hector behind him on the main floor. He was still trying to stare him down.

Roberto spit bloody water into a bucket. His face was flushed and swollen to where he could hardly see out his eyes. He looked up at Mielo and seemed to slowly be coming around. Then he heard Mielo's voice.

"You're backing off from him, Roberto!" Mielo shouted.

When Roberto heard his voice, he started to pull himself together. He looked closer at his brother's face. Then he pulled up a swollen grin.

"Mielo? It's like an angel has appeared to me. Because it is like Tio and you trying to coach me again. Like the old days at the Mission."

Roberto complained about the sting in his eyes from all the sweat and blood. So Mielo grabbed a towel and wiped his face. The noise of the crowd was building. Mielo could hear them heckling him with loud and rough Spanish words.

Hector stood at the opposite corner. He was pointing at Roberto and talking into the referee's ear. They were working real hard to get Mielo out of the ring. Mielo went over to let the referees know that he was the brother and coach. As he walked back, he passed Sanchez's corner. He saw his coach hold up one of his gloveless fists. Mielo saw that Sanchez's knuckles had been taped to cover up large metal rings on each of his four fingers.

"These are fucking him up." The coach said to Hector as he slipped the gloves back over Sanchez's hands.

Hector looked across and recognized that Mielo had seen the rings. There again was that familiar nasty grin. It slowly crept from left to the right of his mouth. Mielo had seen that face many times and the message it was sending. This time Mielo wouldn't be able to stand up to it. He wasn't on the blacktop back at the Mission. This time Hector held the cards. The only chance he had was to fight himself. He had to fight his way in to get Roberto out.

The referees and Zeta soldiers followed Mielo back to Roberto's corner. They were yelling at him to leave the ring. When he got back to Roberto, a man in a gray suit had taken over his spot in the corner. The man was whispering into Roberto's ear.

"You got to do it in this round. To make the money. You understand *Essa*? This is round seven, understand?"

Roberto glared straight ahead at Mielo. Then he slowly gave the up and down head shake. Mielo cut in, pushing the man aside.

"Roberto, what's wrong? Is Sanchez in your fucking head? Can you hear me?"

Roberto didn't answer. He grabbed Mielo by the head with both gloves and pulled him in close. Mielo saw his mouth moving but with all the crowd noise he could not make it out. He then put his ear down next to Roberto's mouth.

"They're going to kill me, Mielo. Get me out of here."

The bell rang for round seven to begin and Mielo had still not left Roberto's corner. Mielo pushed back on the coaches when they pulled Roberto off the stool and onto his feet. He watched Roberto walk away. He was staggering wildly like he was on drugs or something. Mielo knew this was the round when his brother would be killed. Plan or no plan, he had to do something now.

Hector's soldiers saw that Mielo was causing problems so they stepped into the ring to help throw him out. They quickly had Mielo in an arm hold.

Mielo broke from the hold. He made his way over to the referee and judges to try to stop the fight. Shaking his head and holding his hands straight up high he shouted,

"Call it! He's hurt. He can no fight. Don't you see?"

Mielo could sense the crowd's anger beginning to build. The noise rose so loud that he could no longer hear Roberto or anyone.

A soldier cut in from behind. He pushed Mielo sideways with enough force to send him tumbling over the ropes and into the fight crowd. Those in the crowd grew close and took their turns punching and kicking him. The noise level grew even more.

Through all of this mayhem, the fight went on. Roberto was slow to square off. He was having trouble focusing on Sanchez. Sanchez landed his first with a hard left to the Roberto's right cheek. The hit instantly stunned Roberto. He staggered and swayed back and forth with both arms hanging down. Now, he was an open target just waiting for the final blow.

Sanchez began to dance and taunt Roberto. He and the crowd could sense the crushing defeat of his opponent. Then he cocked his right fist back to deliver what everyone thought would be the finishing blow. All were watching. Junior held tight to the beam above. Even the soldiers were lost in the final seconds of the fight. Sanchez threw and missed and then threw and missed again. Both times he did it with the purpose of teasing the crowd.

Sensing the end, Mielo made his move. Junior watched as Mielo ducked down low and slipped back into the ring. He grabbed the metal stool which Roberto had sat and then in stride he scampered over to the two fighters. Sanchez seemed startled and confused as he stopped to see Mielo coming at him. Mielo then came with a whole body swing as he delivered a solid blow of metal stool to the face of Sanchez.

The blow sent Sanchez face down to the floor where he slammed on the bouncing canvas. Sanchez lay still as blood ran out from the front of his head. The bleeding rapidly spilled its red over the white of the canvas. Sanchez was so much out that Mielo feared he may have killed him.

A hush fell suddenly upon the crowd in the barn. Junior pulled his head back behind the rafter beam. As the shock wore down to the reality of what had happened, the crowd grew in an anger that was rising hard and fast.

Junior pulled his ear pods off. He then backed down the timber truss and slid down a post to the barn floor. He wondered to himself what would be his next move.

Mielo had done what Roberto could not. What many could not. He had finished Alberto Sanchez. A soldier in the Zeta cartel. Mielo realized that the price for such an act would be a certain death sentence for him and his brother. He looked over to Roberto who looked tired but now mentally clear.

The crowd growing so wild was a good thing for Mielo and Roberto. Mielo pulled the pistol from his boot and fired up at the roof. The sound of a gunshot cleared all but Sanchez from the ring. With all this confusion brought on by the gunshot, Mielo quickly made his move. He grabbed Roberto and they both went down on the canvas rolling under the ropes and off the ring.

A bullet whizzed past Mielo's head. It must have been close but it missed. He turned to see Hector pointing and firing another round at him. Mielo took this as a sign from God to get out now.

Roberto followed Mielo as the two dropped down onto the dirt floor. The entire barn had now erupted into a full riot. Spectators were storming the ring. Smaller fights broke out all around. Hector's men fired more shots but this time it didn't have any effect on the crowd. While Hector's soldiers grew more confused by the riot, Mielo and Roberto covered their faces and then pushed on below, crawling on their hands and knees. Roberto was weak and his face was messed up, but still he could kept pace with Mielo.

"Get them, I want both. Don't kill. Bring them to me alive!" Hector shouted.

Mielo and Roberto were low enough to be out of view by most the crowd so they kept crawling along on their hands and knees. When they came to the end of the wall leading to the back of the barn, Mielo spotted Junior standing in front of the door leading into the basement.

"This way!" Junior shouted as he pulled the door back.

"How the fuck did you get in here?" Mielo asked.

"I'm here to help," he said as he held his hand out.

"Go Papa! I will stall them."

Roberto took his hand.

"Junior, go back and hide. If you love me and want to help me. Obey me."

Mielo shut the basement door behind him. Junior climbed back up to the trusses, and he was now directly above where Alvarez was barking out orders. It was near the entrance to the barn. From there he could now see both the inside and outside action.

Mielo and Roberto were now on their feet. They followed the passage and soon were on their way out. Once outside, they dodged through more of the crowd. Running at full speed, they scrambled over fences, tripped over cages that held fighting cocks and knocked over stacks of dog kennels.

Fast behind them were Hector and two of his soldiers who opened fire on them with automatic weapons. When they reached the bike, bullets were buzzing by in all directions. Then, a bullet hit the ground just beside them spitting up dirt.

Then another hit one of the side bags on the bike. Mielo started it up. Roberto climbed on. It was then that one hit Roberto on his right side just below the rib. He collapsed onto the back of Mielo. Mielo reached one arm around to hold him from falling. With the other he steered the bike away speeding south toward the city.

"Go! Go Mielo!" Junior whispered to himself from the trusses above where Hector and his men had gathered. Junior could tell that Hector was pissed off seeing Mielo speed off with Roberto.

"One of them is hit and bleeding good. Follow the blood trail," Hector ordered. "I want them to play with my dogs tonight."

Junior listened from above. When he heard Hector's rant, he decided right there that he would stay until dark. He would stay to see if his father and uncle would be brought back. If they did, he could help them escape. So he crawled higher up the barn truss to hide himself. He then placed his ear pods back in and waited it out, praying for Mielo and his wounded father.

Mielo could hear Roberto moaning from the pain and he could feel the warmth of his blood dripping down his back. He realized that he would not be able to go much further without stopping to care for his brother.

He pushed on with the stolen bike until he recognized an old G-field off the main road. He pulled off and drove along a dry creek bed until they reached a wash out beach. Mielo remembered from past crossings that the area had a small spring and it was surrounded by thick brush which would make for good cover.

Still, Mielo heard Hector's men in pickups and off road bikes racing up and down the main road. They were close. It would not be long before Hector's men would figure out where they were and find them. Mielo slowly pulled Roberto off the bike and laid him on the sand.

"I'm hit, bro. I'm bleeding like a pig," Roberto said as he lifted his hand from the bullet wound on his side. It was covered and dripping with blood.

"Listen Mielo, they will follow the blood trail. You have to leave me."

Mielo did not answer. He hurried off to the spring to soak the rag and fill his canteen. He gave Roberto two long swallows of the cold water while he began to clean the wound. He placed the rags over the wound and then ripped his shirt and tied it tightly around the rags to try and slow the bleeding. Roberto looked up at Mielo through his swollen eyes and cheeks.

"So Mielo is a gangsta now?" he asked with a weak laugh.

"He packs a *pistola*?"

"This is not the time to fuck around, Roberto."

Roberto laughed again trying to calm his little brother, but he broke into a cough that brought up blood. Mielo wiped the blood out of his mouth.

"They may have hit part of a lung," Mielo said.

"Mielo, listen to me!" Roberto reached up and grabbed Mielo's arm. He turned his eyes away from the wound to his brother.

"I will be okay. The bleeding is stopped. Now like you said, I am not fucking around. I can't go anymore and they will track me no matter where we go."

"They will kill you if they catch us," Mielo said.

"No, I will talk them out of it," Roberto teased.

"I know Hector. He wants me alive."

This time Roberto's laugh was a lot weaker.

"He wants me alive so he can fuck with me."

"But for you, the best thing is to go right now."

Mielo thought about Elena and the two little ones. They were now in as much trouble as the two of them.

"Yes Mielo! Get to my wife and the babies. You know Hector has already put a hit out for them." He pressed his fingers hard into Mielo's arm.

"The first place he will send his *Pachucos* is to the slum. You have to go! You have to go now; we are almost out of time."

"I can't leave you again," Mielo said.

"You are saving me if you save my family. I swear, Hector will not kill me. I will find my way out. Now go. *Vamanos!*" He let go of Mielo's arm and waved him away.

Mielo then reached down to hold his brother briefly. Roberto then pushed him away. They glared at one another. A moment of hesitation again crept back to Mielo.

"I will leave this with you," Mielo said as he laid his canteen of water at Roberto's side.

"No." Roberto picked it up and pushed it back into Mielo.

"You will need it. It may save your life. It may save my family's life. Go! Now go!" again Roberto shouted pointing to the bike.

Mielo's eyes began to swell with water. He turned and raced toward the bike. He jumped onto it. It started and then he was off flying down the dry creek bed. Roberto could only watch as a cloud of dust followed slowly behind.

It was only minutes later that Roberto was surrounded by automatic rifles. Hector's men followed their boss's order and did not kill him. They loaded him onto the bed of a pickup truck and took him back to the barn at *El Rancho Pollo* where Hector waited for him. Junior too.

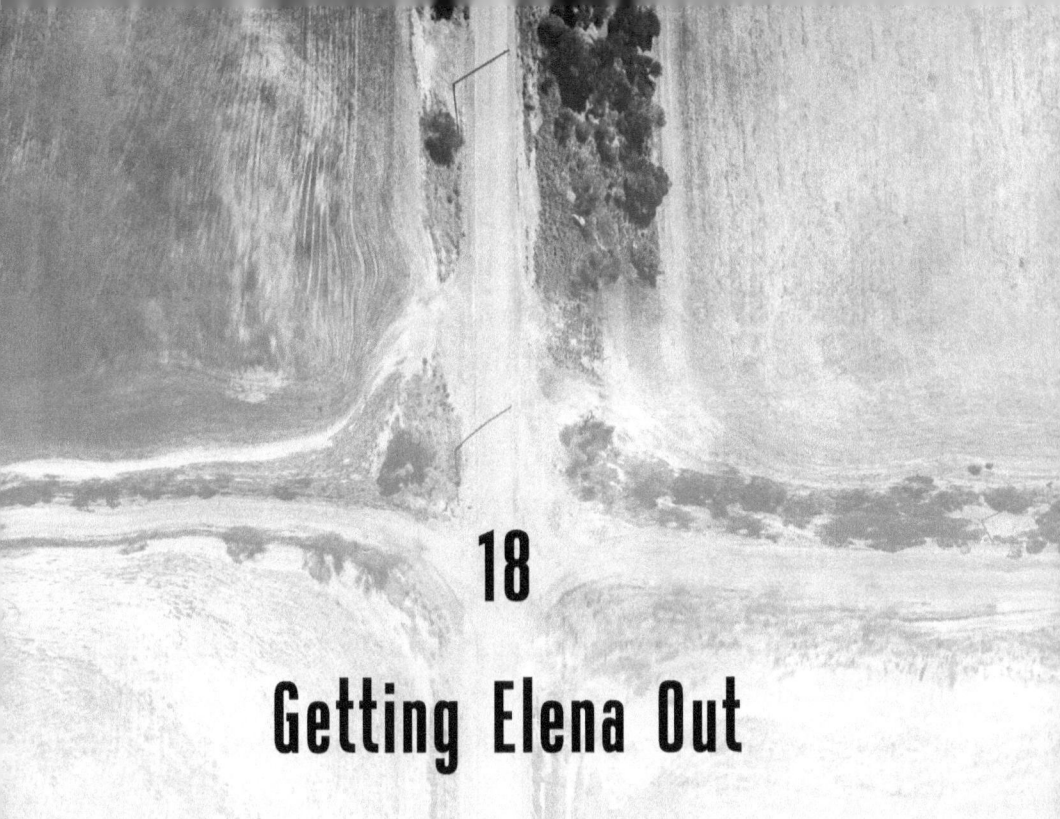

18

Getting Elena Out

Roberto and Elena had lived in many homes as they grew up, but the flat they lived in now was hardly a home, except to Roberto. It had been built by Roberto after his uncle died and turned the small lot over to him. No one really knew who owned the ground. It was all about who was occupying the space at the time and who took it over when someone left. There just wasn't a lot of demand for ground in the slum.

There were also no rules. Most of the homes existed in clusters of ramshackle flats protruding across the hills in random order.

When Mielo entered the slum, he took it all in slowly. Just like last night, it would be a long and dangerous morning. The sun was unfolding itself before his weary eyes. It stood out through a thick layer of smog that was holding still in the east. It was all very orange and the long morning shadows cast by the flats could not hold off the merciless heat. Mielo quietly complained to himself about another hot day.

Just as the break of the morning had been no friend, the long and dangerous night had also taken its toll on Mielo. He had run the entire night racing toward Elena's flat staying barely a half-step ahead of Hector's henchmen. His only leverage had been the good luck of a stolen motorbike. The bike had given him the break he needed to stay off the main roads to avoid the cartel. It also helped him make good time and time was important. When the bike had finally run its course, when the tank had run dry and the wheels stopped rolling, Mielo dismounted and walked the last couple of miles.

He was hungry and his water was running low. He had a small pouch with some jerky meat and half a canteen of water left. This made for his breakfast. He stopped only for a short time to rest while he ate and drank the last of it. Then he looked to the sky to figure his time. There wouldn't be much time for his stop with Elena. He just needed to get her and the two little ones out. They needed to be fast on their way to the first G-field they could find.

Suddenly Mielo thought of Junior. He realized that if he hadn't made it back yet, they would have to leave out without him. Even though it bothered him to have to leave Junior, he had no choice. He had to take Elena and the two and leave right away to protect their lives. It was the right choice. As much as that bothered him, it bothered him more to be the one to put Elena in the same situation. She too would realize a choice had to be made. Not a good choice but the right one.

Rafael was first to see the stranger approaching the flat.

"Papa!" he yelled only to realize it was someone who looked like his Papa, especially from far away.

Rattled by his mistake, Rafael ran back to take cover behind the leg of his mother. Elena stood startled as well. In fact she was frozen at her first glance. Then slowly she melted away into tears as she ran to Mielo and embraced her dear friend.

"Mielo! I can't believe what I am seeing! I thought I was seeing a miracle. Because I never thought I would see you again."

"It's just the same for me," Mielo said.

Mielo struggled with what he was feeling and was slow to respond. He did not embrace her back. The thought of his brother made him feel badly about feeling good in her embrace.

Elena could sense that something was wrong. She slowly backed off and focused her dark penetrating eyes onto Mielo.

All expression drained from her face as she realized why he had come to her flat.

"What has happened to Roberto?" she asked.

Mielo looked away at first. It was a thing he did with his head and his face when he was uneasy. Elena remembered and picked up on that as well. She turned again to look at him more directly.

"Tell me, my friend, is he dead?"

"Not Roberto. No," Mielo said.

"Then why are you here?"

"He sent me."

"Mielo, then tell me what is wrong?" she asked.

Mielo looked away and down to Serena and Rafael. They both looked like her, he thought to himself. He handed his canteen to them.

They both looked back up to their mother, unsure if they should drink.

"Only a few swallows and slowly," Elena said.

Rafael took the canteen and handed it to Serena. Elena and Mielo stepped away so the little ones could no longer hear them. Mielo looked around the flat and asked about Junior.

"He has gone for more water. He will not be back until after dark," she answered.

"Mielo, what has happened to Roberto?"

"He is in trouble. He was boxing and things went bad."

"Tell me more."

"It was Hector. It was a fight that he set up. Hector said he would pay him and that's why Roberto took it."

"He knows I would not want him to do anything for Hector. Hector is with very bad people now," she said.

"He got shot in the side. Things went bad and now Hector is pissed. I left Roberto alive but I think Hector's men took him and they are now hunting all of us."

He reached to hold Elena's hand.

"We are all in danger right now. That's why I am here. I told Roberto I would take you and the children away with me."

Elena's face, even now in the midst of all the distress and with no way to take care of herself, was stunning to Mielo. He quickly turned his head away when she found him glaring at her. After an awkward moment of quiet passed, he told her more.

"It was a trap set by Hector. They were going to make a lot of money if their boxer killed Roberto in Round Seven. But we had to blow the whole thing up. We stopped the fight. Then I got Roberto out and now Hector lost a lot of money."

"Where is Roberto now?" she asked.

Mielo looked down at the ground again.

"I had to leave him. I think Hector got him after I left. I believe he is alive and so is Junior. I don't know exactly where they are, but this all happened just outside of the city at the cartel ranch called *El Rancho Pollo*."

Elena seemed puzzled. It was so much coming at her at one time. She did not answer. Mielo started to continue,

"I wouldn't leave. . ."

But Elena cut in, "Wait. What do you mean when you say, so is Junior?"

Mielo began again. "Junior was there at the ranch. I don't have time to tell you everything. We need to get out of here."

"Are they both alive? Are they okay? I have to know that."

"Roberto told me to leave, Elena. He made me leave. He was injured and could not go on. He wanted me to escape and come for you and the children. He wanted me to get you out."

"I have so many questions still. How bad is Roberto's wound? What about my boy Junior? Is there time for me to put some things together?"

"No, the next people to enter this home will be cartel. If we stay here, we will die. All of us will be killed. Tio Pedro and I have put together a plan. He will help us."

Mielo began to look around for anything he could grab to take with him on the trip.

"Elena. I need you to be the strong one again. There is more hard news."

"What?"

"The Shepherds who leave tonight cannot take children. So we will be alone on our crossing. We will have to carry the two little ones on our backs."

"We can do that. I have two packs for them."

"But. . ." Mielo said.

"Yes. What else? You have more?"

"Elena, Junior is not at the plaza getting water. Like I said, he was at the fight."

"At the fight? Junior?" Elena asked.

"Yes, he helped Roberto and me to escape from the ranch. We cannot wait for him to return."

Elena stood stunned. Her face was struck with pain.

"I cannot leave a child here!" she said.

Mielo was also upset about leaving Junior. Though he had learned to respect Junior's ways and in his heart, he felt Junior would survive and maybe even make it back to them in LA.

"Elena, it comes down to a decision. Do you want to live? Do you want your two youngest to have a chance at getting out? Or do you want to wait for Junior's return and risk all of us to be killed?"

Mielo was now filling his satchel with food from Elena's small supply.

"There is no more time. I will tell you the rest when we are on our way," Mielo said.

It was all beginning to sink in for Elena. They were all in great danger. She quickly understood that what she did over the next few minutes could be the difference between living and dying.

"Do you have any guns, knives, or anything? Did Roberto hide anything?" Mielo asked.

"A *pistola?*" she answered as she reached under the bed grate to find nothing.

"It is gone. Junior!"

"That is good." Mielo said. "Junior needs it more. See Elena, the Lord will watch out for him. I have been with him and in some very bad places. I believe he is blessed and protected in a special way by the Virgin that you pray to."

Elena looked down at the rosary beads in her hand. Tio had given the rosary to her on the day she had been the brunt of a school prank. That prank, so many years ago, that caused her to question Mielo's loyalty as her closest friend.

Even though they were very young at the time, she could never understand why Mielo would betray her for a schoolyard laugh. Now she felt that friendship could be born again. The two of them would have the chance to show one another who they really were.

Elena had reached the point of accepting what was at stake for her and the children. She was grateful that Mielo had come and was willing to lay his life down for them. She quickly rolled clothes into blankets. Then Mielo and she wrapped Serena and Rafael each in a papoose pack.

They left through the back of the flat to avoid being seen. Quietly they scampered down the back streets. Once again after so many years, Elena was heading north to this place called America.

Elena carried Serena and Mielo had Rafael. The first hours of the trip, there were moments where Elena would stop and cover her face. The thought of Roberto and Junior was tearing at her soul. *Watching her weep just made everything harder,* thought Mielo.

When they were far enough away, Mielo stopped under a large tree to give Elena some time to gather herself.

"I am afraid I will lose all of you. So many die," Elena cried.

"Elena, we will cross into America. You will see Junior again. I promised this to Roberto and I promise to you the same."

Mielo slowly placed his hand onto Elena's tender shoulder and soon found himself holding her in his arms. To Mielo, it felt strange. It felt wrong. He was unsettled again by the feelings that rushed to his head, but when he felt the warmth of her body and her moist tears on his neck and shoulders, he knew it was the right thing to do.

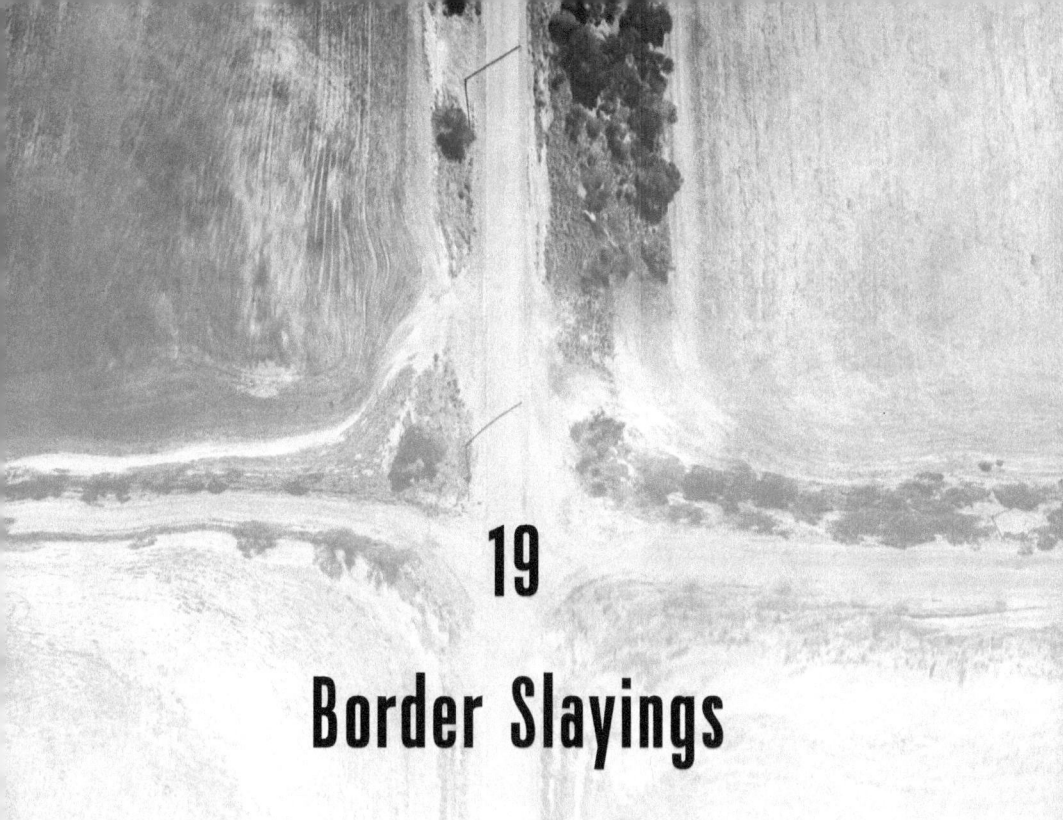

19

Border Slayings

I t was a Sunday morning when Joseph Baca got the call on his cell phone. He was the captain of a border control unit assigned to an area just outside of Campo, California. Today he was on a temporary assignment near El Paso, Texas. His patrol unit was kicking up clouds of dry dust as he sped down the dusty road that ran along the fence line in an area known as the Bush.

He was enroute to a reported homicide specifically at a place in the border where a hole had been dug just below the cyclone fence. This was a place where it was common for migrant crossers to slip through especially on moonless nights. His siren wailed in the background as he listened to the radio dispatcher.

"C-11, no confirmation yet as to which side. Units are on scene now conducting initial size up."

Captain Baca answered the radio, "10-4."

Baca was trying to find out if he really needed to be in such a hurry. He had recently been dispatched several times to this scene only to find groups of lost migrants waiting to plead for asylum in the US. This one did seem to have a different tone about it. He kept his lights going but cut his siren. After all, how many cars were in his way? None.

He continued to fight the rough unpaved road while he pulled his phone from his jacket pocket and speed dialed a number. Then he threw the open phone on his console. He soon heard a ring come through the speakers of his patrol unit and the voice of his second in command, Officer Pete Tatanni.

"Yeah Joe," Tatanni answered.

"Whiskey Tango Foxtrot? Over." which was a not so secret cop-code for *"what the fuck?"*

Baca continued,

"Tell me I am not busting my ass to get there for bullshit?"

After a short uncomfortable pause, Baca looked over at the console where his silent phone lay, "Pete?"

"Yeah Joe," he answered after the short silence.

On the other end of the phone stood Officer Tatanni outside his patrol unit with a shotgun in his right hand and the phone in his other. He found it difficult to answer Captain Baca and at the same time, take in the gruesome scene which lay in front of him. Then he heard Baca's patrol unit closing in on the scene.

"This is a bad one," he said as he ended the call.

Baca got out of his unit slowly. He closed the truck door, stunned by what he was now seeing in front of him.

A man had been inserted through a long upright pole. The pole was at least ten feet tall and brought to a sharp point at the top, like a pencil becomes pointed at the end. The man was suspended naked and the pole had been driven from his anus up and through to his head. His freshly mutilated body dripped with streams of blood coming off of his swollen and shoeless feet. Baca turned to his second in command.

"Holy Jesus!" Baca said.

"Somebody is pissed off," Tatanni said.

"Who's that?" Baca asked as he pointed off to the left where a young boy was squatted down. He had ear pods but they were not plugged into anything. It was apparent that he was not listening to anything. It looked as though he was praying, weeping, and his body was shivering uncontrollably.

The body had been strung up on the other side of the border just close enough for US authorities to see but not act. The man was obviously dead and the only action Baca and his men could take was to notify the Mexican government of the situation.

Captain Baca walked over to get a closer look. Moving in, he surveyed the scene cautiously with his revolver out. It was barely sunrise, but the gruesome act gave clues of what had happened even from a distance. Baca and Tatanni continued to inspect the body.

"Dogs?" Tatanni asked.

"Definitely cartel," Captain Baca answered.

"He was attacked by a pack of dogs. Then they took the time to torture and mutilate him. Finally he was finished off with this. They went to some trouble to get him up there like that."

Baca paused to get a closer look at the victim's face.

"So we would see him this way at sunrise."

"Why the dogs again? Just to make them look like this?" Tatanni asked.

Captain Baca, who was just as puzzled, replied,

"Yes, just to shock us. But why? This is just a typical migrant crosser and he means nothing to the cartel. Why would they want him dead and why such a display? There's a message in all of this."

Helicopter blades chopped through the morning air gradually getting louder as they closed in on the scene. Additional patrol units were now arriving. The scene was building up to a major incident.

"I spoke with the kid through the fence. The victim's name is Estrada, Roberto Estrada. Twenty-eight and that is his son. His name is Roberto too."

"What else does the kid know?"

"He's pretty upset right now."

"See if you can bring him over long enough to find out more about what happened."

"Captain Baca sir," interrupted a newly arriving officer.

Still focusing his attention on the body, Baca seemed to have missed the call from the officer who now repeated,

"Sir!"

Still no reply.

"Joe!" shouted Officer Tatanni, stepping forward. Baca turned quickly to the two officers standing beside him to answer,

"I'm sorry, I didn't hear you."

This time the officer spoke loudly enough to overcome the scene noise.

"Sir, the air crew reports a number of what seems to be more bodies in a ravine about half a mile south. On the Mexico side."

"How many bodies?" Baca asked.

"Sir, they didn't give a number, but said that some may be minors."

The officer paused to glance down to his note pad and then continued,

"They're coming to get you. In fact, there they are right now," he said pointing skyward as the helicopter began its descent.

Once airborne, Captain Baca peered out the port side of the airship with binoculars. Scanning a deep ravine, he spotted several bodies scattered along a trail. Baca opened the helicopter intercom.

"They all appear to be dead and maybe some sort of mass execution? Like something went wrong," Captain Baca said.

"I have never seen anything like this. I've counted about five or six kids," Officer Tatanni said.

"I think we're seeing just part of something much bigger. If you look further down south, you can see what looks like some kind of compound. That wasn't there last time I was out here," Captain Baca said.

"Looks like the cartel has been busy getting organized. They have another one of these compounds being built near our headquarters at Campo near at the California border," Tatanni added.

"I'm gonna need to talk to Washington about this one. There appears to be a whole lot going on here. Take us back," he ordered.

"If they hear or see us looking down into their backyards, they may take a shot or two at us."

"10-4 Captain," the pilot responded as he turned the airship sharply back toward the El Paso sector.

Once back in his office, Captain Baca sat in his air-cooled office. Across from his desk was a young but healthy looking twelve year old boy who looked like he had seen the worst of what had happened the night before.

"You speak English?" Baca asked.

"Yes, very well," the boy answered.

"Do you know that you are not in trouble or anything? You have not broken the law by being here. You are just helping us."

Baca continued.

"You understand that you do not have to answer any questions if you do not want to?"

"Yes, I know all that."

Baca then pointed to a lady who was a staff social worker. He had asked her to be present in the room.

"I have asked this lady to be here so that you understand you are safe and not in trouble. She is here to protect you. You can call on her at any time for anything. Okay?"

"Okay."

"What's your name?"

Junior slowly looked up and directed his eyes at the captain and replied,

"I am Roberto Estrada. They call me Junior."

"Where are you from?"

"South, in Mexico, on the outer part of the City." Junior pointed in the direction south.

"Was the man out there your father?"

"Yes."

"Were you with him last night?"

"Yes"

"I'm very sorry for what has happened. Do you feel like you can answer some questions about what happened to him?"

"Not a lot of questions. I can just tell you. I don't like to be asked a lot of questions."

"Okay then, just tell me what you can."

Junior hesitated at first on where to begin, but then he decided the fight was what started everything.

"There was a fight. A fight for money. My Papa was supposed to fight and he would be paid some money. I don't know exactly how much, but we needed it.

"Instead, they tried to kill him with a crazy man who had iron rings on his fingers. Then, my uncle showed up and stopped everything. It became a big *pinche* mess."

"Where was this fight?"

"I don't know. Outside of the city. In the hills."

"Do you know about the cartel?

"Yes, it was a *Vato* named Hector. He was the boss of the gang. Uncle Mielo just calls them all "Zetas." They chased him and my Papa down. But Uncle Mielo got away."

"Did you see all this?"

"They brought my Papa back to the place where the fight was and then they beat him. I broke in and tried to help, but they just tied me up and made me watch what they were doing to him."

Junior's voice was now breaking.

"They put big dogs on him. Then Hector told them to put Papa out on the stick right? So that SOMOS could see. He said my uncle could see what happens to the people that mess with him."

"What is your uncle's name?"

"He is Mielo Estrada."

Baca wrote "SOMOS" and Mielo's name on his pad.

"Why don't you rest for a while? We can talk later," Baca said.

The social worker had now stepped closer to Junior. She rested her hand gently on his shoulder.

"The rest of what happened is not good either," Junior said.

"Junior, you don't have to talk about it if you don't want," the social worker said.

"They put me in with other boys. Some younger than me."

"Do you remember how many?"

"I think six or seven."

"They made us march like soldiers in a line while these other men looked at us. Like we were for sale or something."

"Then what happened? How did you end up here this morning?"

"I broke away. I stole one of their guns. Then I shot some of them and some of the other boys started to run with me. But they couldn't keep up. They all got shot. All except me. Then they went away. All of them just went away in a truck."

"Okay, so how did you get to here?"

"At first I was lost. Then I knew they took my Papa this way. So I came here to look for him."

Junior finally broke down.

"Then, I found him."

Baca reached across to Junior. Both the social worker and he tried to comfort him as he wept aloud.

Baca spent the rest of the day in his field office writing his report and investigating the facts of the Estrada case. Officer Tatanni sat across the desk from him as they discussed what remained to be done.

"Why does this SOMOS organization sound so familiar to me?" asked Tatanni.

"They're a Catholic organization from California that advocates for the migrants who cross illegally into the US. Years ago, I did a raid in the LA area at one of their illegal holding places called the Mission. I remember some of these kids, well they're all adults now. I think this kid's father and his uncle were there."

Captain Baca shook his head in disgust.

"And I am almost certain that this Zeta boss, this Hector, his last name is Alvarez and he was there too. This guy is no good. Even when he was a kid he was bad, very bad."

"I've heard that name before," Tatanni said.

"This kid says that next of kin for the victim would be his wife in Mexico but she has no phone and doesn't know if she would miss the victim or him for days. He mentioned a priest from LA. The boy said the priest would know the victim. Only problem is he can't remember his name. He just says Tio."

"His last name is Moreno. Father Pedro Moreno. He's pretty well-known in LA. He's the head of a clandestine group of Jesuit priests and others called SOMOS. If we contacted him, he would most likely take the body for burial. Especially if he knows the circumstances. I will see if I can get ahold of him."

"And the boy?"

"He's illegal. He's got to go back. I'll talk to him but go ahead and set something up so we can get him somewhere to get the help he needs."

The next day Junior got word from Captain Baca that he would be going to a receiving center in Texas to be processed back into Mexico. Before that, he would be meeting with the social worker, to help him deal with what he had seen done to his father and the other kids.

"Why do I need to be processed? Mexico is right there." He pointed to the fence outside Baca's office.

"And why do I need to be talked to about what I saw? I know what I saw."

Baca heard Junior but didn't really understand what he was telling him. Like many adults before, Baca didn't understand Junior or what he was capable of doing.

Later that evening, Baca could not find his cell phone. As he was hunting for it, he remembered the last time he had seen it. It had been on his desk while he was talking with Junior. Baca went to his unlocked evidence drawer to discover Junior's ear pods had also been taken. By the time he called Tatanni to report his suspicion, Tatanni was on his way to Baca's office to report his own story about the kid.

Within minutes after Junior had eaten a good dinner, he stuffed his pockets full of the leftovers and a full bottle of water. He then fled from the officers in charge and slipped back under the border fence into Mexico.

Upon learning the story from Tatanni, Baca could only reply,

"I guess this has to be the first time we've had a subject in custody who successfully escaped back into Mexico."

20
Celebrating Saturday

I t wasn't unusual for Fr. Pedro to be at Nunez Park on a Saturday. You could say it was a like a family tradition, a SOMOS family tradition. Even with all the chopping, the barbecuing, and the music going on, everyone knew it was one of Fr. Pedro's favorite ways to network and discuss SOMOS matters.

Today Fr. Pedro took his time getting there because he really didn't feel much like chopping it up. He would have a meal and maybe a few beers before he had to deliver some tough news to Mielo. Captain Baca had been able to reach Tio with the news that Roberto had been executed and that Mielo was on the run with Elena.

Tio had made arrangements for Roberto's body to be brought back all the way to LA for a proper burial. He knew Mielo would need some help so he expected a call from him at some point in the day. He was finding it very hard to wait for the call. He was not certain that the four of them were safe. Captain Baca had also let him know that Junior had run off.

Tio needed to let Mielo know that SOMOS was sending Shepherds out to search for Junior and to help with his mission to cross Elena and the two children. Like his usual self, Tio knew Mielo had a very dangerous crossing ahead of him and was very worried.

There were plenty of people at the park and most of them were connected to SOMOS. They had lots of tamales, tacos, beans, chilies, and beer. Part of them had put together a small group of Mariachis and although they did not have Mariachi suits, they did have some instruments and the voices. Tio had just settled by a picnic table and was sipping a beer when the call came in.

Mielo had found an old G-field where they had all spent the night. Elena was still feeding and cleaning the children. Since it was impossible for the SOMOS Shepherds to keep cell phones charged while making a crossing, disposable pre-paid phones were hidden by other Shepherds to be used to communicate when needed. Mielo had recovered one the night before and now had stepped away to make his call to Tio.

Tio strolled away from the noise of his group but it was hard to escape. He put his finger in one ear to answer as he continued to walk farther away from the noise.

Mielo began the greeting with a tease,

"Tio, what's all the noise? Are you at a party?"

"No Emilio, I am in the park."

Mielo realized it was Saturday.

Tio continued, "It's Saturday. That's just what we American-Mexicans do on Saturdays. We get together with the family and have a picnic. We are just celebrating Saturday. We don't need a reason to celebrate anything else. Just a day for the family. A day to celebrate family. And you, you are the prodigal son? Huh?"

"Sounds like they think it's *Cinco de Mayo*. You better tell them it's fucking July," Mielo responded with a laugh.

The reality of the news Tio had for Mielo suddenly sunk back in and there was a feeling of sadness that came over Tio.

"Emielio, how are you? How are Elena and the children?"

"It's bad, Tio. We are on the run. Hector has turned from bad to evil and he has the entire Zeta cartel chasing all of us. Roberto and Junior too. They are both in a lot of shit. I had to leave them to come and get Elena."

"I know, Emielio. I know most of the story."

"How did you learn so fast?"

"I got a call from *La Migra* in Texas. Do you remember the officer named Baca? He was on the blacktop that day at the Mission. The one who showed Hector mercy?"

"Yes, he's cool. What did he tell you about Hector or Junior?"

The bottom of Tio's lip began to tremble and his words grew harder to get across.

"Tio?" Mielo said.

"I don't have good news for you, Emielio, my dear boy."

Mielo did not answer back. Nothing but silence was at each end of the phones. Mielo could not speak. It was like a large lump was in his throat. He knew that Tio was never short on words. This kind of quiet from Tio was about something scary bad. Mielo braced himself for the jolt that was on its way. Tio took a long slow breath and then delivered the dreaded message.

"Roberto, he did not make it. He was killed yesterday at the border near Texas."

Tio let Mielo have a moment for the news to sink in. Mielo suddenly felt weak. The words he had heard seemed unreal. He had just talked to Roberto and told him he would get his family out.

Elena had sensed that something was wrong and came closer to listen to the conversation. Mielo was dizzy. His hands were too weak to hold the phone.

"I am sorry about this, Mielo," Tio said.

Mielo dropped the phone onto the dirt. Elena could see what was happening. She read Mielo and knew it was bad news from Tio. She picked up the phone.

"Tio? This is Elena."

"Elena, sweet girl, is Mielo okay?"

"No. What is wrong?" she asked.

"Elena, I am sorry to tell you this way."

"Roberto?" again she asked.

"Yes. Yesterday at the border."

Mielo could see Elena shaking as their eyes quickly fell upon one another. Even though Mielo had not seen her in over twenty years, he knew right then at that moment that he didn't need to say anything. He reached out just in time to break the hardness of her fall. She had collapsed down onto the dirt.

"Mama!" Serena cried.

She did not respond. She was out. Helping to hold her head up off of the ground, Mielo wiped her brow and face with his bandana as she began to stir back awake. This time there was nothing Tio could say to end the silence on the phone and in their hearts.

"And what about Junior?" Elena asked with streaming tears.

"He is alive. Last report was that he ran from *La Migra*. That's all I have on him," Mielo told Elena.

"Can you call us back, Tio? We both need some time."

"Yes, Mielo. But we cannot wait too long. We have to plan your way out of there soon. You are all in very bad danger."

"I know. Thank you, Tio."

There was just too much agony between all of them to continue on the phone. The bond of life and death moments from their childhood and now as adults was so strong. Mielo and Elena held one another like they had on that day at the river, the day they had all became orphans.

It took some time for Mielo to get himself back together.

When Tio phoned back, Mielo was able to compose himself enough to get the details about Roberto.

"Hector has spilled a lot of orange juice, Tio. He is bad. The worst I have ever seen. I don't think there is anything you can do for him anymore. I don't know how you can keep taking up for him," Mielo pleaded.

"It is now up to God to take over and help him to see his wrong and then to clean up the mess he has made. If he does that, then the Lord will save him," Tio replied.

"He is shit! How can you say that about that *pinche* sewer rat? He is nothing but *mui malo* like Sister Ana Rita used to say. Tio, there is nothing there but evil and hate in him. He is the devil's own and if I ever see him again, I will kill him for Roberto, for Junior, and for God who you have said yourself hates the evil."

"No Emielio." Tio was now shaking his head and pointing with his glasses in hand.

"It is not our place to deliver the wrath of God. Only God can. Hector will someday meet his God. We must not let the world decide. God will have the final say on Hector. If you kill him, then you will become like him. And Emielio, you are not him," Tio said.

Mielo worked with Tio to try and understand all that had happened. By the end of the call, they had agreed on a plan to get all four of them out. Mielo discussed the cartel complex now built over the tunnel near Campo. Tio agreed that the tunnel near Campo would be the best way for them to cross. Mielo told Tio about the children that he suspected were held there. Tio said that the US authorities were aware of the possibility of children being held and trafficked out of there. Both Tio and Mielo agreed the investigation by the US might be the perfect distraction Mielo needed to enter and try to cross through the tunnel.

Tio spent time on the call to help Elena too.

"Elena, we cannot wait so we are going to give Roberto a proper Christian burial here. The priests back at the Mission will hold a mass for him and for anyone to attend and pay their respects. Then when you get here, again we will say a mass and have a private ceremony. Don't worry. We have taken care of everything."

Finally, Mielo put Tio on the phone speaker so they could all share their plan and the loss of Roberto.

"What about Junior?" Elena asked Tio.

"He was alive. Elena, he was with Roberto through all of this. No one knows where he is now."

"It doesn't surprise me to hear that he ditched *La Migra* and ran back into Mexico." Mielo quipped.

"That boy. He's crazy," Elena said shaking her head.

"Crazy good like his father," Mielo said.

"He has seen too much. Too much for a boy his age. We will find him. We have already sent SOMOS Shepherds out. They will find him," Tio said.

"Elena has prayed to the Virgin many times for her baby boy. And even though he is in the greatest of danger this very moment, I have seen it. He is protected by angels. Tio, your Shepherds may find him, but only if Junior wants them to find him and he may not want to be found." Mielo said.

21

Tio's God

The next day Mielo sat with Elena to go over the plan for the crossing. It was hard for them to keep working without the sadness of Roberto getting in their heads and slowing it all down. There were times when Elena could do nothing but sleep or sit and think about Roberto. Then she would think about Rafael and Serena. They needed to get them out of Mexico and to do it for Roberto. The most important thing for them to do was to not sit around feeling badly about things, but to help the family that Roberto had left behind. That would have been Roberto's way of thinking for sure.

Mielo was still really angry about what had gone down and there were times when he wanted to just go after Hector bare fisted. He wanted to take a hold of him and finish him with a blade or something.

But Tio's words would make him think better about it and make him stop. Mielo remembered what Tio had told him about death. He said that, *"death was nothing but a punk."* This was something Mielo understood and it hurt because there was nothing he could do about it. Tio was right. Death was a punk. Especially Roberto's death.

Tio continued to call him and Elena for the next few days. He would call and talk about the "Holy Book" and what it said and he would tell Mielo about men that were his *compas* who had gone through what Elena and he were going through. Some of them were holy men who were still alive, but Mielo was pretty sure the *Vato* from India that Tio kept bringing up was dead. Tio said that a holy man from India once told him,

"If somebody knocks your eye out and you go back to knock his out, or if you get your tooth knocked out and then you go back and knock his out. Then after a while the whole world is blind and needs dentures." Or something like that.

It was kind of crazy the way Tio would say stuff, but Mielo understood what he meant when he said those kind of things.

"You just can't keep punching each other in the face because not only does that shit hurt, but in the end nothing gets done. You just bleed a lot and that's it," Mielo said to himself.

He remembered that most of his friends around the Heights would say that Tio was full of bullshit and that if someone messes with you, then you should go after him and mess him up. But, Mielo was getting old enough now to know bullshit when he heard it.

When he thought through both sides, it was Tio who was right. Sometimes it made him mad when Tio was right, but most of the time he was. Right then he pledged to himself and to

Roberto to focus everything he had left inside of him on getting Elena and the family out. And that will be it.

He wasn't going to waste his time looking to kill Hector or anyone in the Zeta gang. Besides, Mielo knew he wasn't a killer. He knew he could not clean up after that kind of spill. Hector and he would see each other again. Maybe it would be in heaven or maybe in hell or maybe just on the street. But whatever happens at that place and time, would be up to Tio's God.

So Mielo stayed in the G-field to rest up and went back to work getting ready for the crossing with Elena and the two little ones. From passing Shepherds, Mielo had gotten the word that the border was now getting hot. *La Migra* was working more along the fence lines and they were in the air. There was a lot of talk of the gangsters taking kids and shooting anyone that tried to fight them off.

All this talk about the kids just made Mielo more certain that the tunnel crossing was the best way to go. He would just have to make sure it was open and that the Zeta soldiers weren't working it when he went in.

Mielo and Elena stayed up late and talked about the old times. Elena wondered why *La Migra* was not working with the Mexican government to stop the gangsters who were stealing kids and killing everyone including a simple man like Roberto who just wanted to find a better way to live. Why did no one care?

Mielo's mind drifted off to the day when *La Migra* agents raided the Mission and came in and took everyone away. He thought about the *pinche* redheaded one who tore his shirt. Then he remembered the one called Baca. He stopped that asshole agent from punching Hector while he was in cuffs.

That was the only *La Migra* agent who ever showed any respect. He wanted to do things the right way and to treat them like people and not like animals to be rounded up and put in cages. It was strange to him that Baca was still out there and that he helped take care of Roberto. In some way that made him feel better. There were some good people out there.

It must have been what Tio calls "God's grace" that sent Baca to help take care of his brother. Tio's God had sent this man and it seemed like that man really did care. Mielo was starting to believe that there really was something called angels and that Tio's God was maybe even for real. Maybe this God or someone would help him on his journey back to America. Mielo needed to believe in something, something that was good.

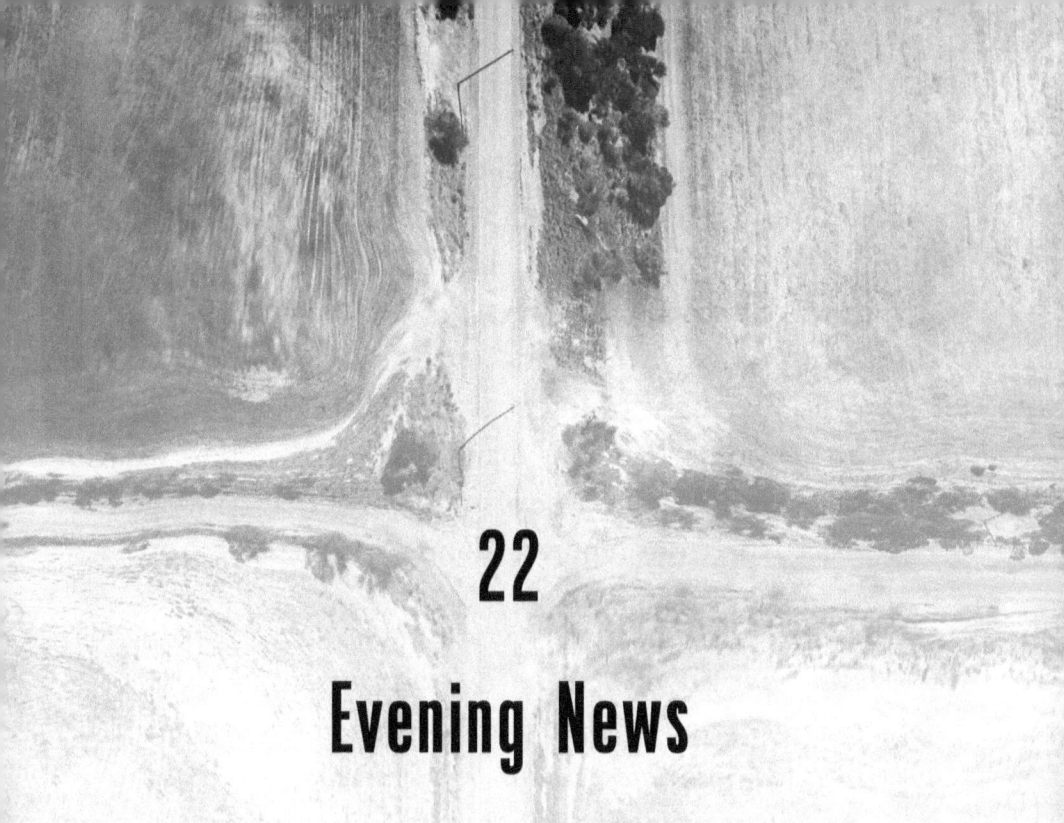

22

Evening News

The office was posh and the panoramic view of the downtown Los Angeles skyline was exclusive. The city glimmered with night lights as the sun was fading to the west. It was the offices of Marcos Ramirez, an attorney and assistant to Armando Vega who was also known as "*Z-1*." This was a name given only to the high boss within the ranks of the *Los Zetas* Mexican criminal syndicate. The Zetas were regarded as one of the most dangerous of the country's cartels. While their primary business was drugs and guns, sex trafficking had recently become highly profitable, especially the trafficking of young children.

To the left of his window view and above the bar was a large screen television which was usually concealed behind custom Cherrywood sliding doors. This evening, the television cabinet was open and the TV was set to the nightly news. It was news that both Mr. Ramirez and his client, Mr. Vega, were very interested to hear. The news began with the local anchorwoman leading with the story from El Paso, Texas.

"Tragedy today at the Texas and Mexico Border. For those of you who may have young ones watching, this is a short but important warning that you may want to take steps to avoid them seeing or hearing our next story. For the story, we go to El Paso, Texas, where our reporter Donna West has the story."

> Hello from just north of the Texas border near El Paso. Early this morning US authorities found the body of an unknown migrant who had been brutally tortured, mutilated, and then murdered.
>
> This appears to be more bodies on the southern side of the border. Information is still being gathered but it appears the victims were all male, were Mexican citizens and possibly migrants who apparently may have been trying to cross the border. The number of confirmed deaths remains unknown at this time. The bodies were discovered early this morning by Customs and Border Patrol agents. For some unknown reason, the body of the one victim had been propped up on a wooden post. Due to the condition of the victim, we are unable to bring you film of the crime scene.
>
> This all occurred on the Mexican side of the border and as of this time, there is no clear motive behind the deaths. Another disturbing development which as of this time has not been confirmed, is the story that most of the remaining bodies were children.

Earlier Captain Joseph Baca, the lead officer for this territory, had this to say at the press conference:

"The only suspicious death we can confirm at this time is the one where the body was posted and displayed right at the border. We do not have enough information or evidence to confirm the other bodies were homicides or otherwise the result of an accident.

Since these incidents have occurred on the Mexican frontier, we have no jurisdiction and have not heard from Mexican authorities as to their plan of action at this time."

Suddenly, a phone call came in, breaking Ramirez's concentration. Ramirez immediately muted the news cast and picked up the call after the first ring.

"Yes Mr. Vega. Yes, I have. I'm watching it right now."

A short pause ensued.

"Yes, I too think so. It is a terrible tragedy."

Another short pause.

"I plan to meet with him in the next couple of days, sir. I am sure that this is just a misunderstanding."

Finally another pause as Ramirez took in the last of the concerns of Z-1.

"I will deal with it this week. Yes, I have it under control. Thank you sir," Ramirez said as he ended the call.

Marcos Ramirez is in a very dangerous business. That's why he is paid so highly. Sitting at his desk, he slowly returned the phone to end the call. He has been Vega's number one man and he has single-handedly set up much of the organization's structure for processing the minor children through Zeta hands. It has become highly lucrative to both Ramirez and Vega. Ramirez has himself appointed Hector Alvarez as the point where the operations occurs. Up to now, Hector had been reliable and smart about managing the whole process. Most recently however, Alvarez had become a problem. He is killing indiscriminately and drawing attention to the cartel by his careless acts of violence.

Staring at the screen now on mute, Ramirez contemplates his situation and the amount of money he stands to gain by continuing this job. He sits back in his chair, recognizing that this may be the last time Hector acts as the liaison between the organization and the soldiers who carry out his every order. While he continues to control the interest of big money customers with an attraction for young sex mates, Mr. Vega has just reminded him of who is in charge and that if Hector continues to be out of control, it may be necessary to take him out.

"Each time Hector fucks up, the Feds get closer to learning what this is all about," was the last comment Vega had made on the phone.

So for now, Ramirez's number one priority was to get the Zeta gang back under the radar of the US authorities and more importantly, he had to get Alvarez to work under the radar of the American press.

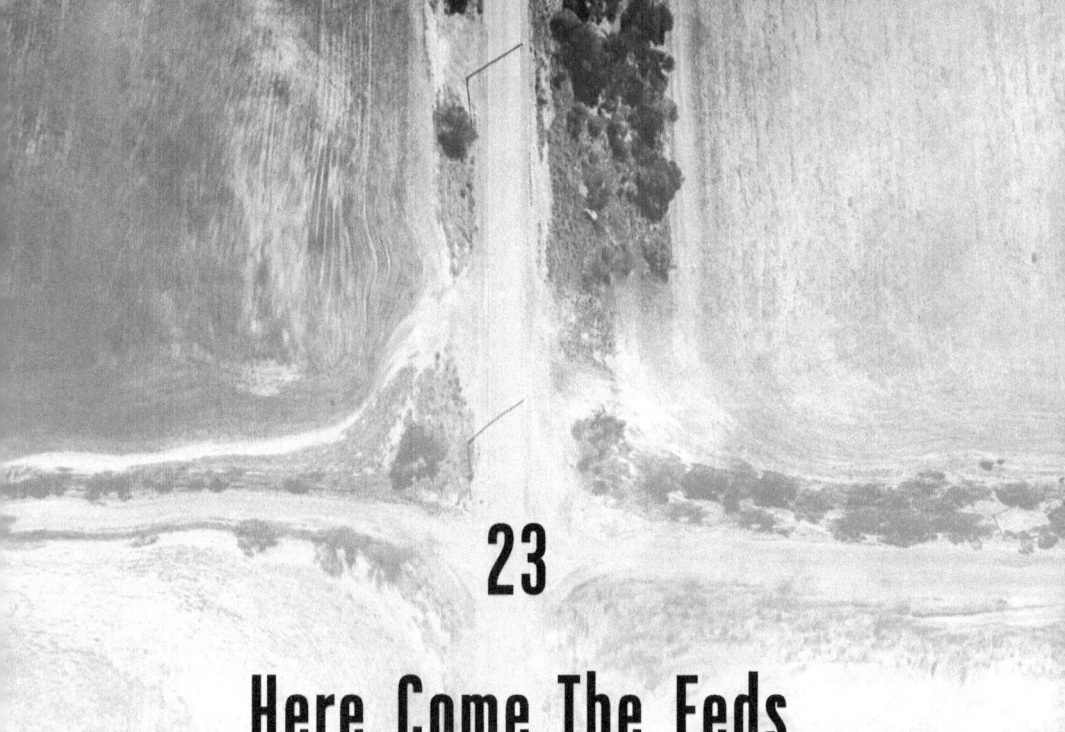

23

Here Come The Feds

aptain Baca sat back at his desk at the southern Texas border patrol headquarters. Tapping his note pad with his pen, he could feel the "calm before the storm" as he thought about all that he had seen yesterday at the border. Suddenly his desk phone rang out.

"Baca," he answered.

"When? What Time? Okay."

He held the phone down on the receiver and then released it to dial out.

"Ya Carol, let the squad know we're expecting Washington today. Not sure who will be in the entourage. Also no idea what or when to expect them, but I am sure it will be loads of fun," he said sarcastically.

Looking out his window, he continues to speak into the phone,

"Son of a bitch if they're not already here. So much for the heads up. Let them in."

Baca hangs up the phone and goes to the window to get a better view.

The security gate rolls open and in comes a black sedan with federal badging. It is escorted by two black armed utility vehicles. Officer Tatanni bolts into the office.

"Here come the Feds!" he announced.

"Yes, I see them," Baca said.

"Who is it? You know we have investigative authority over this incident. This is ours, isn't it?" Tatanni asked.

"Washington? Maybe Helms? Maybe our good deputy secretary? They really didn't call me to talk about the details."

The door opened and in walked a tall and trim Caucasian man followed by a Hispanic woman. Both of them were well-dressed in black and white suits.

Baca was acquainted with Jordan Helms; he had worked with him when Helms was head of immigration. Baca had been promoted under Helms and both men had a mutual respect for one another. Baca was relieved to see him because he knew he was a competent statesman and wasn't full of the usual federal bureaucratic bullshit.

Helms also understood how to play the game well. He had been appointed Deputy Secretary in the state department just a few years earlier and was well-connected as high up as the President. Within the ranks he was known to most of the staff as a "fix it" man. He was sent places to fix things and then move on. He had been sent to investigate the Mexican incident and if there was indeed a problem, he was to negotiate a rapid resolution.

The woman with Helms, on the other hand, was unknown to Baca. She looked FBI and her photo badge said "SUAREZ." She was obviously Hispanic. Suarez took a long look at the face of Tatanni and then Baca.

"Yep, the fucking Feds are here. But don't worry, Captain, we're not like most of the assholes you're used to working with." she said with a smile as she extended her hand out to shake.

"We're worse," she added as she shook hands with a small chuckle. Jordan Helms then began his greeting.

"Joe, nice to see you. Wish it was under better circumstances. Sorry to just drop in without much warning. I was already in Texas and when I saw the news and then Washington called. I mean this one is coming straight from the top. We just made a right turn instead of a left and here we are."

Helms was a tall and well-groomed man whose presence seemed to fill the room with an air of importance.

"This is Agent Marty Suarez. She is a senior agent with the FBI who has worked with me on several assignments. I asked her to join me as the primary investigative authority; however, she reports to me directly so you don't have to deal with the bureau.

"She speaks fluent Spanish and is an attorney specializing in immigration and naturalization. She will be my assistant on this assignment and lead the law enforcement entourage as assigned."

"As assigned? That's impressive," Baca said.

"Joe, can we settle in and use this office as the command center?" Helms asked.

"Are you asking my permission? Or just being nice about taking over this mess," Baca replied.

"Captain Baca, all egos aside, I am not old school. My team recognizes that we can't get anything done here unless we work both with and through your agency and men. Just for the record, I was ICE for over seven years. I did my time in Houston. I am here to simply help make things happen for Deputy Helms and to offer what I can to help your squad."

"Hum, it's Ms. Juarez right?" Baca asked. She nodded her head and answered, "It's pronounced Suuuu-arez with an S. It's Hispanic like yours, but you can call me Marty."

"Okay Marty, we do appreciate your assistance and I am certain we will need you to make things happen for us as well," Baca answered with a smile.

"Thank you, Joe," Helms added.

"You both can expect the full cooperation of this office and my men. Of course, I hope you understand that our priority will continue to be protecting the integrity of the border. Other than that, we will do whatever we can to assist in resolving this situation. Jordan, please take my desk and anything you may need to conduct your operations."

"Thanks again, Joe, and now I will need to speak to you privately."

All the other officers and agents except for Suarez left the room. Helms took a seat at the desk. Folding his hands, he placed them squarely on the middle of the desk.

"I don't have to tell you that what is discussed in this room is highly classified and privileged. That being said, now tell us what we don't know."

Suarez sat beside the two and listens in.

"We've had zero access to the scene other than the fly over and that was not taken lightly by whoever is in the compound—*Los Zetas* Cartel or maybe even Mexican militia types."

"Do you have good numbers?" Helms asked.

"No. What I saw was approximately six to seven bodies with no attempt to conceal or burn them. They were small bodies. In regard to the man who was killed. It's been my experience that they almost always burn or bury. In this case, they went out of their way to make sure everyone knew what was happening. This was some sort of message. I'm not sure who the message is intended for or why," Baca answered.

Helms looks at Suarez who opens her briefcase and pulls out some documents. She hands a photo to Baca.

"Have you ever seen this man before?" she asks Baca as he studies the photograph.

"I have seen him before. Can't place him though. Tattoos look like cartel, probably Zeta."

"Hector Alvarez. He is large in the *Los Zetas* Cartel. Answers only to the second in charge, an attorney in LA named Marcos Ramirez. Alvarez is a ruthless and reckless killer who is usually with band of anywhere from ten to twenty Zeta soldiers at one time. All of them are connected to the number one Zeta, Z-One, the boss, Armando Vega," Suarez said.

"So this is about the Zs?" Baca asked.

"Yes, but the other big targets are the money behind all this perverted trafficking of young kids. We have been monitoring these activities for more than two years now. It has only been recently that we have discovered how many there have been. We estimate up to a hundred kids have been taken just this year alone," Helms said.

"But now and with your discovery, we have a better idea of where they are being held. The thing is that only recently have they been more and more brazen about it. Like they are boasting. That doesn't fit their MO," Suarez added.

Handing another photo to Baca, Helms leads on.

"Joe, have you seen or heard of these two men? They are quite well known in the business circles here in Texas. This one is Marcos Ramirez and this one is Mr. Magnus Porter."

"Porter, I know that name. Isn't he the one with all that money? One of the wealthiest men in the nation? I work more in California than in Texas and I know he's a big donor to a lot of California politicians," Baca answered.

"That is spot on. Glad to see you are paying attention to your politics around here because that too is what this is all about. We suspect he works with the Zeta attorney Ramirez to access the kids for sex. He may be the leader of a ring of men who like to have sex in Mexico with children," Helms said.

"Porter channels his money to Vega through Ramirez who controls Alvarez. But I think Ramirez has lost control of Alvarez. We think these killings were not part of the plan. That something has gone wrong. This is where the cartel has made their first mistake," Suarez said.

"I do think Porter, Vega, and Ramirez are all very concerned about the brutality of the killings and the consequent attention it has brought on them from people like us, and the US press. Although, I'm pretty sure they are most concerned about their money," Helms said.

"Then, it's not just about stopping these kids from being used to cross the border, it's also about stopping this sex trafficking ring," Baca said.

Suarez and Helms shook their heads in agreement.

"This is just so hard to believe," Baca said.

"Yes, Magnus Porter has millions that he and the cartel have made off of this perverted shit. This not going to be easy. Again, Porter is well-connected and we will have to be on our game. We have to play everything by the book to make this stick," Helms added.

"There's another part to this story," Suarez added.

Baca looked intrigued, "More?"

"There's an underground organization known as SOMOS. Have you heard of them?"

"Yes, of course, they're not so underground these days."

"Yes, they have been a major player in this operation. They were the first to discover and report these activities and most of our intelligence comes from people inside their organization who have passed it on to us."

"I'm not surprised. They're good people," Baca said.

"Yes, now this is what we believe. We have learned that the dead, mutilated, and exposed body was that of a SOMOS affiliate named Roberto Estrada."

"It was. We talked to his kid. His name was Junior. We got some good stuff from him but then he ran off on us," Baca said.

"Did he say where he was going?" Suarez asked.

"No, he just went back into Mexico. Free and on his own. I guess you could call it an escape. But we really didn't consider him a threat or anything and the last thing we expected after what he had been through was for him to run back into Mexico."

"Again this is top secret," Suarez continued.

Baca nodded his head in compliance.

"That kid has been our lead source on all this. And most of it has been very reliable and on target."

"We lost contact with him the day the murder of his father took place. We are almost certain that these killings were Hector Alvarez's way at least in part, of intimidating him and SOMOS to stop reporting on the cartel and their sex venture."

"All that you say matches up with what he told me. And it also explains how those seven dead bodies ended up in the ravine we flew over. It was only minutes from their compound."

"Yes, their compound," interrupted Helms.

"They have another that has just been completed near Campo in California. We will need to get to know both compounds and see what's both in and under them. We believe there are tunnels under both. They may be hiding a bunch of missing kids," Suarez said.

"Just as we said, Joe. We are going to need each other's help on this one. Joe, no disrespect intended, but your operation has its hands full with normal conditions here at the border.

"This is huge, with huge ramifications and if we get to the bottom or top when you think Magnus Porter, we need to be absolutely clear and preponderant. As I said, Porter is well-connected from here to DC with important buffers who can take all of us down in minutes," Helms said.

"Sir, you can count us in. We're here to help you in any way possible," Baca replied.

"Thank you. Again, our role in this will be to grab as much intel as we can while your team works the normal channels. You may need to help us out with the Campo station in California as well," Suarez said.

"That is fine. I have worked that station and I know that area well," Baca answered.

"We will need to be as covert as possible. We will try to take Alvarez out alive. But we're not here to negotiate with him," Suarez said.

"Meanwhile, I will be the good statesmen. I will be in contact with the Mexican consulate trying to be nice about what we are doing in their country. We will also try our hardest not to piss them off any more than they probably are right now.

"Furthermore, I have the Secretary of State who wants a briefing on this situation by 1800 hours, so she can brief the Press Secretary who will in turn brief the president. Because of the press, this is now a big deal. Now, let's get to work, shall we?"

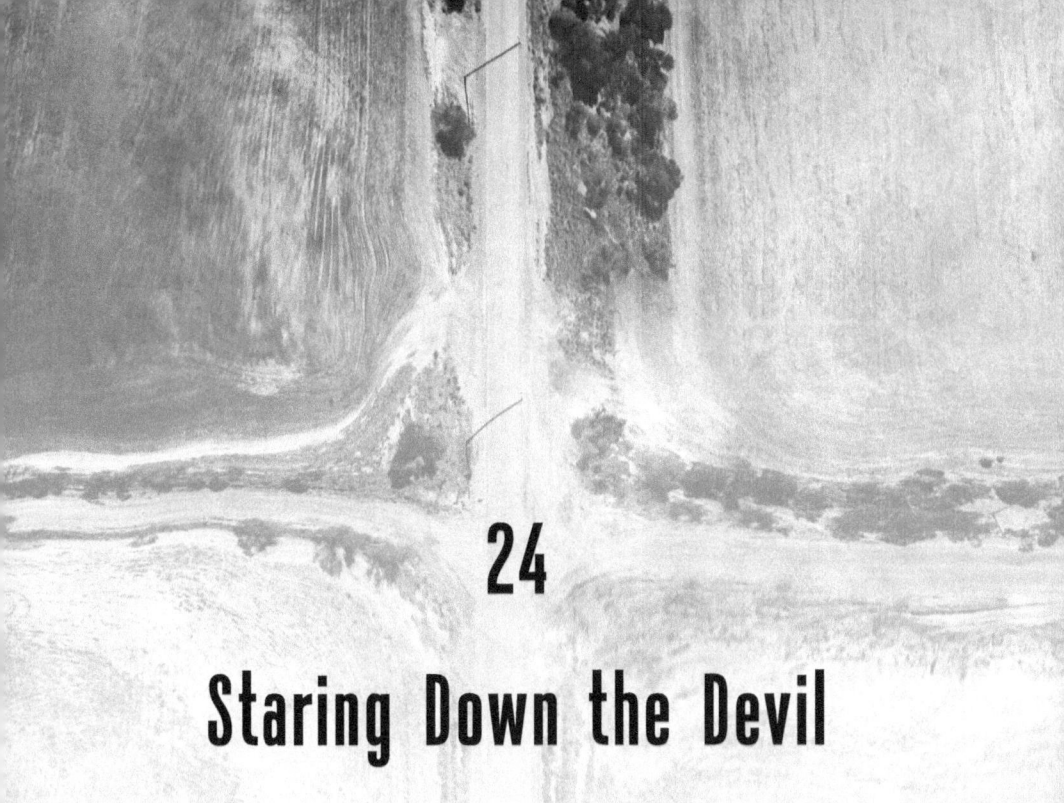

24

Staring Down the Devil

Marcos Ramirez sat in his car at the designated point just off the dirt road south of an area controlled by the *Los Zetas* known as the Sangria de Christo Paseo. He parked his silver Mercedes sedan with black-tinted windows away from the public roads and far out in a deserted trucking lot. Before he parked, he set up a team of Zeta soldiers loyal to Vega. He posted them within a mile so that if his meeting went south, he could call in for a rescue.

While he talked to his office on his cell phone, he glanced down at his gold watch. He had looked at the same watch twice before over the last few minutes. He was waiting for Hector Alvarez, waiting for a face-to-face with him. Alvarez was always at least fifteen to twenty minutes late. Ramirez knew that this was just the way it was with him. Today was an especially irritating morning and he was in no mood to put up with Alvarez's games. Yet he knew that every second he was with him was extremely dangerous and that also made him very unsettled.

Soon, a black Range Rover with tinted windows rolled up beside him. As the side windows slowly dropped, Ramirez could now see three men seated inside. The one in the back was Alvarez. The other two were cartel soldiers. They got out and stood guard, leaning against the Rover with their hands in their coats. Ramirez stepped out of his sedan and into the vacant rear seat of the Land Rover. Now seated beside Alvarez, Ramirez could see that he was drunk and high on something. Judging by the constant sniffling, it was probably cocaine. The two then began their meeting.

"Hey Ramirez, why do you pick such shit holes to have our meetings? I could have met you in Los Angeles. We could have done a McDonald's or something so that I can have some authentic American food while I listen to your fake ass Mexican accent."

"I have important things to discuss," Ramirez replied.

"Of course you do, begin," Alvarez said.

"There was supposed to be no spectacles. Why all of the killings? Why all the high profile shit?" Ramirez asked.

Alvarez opened up his usual grin and answered.

"I do what you and the boss tell me. I take the kids and sell them off. You tell me to scare all the others away and then you pay me. No one can be afraid of wolves if they can't see them. The wolves must come out. They must be seen.

"I have scared all the problems, the Feds, and the people like SOMOS away. Now no one sees what we do. Has it not worked? You and I have been paid and the Boss? Z-1 is happy, no?"

"Look. No, we are not happy. The shit is in the papers and on the TV. The American TV. That makes *mui* attention on all of us. It's too much. The American press makes the American law interested in us," Ramirez said.

Alvarez dropped his grin, contorting it into a penetrating glare. He said nothing, but continued to eye Ramirez who now looked away.

"No more for a while," Ramirez said.

"You want to stop?" Alvarez snapped his head to the side, then followed with,

"Once you stare into the devil's face, you cannot turn away. You have to face him straight on. The devil, you have to stare him down. Do you know what I mean?" Alvarez asked.

There was another uncomfortable pause as Ramirez slowly looked back up to Alvarez. Alvarez continued his rant,

"You know, I once cut off a man's head and a very strange thing occurred. The man's eyes continued to stare at me."

He held his finger up.

"Yes, I cut his neck and his head fell off, rolling along the floor. His face was covered in blood. But when the head stopped rolling, the eyes were locked wide-open. And they were looking right up at me. Now that man had tried to stare down the devil."

Alvarez then belted out a long laugh. Ramirez again looked away, turning his head down with his eyes fixed at his feet. *This guy has gone fucking crazy*, he thought.

"I will need to talk to my people. But I think we will continue to kill when we want to and how we want to. Tell Z-1 that is why I am being paid, right? There was no end in my contract, right? I am *Culebro,* the Snake."

He was making no sense to Ramirez. He could now feel his muscles tense as he realized Alvarez was going rogue on him and on his boss. This was a death cry from Alvarez. He didn't care what would happen to him. He was defiant to the boss and he didn't care about what price he would pay for his defiance. Ramirez could feel the evil rising up. He needed to leave, but he knew it would be certain death for him if he suddenly bolted from the Rover.

"We are not telling you to stop. Only to take a break and drop back and let things settle for a while. We have what we need for now. No more need to steal or to kill anyone," Ramirez said.

"First you tell us to steal the kids. Now you want to do nothing. My men are in the desert right now. They have orders. The dance is not over. The taking of the kids will not stop. Not until I say. I will be in contact."

Ramirez took the warning and stepped out of the Rover, saying no more. Alvarez peered at Ramirez as he rode off.

Back in his sedan, Ramirez contemplated the difficulties of his situation. What he had considered to be a simple miscalculation had now become out-of-control and larger than he had ever expected. Alvarez had made a big mistake. He had crossed the boss. It also appeared that Alvarez's men were also defiant and following him. They were all part of a bigger rogue scheme. When the boss understands what has happened, all of them will be in great danger. There will be a blood bath. The meeting had gone wrong, very wrong.

25

Consulate Meeting

Deputy Helms sat on one side of a long and gleaming wood conference table. Two secret service agents stood behind him. At his side was Agent Suarez. Directly across was Representative Ricardo Morales of the Mexican Consulate and two of his assistants. Behind them were the draped and proudly displayed Mexican and US flags. Helms began the meeting.

"Representative Morales sir, we appreciate the opportunity to meet with you this morning and I assume that you have been briefed or have seen the latest news reports on our situation which has developed over the last two weeks at our border near El Paso, Texas?"

"Yes, of course, and we have taken measures to investigate this matter and will act as soon as possible to mitigate any further activity," Morales said.

A short period of silence forced an awkward tension in the room. Helms continued,

"That is very good news indeed. Might I inquire as to what your country is planning in response to these incidents?"

"As I have previously stated, we have taken measures to investigate this matter and will act as soon as possible to mitigate any further activity. Mr. Helms, if you are asking for my country to provide you with a detailed plan of what, when, and how we plan to react to these incidents, then I will need to consult with our military advisors. I am not prepared to give you that information at this time."

"No. Your initial response is adequate. I too have others who wish to be consulted as well and to whom I will need to report. Obviously, the more I can report, the better the understanding we will have about how to deal with it."

"Deputy Helms, I too report back to my superiors. I am also looking to discover what a US airship is doing well across the border?"

"The crew on that mission was performing. . ."

Agent Suarez interrupts,

"Representative Morales, I am the FBI special agent assigned to this mission. At this time, some of our cooperators in your country have presented substantial evidence to believe that a heinous crime has been committed.

"These are credible people with reliable reports of what they saw. Several children were killed in a mass-style shooting with automatic weapons."

"Cooperators?" interrupted Morales.

"I have not seen or heard of any official cooperation with your country regarding this matter in particular. This sounds more like an act of impulse. Perhaps a reason to enter our country to gain intelligence on a matter that, as far as I can tell, has not been confirmed. Nor for that matter, can we say that if it had indeed occurred, how has it impacted your national security or sovereignty?"

Helms now gave the look to Suarez to try to slow her down. He interjected,

"Sir, you are right. We are not here to pass any judgment. There is much more to learn about this situation and we do not intend to indict anyone in any way from the Mexican government. It was a very unusual event. And it is true that we may have overacted by entering into your country without actual permission. But I do have to advise your country that US policy has always been and will continue to be that we are always looking out for violations of human rights. Which includes anywhere in the world, including our own country and our closest neighbors."

Another pause of nervous tension filled the room as Morales attempted to regain his diplomatic composure. He then stood and extended his hand to Helms.

"Deputy Secretary Helms, Agent Suarez, you have been very helpful and we thank you for providing us with your perspective. I will be very pleased to report your concerns to my superiors. We will issue a statement to your state department within the next twenty-four hours. Until then, thank you for your assistance in this matter."

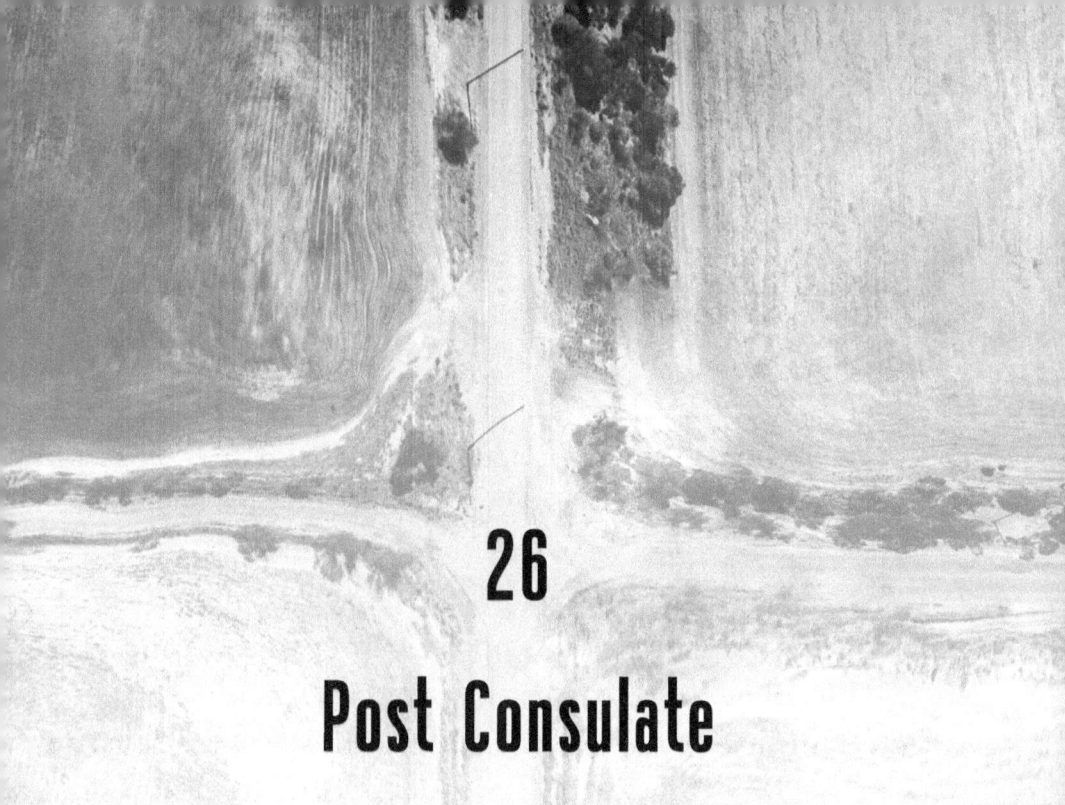

26

Post Consulate

Back in the car and on his cell phone, Deputy Helms briefed the state department as to the outcome of his consulate visit.

"I don't have anything else to report. Yes, I have her with me now. Of course, there is always something that can be done. I just do not have any idea what that will be yet. Yes."

He hung up.

"Well, that seemed to have gone well," Suarez said.

"Your sarcasm is in reference to the meeting or the phone call?" Helms replied.

"I was referring to the meeting, although the call sounded interesting."

"Yes, I meant to thank you for your help." He responded with his own twist of sarcasm.

"This may be much bigger than we initially thought. The department is nervous and hungry for more information and a quick resolution. The press is really starting to dig in on this," Helms said.

"What about a recon mission on the main compound? Captain Baca and I could put a team together to slip over. We could cause some trouble while we look around. We have a pretty good idea of the layout of the compound. We could also do some head counts on bodies or whatever else we run into," Suarez suggested.

"Have you talked to your bosses?" Helms asked.

"Yes, I am the agent in charge. Straight from the top. They support whatever efforts you support. I cover your ass and you cover mine. Then we both cover Baca and his team."

"I am pretty sure this director is dirty. This Morales is in on some of this. With Mexico you never quite know. It isn't unusual to find one person at one level of the government corrupt and then the next a straight shooter.

"Either way, I think they are little embarrassed about how little they knew about what is going on. Either that or how scared they are that we are on to them.

"I may need to go somewhere above Morales to get the real help we need. I do think this is going to escalate and I have been given the go to do what I have to do to get to the bottom or top of this before it becomes a major military operation."

"So we have an agreement? Covert action on the compound?" Suarez asked.

"Yes. But I think there is more going on at the California border. Part of the phone call I just had was new intelligence about kids being held at a similar compound with a tunnel beneath it. There is a lot of activity with the cartel going on there. It is believed that this is Alvarez's new hold up.

"The compound is near the small town of Campo. Captain Baca knows that area, so see if he and some of his men can go that way with you.

You have my go. But try to keep it at a criminal level. We don't want this to escalate to military action. That's very important. If you see any military, stand down. Otherwise do whatever it takes to bring these Zetas down and get the intelligence we need."

27

Grieving

Mielo realized that getting Elena and the children across the border was going to be complicated and long. Like the trip with little Sal. Campo was straight north, but it would be an even longer trip because they had started the trip much deeper south near Mexico City. Having two children and an attractive woman with him also made it much more dangerous because of the value the cartel would put on all of them. These risks led Mielo to decide on traveling mostly at night and to using a less traveled route which cut through long trails of high desert and an occasional small mountain range. The route would not offer much to see except dirt, sage, and cactus.

There was a song that Sister Rita had taught to Mielo and he would sing it with Elena when they were young back at the

Mission. It was called *El Rossinyol,* which in English meant The Nightingale. Elena was known throughout the Heights for this beautiful song and this was the reason she herself was often referred to as *El Rossinyol.* As they made the first leg of their long journey to America, Elena walked beside Mielo singing that song. To Mielo it was like walking next to an angel. It gave him the strength he needed to do what he had to do.

He thought about Roberto a lot. He thought about how hard it was to see Elena's heart being broken again. He too was broken up over Roberto's brutal death. Tio had always said that they need to look for the good things in bad times. He did feel good that it had fallen to him to get Elena and the children out. He just could not see anything good in the work that lay ahead for them. It was all hard. His mind went back again to Tio's words about death. That it was a punk.

When evening grew close, Mielo had reached a G-field outside the city of Zamora. He felt they would be safe there and knew he could resupply, so he decided to stop and set up camp for the night. The day had been hot and the wind had been blowing dust into the dry air for most of it. Mielo was able to hustle a bucket of clean water for Elena and the children to clean themselves. Most of the other crossers were sheltered under a grove of wild trees. Elena set up camp close to them. They all sat before the fire eating a meal of beans and tortillas. In a short time, the two children drifted off to sleep, leaving Mielo alone by the fire with Elena.

For a moment Mielo froze, unable to think or do anything but look upon Elena's face. It was like a spell that only she could cast and it was once again upon him. It was the same as back when they were kids at the Mission. Only now it was stronger. He had a strong desire to touch her and hold her. He had tried for so many years to force the thought of her from his mind. But, losing her and Roberto the day of the raid had given him a pain that he could never get over. She had been taken when they were so young.

The only thing that came close to the agony of that day was the when Tio gave him the news that she had married Roberto. After that, whatever hope he had left for Elena had been ripped out from under him.

Now the sweet song of the nightingale had once again caught up with his heart. It seemed as though he had forgotten nothing and his soul was as fresh again as when they were children.

"Mielo, it's been good to be with you after so long. I am sorry that it has been because something horrible has happened."

"I too am sorry that I didn't stop to help all of you sooner. And for the thing I did to you back at the Mission."

"What thing?"

"You know, when we were kids. The prank about hell's elevator."

Elena began to slowly smile. Her hair blended into the dark black of the sky while her face glimmered against the flames of the stout fire.

"But I am most sorry that I didn't stay to help Roberto get out."

Again, Elena had a small and gentle smile that glimmered with the flames' light.

"Mielo the prank was forgiven and forgotten by me long ago. I understand why you could not come to see us all these years, so that too has long ago been forgiven. The last that you bring up, well I think that is something we should talk about."

Mielo turned his head to face Elena.

"Si. Let's talk," he said.

"Mielo you need to sit and think about it as a whole and not just what happened in those crazy moments before Roberto was taken."

Mielo sat still while he let Elena's words sink in.

"I wasn't there but I know what Roberto said to you. I know that he would want his family to be protected and cared for by a person he was close to and trusted. He told you to leave him there and to go to help us. That's what he said, right?"

Mielo affirmed her story by slowly shaking his head.

"Why would he say that? Why would he ask you to leave him when he knew the risk he was taking? Roberto not only chose his family over himself, he chose you too."

Mielo sat mildly stunned.

"He knew you would get it. He knew you would understand and do what was right. So you have to accept that he is dead and is terribly missed by all of us. But you helped him. He was able to die with dignity and show his love for his family."

Elena then drew her head down into the shadows of the flickering light.

"Mielo you didn't betray him, you helped him."

Mielo again said nothing as he stared at the fire.

"My heart aches for Roberto but now my thoughts go out to my baby boy. I am sad that we had to leave Junior. I pray for him. I pray to the Virgin that he will be safe." She paused.

"All this talk makes my eyes wet again. It just happens. I cannot hold it back."

She again was trembling. Mielo helped her to lie down on her blanket. He then covered her with his blanket. She slowly drifted off as her eyes closed.

Off by himself, Mielo thought that the night had fallen too soon. Then he thought of Roberto. Was he really dead or was all of this a dream? He really missed being with Tio. He wished he was back home at the Mission. He thought of Tio again. Death really was a punk.

28

El Rossinyol

Mielo's satchel held some crackers which he had rationed out to all of them along the way. However, it was the water that he was most concerned about. It had to last for at least two more days and the weather wasn't helping. For the first few nights, they had traveled in higher than normal heat and humidity. During the day, it was hard to find shade to rest under. His water supply was dropping fast to where he was now rationing swallows and going without, himself. Elena was used to going without water and could outlast even Mielo, but Rafael and Serena were having a rough time.

Mielo had crossed these mountains many times and knew exactly where to go and when to drink. He was quickly learning it was different when you had young ones along. Serena was slowly growing blisters on her feet and Rafael was not far behind her with the same problem. Neither one had complained, but the limping made it obvious and the slowing pace forced Mielo and Elena to carry them on their backs for most of the night.

The air was also very thick and dirty from all the cars and cities not far below the mountain ridges. It would be at least ten more miles over rolling hills to reach the next stop which was a small camp just outside of Guadalajara known as Hermon.

Mielo knew that a Red Cross wagon usually stopped there in the morning and Mielo was hoping to catch up with it. After Hermon, Mielo would face his next big challenge. Because the walking had been so hard on the children and turned their feet bad, Mielo had decided that jumping a train would be their only way to make it to the tunnel. It was a chance he knew he would have to take.

They would be leaving Guadalajara by train to make up some time heading north. Still he knew he would have to find a place where they could rest before entering the tunnel.

They would all have to make a running jump to get on the train. The train they were jumping was known by the migrants as, "El Tren la Muerte" which translated in English to mean "DEATH TRAIN."

There was enough to be scared about with this train jump without knowing what the others called it. *I won't tell Elena or the children that little fact,* Mielo thought to himself.

But if truth be told, he really was scared. It was hard enough to jump the train with adult crossers. This time, it would be with two children. And now the weather was beginning to change for the worse. If it rained, the jump could be almost impossible. They needed help. If Mielo could get a throwaway phone from the Red Cross wagon, he would call Tio from Hermon to see if he could send help.

Mielo wanted to get to Hermon before daylight, so they stepped up their pace. The sun was easing over the crests of the foothills and dropping light into Hermon. Mielo could see the Red Cross wagon setting up just below. They continued their descent down the switchbacks of the mountain trail until Mielo could see where the wagon was parked. He left Elena standing in the line with the children while he tried to buy a phone and search for water or anything that might help them further along.

"Where are you heading?"

Mielo turned to find a lady speaking perfect English. She was a middle-aged white lady with a large sun hat sitting on the steps of old shanty cabin. When Mielo looked, she looked back with a bright and broad smile.

"You're SOMOS, aren't you?" she asked.

"I'm sorry, I didn't see you. Your voice came out of nowhere and surprised me."

"Are you a lost Shepherd?"

"Now, again I'm surprised you know I am one of them," he answered.

"It is clear that you are crossing the woman and the children, and that you are not the husband or the father."

Mielo continued to be amazed as he listened.

"The children and the mother do not cling to you like most good fathers. I could tell you are a professional crosser. But you're not connected with the bad hombres, the cartels.

Only SOMOS would try something that crazy. Try to cross with a woman and two children. But only SOMOS does anything good for these people around here," she said.

"Alright then. I will tell you what I have learned about you," Mielo said

"You are a good observer and a wealthy American who plays the guitar," he replied, looking at a large acoustic guitar leaning against her cabin porch.

"I am not the only one who is a great observer," she said. She picked up the guitar and gently began to strum.

"I am an American, not particularly wealthy but I get along. There will be a protest demonstration here this morning. You may want to be there," she said as she laughed and then stopped to take a drink from her coffee cup.

"How rude of me. Would you like some coffee?" she asked.

Mielo accepted and sat down beside her in the cool shade of her morning porch.

"What will you be protesting about?" Mielo asked.

She did not answer.

"How is the Padre? How is Father Pedro doing? she asked.

"You know him? From Los Angeles?"

"Of course, I marched with him in LA for years. He is part of the reason I came here. My name is Jona and I have been a friend of the Padre for many years."

She held out her hand to Mielo,

"Father Pedro Moreno, the crazy Jesuit from the old days back at Columbia University. We marched together in New York, San Francisco, and when I finally settled in LA, he purely by chance was there as well. I think he and I are kindred.

"It did not take me long to support his causes for the California migrant. It first started with the *braceros* in the San Joaquin valley. He worked with Chavez. We broke up a lot of bad stuff. Working conditions back then were terrible."

"He never talks about that stuff to me," Mielo said.

"I fell in love with all of these people long ago, beautiful people so full of tradition and so dedicated to their families. So now here I am. I am like him, I try to do what I can to help."

"So you are here to speak out against the way they are treated now and to help them?" Mielo asked.

"Yes. Stick around and you shall see all the people." She pointed over beyond the Red Cross wagon.

"See, some of the people are gathering over there."

There was a crowd handing out food and coffee to a line of migrants and other crossers. Elena walked up, holding Serena who was asleep and beside her was Rafael limping slightly. Jona looked up and down at the children and then to Elena. She then greeted all of them with her gentle smile.

"It is such a privilege to meet all of you," she said, holding her hand out to Elena. She then kissed Serena on the top of her head, then kneeled down to hug Rafael.

"This is Elena," Mielo said.

"Yes, I know and these two are Serena and Rafael," she answered back.

Elena looked at Mielo, but he too was confused as to how the lady knew all their names. Mielo was suspicious he was always careful about unfamiliar friends while on a crossing. He had learned the hard way that it was not always good when people know your name before you know theirs. Then he thought of what she said about Tio. She said he was a friend and maybe he and SOMOS had sent her to help.

"It is nice to meet you too," Elena responded.

"Elena, I have heard that you can sing like a Nightingale. I would like you to join us later when we hold our demonstration out here at the stage."

She pointed to a grassy park with a makeshift wooden stage. There was a group that was beginning to grow standing around it.

"Now Emilio, take her and the boys inside to meet Martha, my assistant. She is a nurse who will feed you, provide a cleanup and apply the medicine you received from the Red Cross to the children's feet."

She then looked down at Elena's feet.

"Dear girl! Martha will tend to your feet as well," she said.

Mielo looked down to Elena's feet and saw blood streaming from her blisters. He then realized that she had traveled all night this way. Her feet were worse than anyone of them. She had never complained, not once.

They entered the small cabin and met Martha the nurse. She made Elena lie on the floor while she cleaned and bandaged the open wounds on her feet. She then allowed her to rest while she bathed the two children. They all had some cold cereal and fruit. Elena had her own bath and it wasn't long before all four were asleep next to one another on the floor.

When Mielo later awoke, it was early afternoon. Martha had washed and cleaned his clothes. He washed his hands and face and cleaned himself as much as possible. He then saw Elena too. She had awakened to the music which had been playing outside.

"Listen Mielo! They are singing *De Colores!*" Elena said.

Soon the two children were awake. They all sat beside Elena on the front porch and listened. Elena gently sang along with the distant music. The children told Elena they wanted to stay there forever.

Suddenly, the music stopped. Elena could then hear the voice of Jona on the loudspeaker.

"That is Miss Jona?" Elena asked.

"Yes, she is some kind of protestor like Tio used to be," Mielo said.

Elena looked confused.

"What is a protestor?" she asked.

Mielo didn't exactly know how to explain it to her but he tried.

"It is like Tio was when he used to go downtown and walk in the streets and carry shit and yell about how fucked up things were for us. Only we were small and couldn't walk with him."

"Mielo, how did she know our names? How did she know I sing? And why did she clean and feed us?"

Then she paused thinking some more about it. She pulled an angel medallion from her pocket.

"Do you think she is an angel? An angel from the city of angels? She said she was from Los Angeles!" Elena asked.

Mielo remembered about all the angel talk Elena did back at the Mission when they were kids and how Tio would play it all up like they were for real.

"I don't know, maybe so," he replied.

Martha entered through the front door.

"Elena darling, Jona has asked that you join her outside and sing with her. Do you feel you can do it?" she asked.

Elena looked at Mielo as though she needed permission.

"You never need my permission to sing. It is your gift. Go give it away. Be thankful for what we have received here. It's your chance to give back," he said.

When they stepped outside, Mielo was amazed at the size of the crowd. Even the *Policia* were there and for some reason they were leaving everyone alone. It was like everything was okay— even though these people were trash-talking the governments on how they treated the migrant.

Then Mielo heard Jona speaking in broken Spanish.

"I'm going to bring in a special friend to sing a song. She is a friend to all of us because she is a friend to our cause. They call her, The Nightingale. She will be singing an old song with me. Some of you may know it, it's an old Mexican folk song we both learned as children. It is called *Rosa de Castilla* which as many of you may know means the Rose of the Castle."

Then it just took off like fire. The music started and Elena sang the song as she had sung it a thousand times. Even Serena and Rafael seemed completely overtaken by the smooth power of Elena's delicate voice.

After the demonstration, Mielo decided there was time to let Elena and the children rest into the night, giving their feet a longer time to heal. As the early morning fell, Mielo was up and soon planning to leave. Martha was packing Mielo's satchel with tortillas, dry beans, and water.

He had been able to make a call to Tio earlier that day. Tio had agreed to have someone meet him at the rail yards near the small town of Chacon.

Mielo stepped out to the front of the cabin to get a look at the weather.

Jona came out from behind him. "You have been in contact with Pedro?" she asked.

Mielo jumped slightly taken back.

"You have a way of surprising me that throws me each time."

Jona laughed.

"He knows of your change in plans to jump the train. He sent this."

She handed him a small and wrinkled piece of paper.

"It's the time and name for the meeting. This boy is not with SOMOS but I know him."

"He's a boy?" asked Mielo.

"He is young, but he can be trusted and he knows the trains." She pointed to the paper.

"This is what you say to him and this will be his response. That's how you will know him. He will help you."

Jona then took hold of Mielo's hand.

"They expect it to rain tonight. Do you think it might be a good idea to delay the jump until the rain stops? she asked.

Mielo shook his head no, knowing that he was about to get some serious words from her. She and he both knew that it was going to be very dangerous and the air did smell like rain. Mielo prepared for a long story about something he already knew, like the ones he used to get from Sister Rita back at the Mission.

"Emielio, you know she is a woman and her feet are very bad. How do you expect to get her and the two children on? They won't be able to get up to speed for the jump. Perhaps you should stay another day. You could wait out the rain and think this through a little more."

Mielo's mind flashed back to that day at the river. When just before they made the tragic crossing, the sky let loose with a heavy downpour. He recalled how much courage Roberto had, saving the boat and the four of them. Deep inside he was scared, but he had to move on. The chances of the cartel catching up to him, especially after Elena had performed publically here, was by far a worse gamble.

"I can't. I don't know how much Father Pedro has told you but we are being hunted by the Z's. We have to keep moving to stay ahead. Even staying here for this long and Elena out on the stage has been a big risk. If we are meeting someone for help this morning, we should be leaving within the next few minutes," he said.

Jona again began to plead with Mielo.

"But Mielo I can. . ." she started to say when another voice cut in,

"Thank you, Miss Jona, for all your help and concern for me and the children. But I can jump the train. We will all make it," Elena said.

Jona persisted with Elena.

"My sweet girl, this is very dangerous. It will likely be wet and slippery and if you miss, you could be cut to pieces and the children? What about the children?" Jona asked.

Elena looked at Mielo. "I trust Mielo. God and the Virgin will protect us."

"I do have a plan, Miss Jona. Thank you for your help though," Mielo added.

"Father Pedro was right about you two. There's something special. It's like you are angels sent to inspire all of us. What you are doing is incredibly dangerous, but also incredibly brave and somehow I too have the feeling that you are blessed and that you will make it."

Both Mielo and Elena said nothing.

"Well then, I will not try to stop you anymore," Jona said.

She then kissed each of one of them and soon they were once again on their way, On their way to the Death Train.

29

The Jump

I t was just before midnight when they reached the rail yards and so far there had only been a sprinkle of rain coming down. With the heat and humidity of the last few nights, the rain was a mix of blessings and curses. It felt refreshing to their bodies, but it would make the jump much harder.

Mielo was uneasy about leaving Elena and the children, but he needed to search and make contact with his SOMOS help. Walking the rail yards at night was dangerous and he didn't want to expose Elena and the boys to it. So he sat them down next to the rail line near a switching plate and told them he would return soon.

Mielo wandered the yard looking for his help. It was now raining steady. Jona had said his contact was not SOMOS.

Maybe he was not reliable or had forgotten or maybe he was just off somewhere drunk. He was about to turn back when he saw a dark figure of a man with a hoodie on. It was difficult to make out his face, but he was alone and seemed to be straight up.

"Hey," Mielo said to him.

"*Que esta pasondo?*" The man answered with a nod.

"You speak English?" Mielo asked.

"Only when I want to," he responded.

Mielo could tell from his answer that he was his contact. It had been written on Tio's paper. Not only did he look young, but he was a white boy. That would explain why he was so hard to find. A white boy wandering these yards alone was easy bait.

"You can help me get the mother and two kids on the train?" Mielo asked.

"Billy is my name," he said, extending his hand.

Mielo shook hands looking him over.

"I know what your thinking, what's a white dude with a red neck name doing out here in the middle of this shit. Your friend Father Pedro. He saved my life when I was a kid. He knows I have jumped a shit load of trains around here. I guess you could say I know my shit about doing this. That's about the whole short version of the story. He asked me to help and so I'm here."

"You know the Death Train?" asked Mielo

"You mean *El Tren la Muerte?*"

"Yes, I've jumped it many times. I know it well. It's not easy, even if you are alone."

He looked down at his watch, then up at the storm clouds.

"This is some wet shit and you don't have much time. But if you are ready, I am ready. Where are they?" he asked.

"Back by the switch. The woman has bad feet."

"They all have problems with their feet or their fucking shoes. We just have to make a go. Take me to them," Billy said.

When Mielo took him to Elena and Billy finally saw the three of them, he looked at Mielo and said,

"You are a fucking crazy SOMOS Shepherd. They didn't tell me they were so young. And the woman, she's fucking hot which is a big problem even with fucked up feet."

Elena moved toward so she could hear their words.

"Is there any way you can wait for me to come back? Maybe a day or two? With the rain and all this."

He swept his hand in the air toward Elena and the children. "This is just something I don't think we can do. You and I could make the jump with the kids on our backs. Maybe we can make it with the kids, but not the woman. Maybe we can come back for her. Is there a place she can stay?" he said.

"No!" Elena interrupted.

"I can make it to the train and I will make the jump."

She was shaking her head and her face was stern.

"I will not leave my children. I already lost one and I could never bear the loss of the other two. They will not leave here without me."

She stood face-to-face with Billy.

"Mielo, I will follow you to the train. I will put the pain out of my mind and I will do the jump. I will make it. I have prayed to the Virgin and we will all make it."

Billy looked at Mielo.

"Who is the Virgin?"

"This is Elena." Mielo said introducing her.

Billy reached his hand out to her.

"Nice to meet you."

"You as well," Billy said.

"Thank you and thank you for helping us," Elena said.

"Can you run with your feet that bad?" he asked.

"Yes, I can keep up."

Mielo looked over to Billy who seemed to be taken back by Elena's fierce resolve. Mielo had seen it before and had resigned himself to not even try to change her mind. So it was settled.

"Okay then. I believe you. For some strange fucking reason, I believe you," Billy said.

He then looked to Mielo.

"We need to find shelter and lay out the plan. We don't have much time. Maybe an hour." He said as he wiped the rain drops off his pocket watch for the second time.

"We have exactly forty-six minutes."

Planning with Billy made Mielo realize just how difficult and dangerous this part of the journey had become. He too said a small prayer to the Virgin to ask Tio's God to help. Between Tio's God and Elena's Virgin, he figured he had it all covered.

The rain turned to showers as they gathered with the others along the end of a long curve in the tracks. Billy had Rafael and Mielo had Serena wrapped tightly into the papoose backpacks. Elena had only herself to carry.

They kneeled down at a point where the train would be between slow and fast. The time when jumping was possible was only about two to three minutes. This was also where the Rail Guards were no longer watching the track for jumpers. Even with the bad weather, there were still many crossers waiting.

In the past, many had lost their lives at this spot. They had missed their step or were knocked off by the others. Mielo had made many jumps before, but with the rain and the extra weight and so many people to crowd around, this would be his hardest.

They could hear the train long before they saw it. Soon it came around from behind a long row of trees. They ducked down with all the others as the locomotives first passed. Then on Billy's que, they were all at once running as fast as possible toward a grain car that looked empty. Elena could see people stumbling and falling all around. Then there were those who tripped others or threw them to the ground. At first, Mielo was beside Billie but soon there were so many and he was so focused on the jump that he lost sight of Billy. He could still see Elena. She was directly behind him running on her bloody feet. He could feel the extra forty pounds of Serena slowing him. He was rapidly becoming weak and winded. There was not much time to be choosy about where he would make his jump. He closed in on the grab bars at the rear of the grain car. As soon as he could see the bars clearly, he made a leap with both hands and feet.

His left foot landed but his right slipped off the wet bottom rail. The same happened with his left hand but his right hand then caught a firm grip. Since the one hand and foot were on opposite sides, he was lucky to be able to balance his weight and pull himself up close to the railing. He clung tightly and brought in his other arm and leg. Serena also held on well. Mielo and Serena had made it but where was Elena and Billy?

Mielo had to move out of the way or be run over by those behind him. So he began to shift sideways onto the outside ladder while he watched for Elena. The rain was coming down in sheets that was blinding him.

Suddenly, Mielo felt a load as he looked down to see Elena holding on to his left leg. The pulling forced him to strengthen both grips as he could feel Elena trying to pull herself forward and off the ground. The ground itself was now beginning to move faster as Mielo looked down into Elena's frightened eyes.

"Mama, Mama!" screamed Serena.

Mielo's grips were weakening. But there was nothing he could do. He had to use both hands to hang on and Elena had his leg. As the train moved on faster, there were less and less jumpers and Mielo could see Elena was making good progress. She had now climbed to his waist.

But just before she reached to grab the ladder railing, out of nowhere a man jumped onto her. Holding her tight, he began to make her slip back down to Mielo's leg. Barely hanging on, Mielo could see the strain tearing Elena's grips from his leg. The train was now up to full speed and the wind was also adding to the pull on the finger grips.

When she slipped to the lowest point, Mielo could no longer do nothing. So with one swift move he raised his one free leg, his stronger one, and with one swift swoop he landed a kick square into the face of the man who held Elena. To Mielo's horror, both Elena and the man dropped further down, both barely able to hold their grips.

Mielo then put one more kick this time into the hands of the man. The blow was strong enough to cause him to release. Mielo watched the man's eyes fix upon him as he dropped into the darkness, disappearing beneath the train. He had seen that look before, the day he crossed the river as a child.

The sudden release of the man gave Elena a lift. She was able to renew her grip on Mielo and the other hand caught a firm grip of the other ladder rail. Mielo pulled her by her arm and she was soon over and aboard the train. Once they dropped down into the empty grain car, Elena, Mielo, and Serena all collapsed upon each other. They clung together beside a small outlet at the corner of the grain car. Exhausted and relieved to have made it, Mielo and Elena rested holding one another with Serena sheltered between them. The warmth of their bodies together held off the cold of the steady rain.

Once Mielo had regained some of his strength, he slowly climbed to the top of the rail ladder. He looked for Billy and Rafael, but the rain and the wind ripped at his face. He dropped back inside and down to the floor of the grain car.

"Can't see anything. We will have to wait until we can see again," he said to Elena.

Mielo reached over to her.

"They are on. Billy is a very good jumper," he added.

Now that they were out of the rain and wind, they could no longer hold their eyes open. They both joined Serena and fell fast to sleep.

Daylight was breaking when Mielo woke to see Elena cleaning the scrapes and wounds he had received from the jump. To his relief, he saw Billy and Rafael had made the jump onto another car and while they had slept, they found their way to them. All were aboard and safe for now.

Mielo had lost his satchel on the jump so they had no water or food. Because of the overnight storm, there were many puddles of fresh water. There was still a half-day ride to the small village of Chacon near the Yaqui River. It was the end of the road for most of those who were to cross.

It was where they too would get off and continue by foot. At that point they would be twenty-five miles from the tunnel entrance and ten miles from a secluded hilltop resting place that Mielo had learned about from SOMOS.

Mielo had decided that it would be worth the extra three mile hike to go there and get a much needed rest. First they would need to make it off the train.

Throughout the rest of the trip to Chacon, Mielo's mind kept drifting to the image of the man's face that he had kicked from the train. He was seeing him both in his mind and in his dreams as he dozed on the train. He was pretty sure that the man didn't make it. Even though he had to kill those two cartel soldiers back when he got little Sal out, this was different. This man was not cartel. He was just a normal guy trying to get somewhere, just like him. He didn't like killing anyone, but this one felt bad. Bad like never before.

It was difficult for him to accept, but he told himself that Elena, Serena, and he would have all died. He thought about Tio's story and how he had spilled some orange juice. He was sorry and he told God that he would clean up the mess someday. For now, he had to get Elena and the children to their home in America.

30

Chacon

The rain had stopped and things had dried out by the time they reached the village of Chacon. The drop from the train was much less dangerous than the jump. The train had slowed enough for all of them to land on their feet.

What remained dangerous for all were the coyotes who were there in numbers to greet and recruit all the migrants to cross with them. It was sad to see it all. Most of them went with the nasty coyotes and followed them blindly to their wagons. Mielo felt badly for them because they did not know what they were walking into. Mielo pushed through the village quickly keeping a low profile. There were many cartel soldiers and Mielo led his group away and around any of their recruiters. He had Elena hide her face and cover her hair to disguise her sex and natural beauty.

Elena had told Mielo of another dream she had while sleeping on the train. She said she saw weeping mothers who had been raped, beaten, and robbed. There was also children who had been taken and abandoned. Both Mielo and Elena watched as many of the crossers were going with the coyote recruiters who were making promises of buses to carry them and bridges to cross over rivers. The truth was that the men were on their way to their own deaths and for the women, there would be rapes and beatings.

As she passed through Chacon, Elena realized that she was seeing her nightmares become reality for the others. She and Mielo both knew there was nothing they could do. That was the hardest part of it all. Watching the fate of so many with so little and nothing could be done to help them.

Billy stayed with them until they were safely beyond the line of the recruiting coyotes. He was also able to get a small bottle of water and some crackers from a friend he had met to take him back home. He gave it all to Mielo and Elena. They thanked him for his help and once they were back on their way, he disappeared into the hills behind the village just as fast as he had appeared. Mielo thought to himself that he had again been helped by another one of Tio's angels.

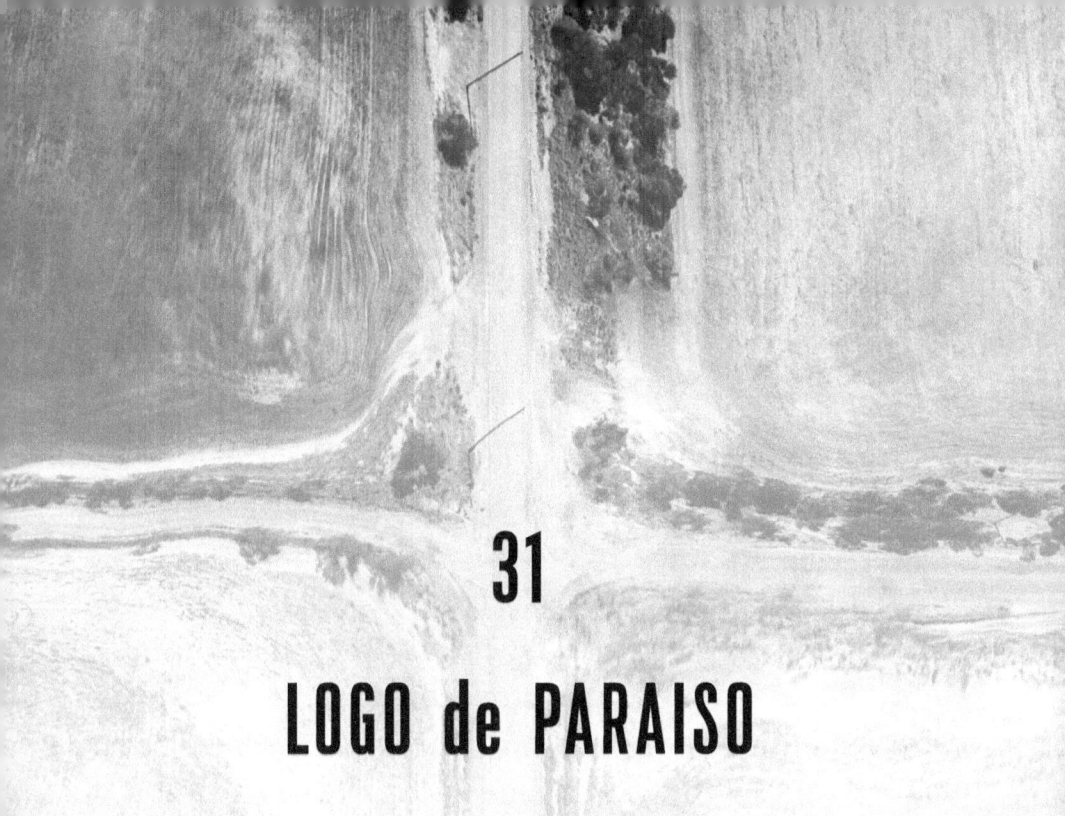

31

LOGO de PARAISO

After leaving Chacon, they ascended to an area high above the desert. The area was called the *Altiplano* which was between two mountain ranges close the Pacific Ocean. They had not been traveling by day so the heat, even with the ocean breeze, was difficult to tolerate for both Elena and the children. After two long days of walking north towards the border, they began to descend into a small canyon known as *Logo de Paraiso*.

This had been a SOMOS holding point that few if any knew how to find. It was a place with plenty of water and it was secluded so that made it very safe as a place to rest up. When Elena turned the corner on the final small rocky path descending into the canyon, she was stunned by the beauty and grace of what lay at the canyon floor. They all stopped to take it all in.

"Mama, can we go to the water?" Serena asked.

Elena looked to Mielo for advice.

"Yes, it is safe to swim and drink. It's not very deep, even out in the middle of the lagoon.

Just stay away from the deep end, where the falls are," Mielo said.

Elena repeated the warning in Spanish. Then both children ran across the flat granite beach and into the water.

"How did you know of this place?" Elena asked.

"This is a secret among the Shepherds of SOMOS. We only come here when we have to. There are others that know of it, but it's not on the maps. The cartels and most of the world don't know about it. We never know for sure if the water will be here. God and the rains decide," he answered.

At the end of the descending trail, there was a small rock to step or jump over. Mielo offered his hand to Elena just as she slipped on the granite. Catching her fall, Mielo's face came within a few inches of hers. Elena was in his arms for only a moment, but in that moment, she looked down upon his lips and then back up into his eyes. For the first time since they were kids, they were reminded that they were to grow to be more than just close friends. Then thoughts of his brother's recent death rushed into both of their minds and their hearts turned their heads away.

"It is so beautiful here," Elena said, trying to clear the nervous tension between them.

Taking in all of the moment, Mielo was moved by the beauty of what surrounded him. When they had reached the shore of the lagoon, Mielo just sat upon a large flat rock. He was fresh out of cigarettes but still was satisfied and filled with a new confidence. Elena looked back at him as if to tell him the same. She foraged on the small beach with the kids at her side and Mielo could only watch her. He took in the power of her silhouette as the sun reflected it off the water.

As the long shadows began to fall in the ravine, Mielo built a fire on the shore near an outcropping that protected them from the breeze. They ate the crackers which Elena heated and fed from the fire. Elena then bathed in the water far off and alone by the small waterfall. When she returned, she cleaned all the clothes and laid them on the rocks to dry. She then settled Serena and Rafael down beside the fire while she sang a quiet song. Mielo entered the water to clean himself.

"Mama, is Uncle Mielo our papa now?" Rafael asked.

Elena paused and looked around to see him coming out of the water but still far off enough away that he could not hear what they had said to her.

"No *hijo*, he is like a father. But you can only have one father in this world. Roberto was your Papa," she said.

"But mama, he can help. He can be our father until papa returns?" Rafael added.

"Your father will not return. Mama has told you about his accident. He will not return to us. Only as an angel someday you will see him. He is with God. Now sleep, you must go to sleep. We have to travel far again tomorrow," Elena said.

Mielo sat on the large rock which was still warm from a long day of sun beating down on it. He could see Elena continuing to dry herself off in the same sunlight. Her dark hair was wet and glimmered in the light of the falling sun. She wore a simple but clingy white frock that set off her delicate frame. Although she was unaware, Mielo watched as she bent over to check the fire.

"Your feet are better?" Mielo asked.

"Si, clean helps them and the medicine has helped them to heal."

"Come, feel the last of the sun's warmth," Mielo said.

She was slow at first, but then moved over toward him. She sat with her knees up beside him staring out at the water.

"You are thinking of Junior?" Mielo asked.

She looked at him.

"Si, I am worried for him. He is so young to be alone."

"I can tell you that he is good. He may have a hard time like all of us, but he will do well. I have seen him work. He is smart and fast," he said as he smiled to himself.

"And you, Mielo? I am thinking about you too. I can tell that you are having a hard time from what you did on the train, with the man."

Mielo looked away.

"I had no choice. It's not my way to kill and I have not had much rest in my mind since," he said.

"It was you who told me that Tio would tell you that death was a punk. But in this case, the death of one to save all of us gave us a chance. It was the same for Roberto. He gave his life to help all of us to have a chance. It is wrong to kill anyone but sometimes our choices are not really choices. They come down to what is most right."

She lifted his hand with hers.

"I've heard you say that death is a punk. A punk that we all must face at some time. Last night was your time. It may not be your last. But even God's angels had to destroy the bad and the evil. Now it is time to let the punk alone and move on."

Elena looked at him with a gentle smile shaking her head and with tears now streaming.

"Roberto would have liked this place. Yes, and he would have thanked you for helping us. I too, I wish to thank you. I would be with the coyotes and they would be making me do all that they wanted and the children would all be dead if you had not come to help," she said.

"You are my only family now. I will be with you until you cross and will always be there for you," Mielo said.

Mielo thought maybe what he had said suddenly made her feel good about what they were doing because she just rose from the beach rock, dropped her frock and ran to the shore splashing head first into the blue water. Mielo soon followed her. It was like they knew this could be their last chance to feel good. They would steal from this lagoon, steal the last drop of grace the water had to offer.

They both swam across the lagoon to the deeper area of the waterfall. Elena disappeared under and surfaced within inches of Mielo. When she came up, she opened her eyes to find him with his head back rinsing his hair in the waterfall. He then dropped his head forward and out of the water to find her face very close. With the water falling behind, he moved closer to her and held her hand tight under the water. This time she did not resist his touch.

"I mean no disrespect to my brother. But I have waited from the moment I met you."

Even in the water, her hands were warm. They trembled as Mielo looked into her wet eyes.

"I know it has not been long enough and I have not yet grieved my husband's death. But I know of no other man that I can be with. My life is in your hands, Mielo. My children and I know that this trust has come from God and so have you."

"Tio used to say that God tells two hearts when it is time to surrender their souls to one another. Elena, I surrender to you."

Elena looked down upon Mielo's lips. Without thinking any further, she moved her head closer to offer a kiss. Mielo moved in to press against her. He could feel the heat of their bodies against one another. This was the kiss that answered one of the deepest longings Mielo had ever known. They held one another and slowly drifted back into the cool water of the falls.

32

Laying Up

Leaving Logo de Paraiso made for a sad evening for all of them. Elena said it had been like, "visiting heaven but only for a short time." They did leave that evening heading towards the final destination of their crossing which was just fifteen miles ahead near the town of Campo on the California-Mexico border. That's where they would breach the Zeta tunnel and if all went as planned, cross into America.

After two long nights of walking, Mielo found a small cave under a hill with a large sage tree. It was a hiding spot for *SOMOS* Shepherds but Mielo had never stayed there. If he could get into it, he knew he would find supplies and maybe some food. He first checked out the cave for snakes and then they all settled down deep in a cool crevice inside the cave. Under the shade of the overhanging sage tree, Mielo felt they were well-hidden and safe from all the crazy action going on outside on valley floor below.

After the children fell asleep, Mielo searched the cave for supplies. He discovered a satchel full of dry beans and rice. He gave the food to Elena who had started a small fire. As she prepared the food, Mielo sat down at the opening of the cave and went through some of the supplies left by *SOMOS*. He pulled a set of binoculars, tossed a disposable cell phone that no longer worked and pocketed some ammunition for his pistol.

His mind was deep in the thoughts of how to go forth from there. He needed a plan, a plan to get out of there soon. Tio had told him to wait at the cave and that he would send help, but there had been no sign of a *SOMOS* contact. Mielo was ready to make a move on his own but knew he would have a much better chance of crossing the tunnel if he had help. He would wait it out until someone from *SOMOS* showed.

The cave was at one of the highest points in the hills overlooking the northern Sonora desert. Below was a good view of the sagebrush-covered desert floor and they could see the lights of the town of Campo which only two miles off. Just west of Campo was a shipping center with several warehouses known as Tarlow. Tarlow was where they would exit from the tunnel. They were less than a mile from the tunnel entrance and with the binoculars, Mielo could make out the Zeta compound which was built over the tunnel entrance and now looked completed.

Mielo did not know how long he would have to wait and who would make contact with him. The latest word was that the Zeta soldiers had set up business at the compound. They were reinforcing the tunnel walls and they had taken over everything.

With food in their belly, Elena laid the two children down for a rest as Mielo set out to collect some dry wood or any food that he might run into. Just below the cave less than a mile east, Mielo spotted a large encampment of migrants settling in for the night. He wanted to stay away from them because they were probably led by a cartel band. So he ignored the camp and went back to the cave where he sat beside the fire.

Elena soon sat down beside him. She took his hand and their eyes slowly met. Her eyes began to swell into tears. Mielo thought to himself how tough it had been on her. She had stood up to everything that had happened to her. She had walked all those miles on bloody feet without complaining. She had taken on "Billy the kid" when he told her she could not jump the train. Now she was willing to do whatever she had to do to get to a place where her children would finally be safe.

Mielo reached up to lightly touch the bottom of her chin with his fingers, turning her face closer to him.

"I am sorry for all that has happened to you, Elena. We cannot change what we do not control. There are evil people in this world who do not care about anyone or anything."

Her eyes again were growing wet as she answered.

"I am beginning to doubt myself. I am starting to think I do not deserve to go on."

"Elena, it is the evil taking over, trying to convince you that you have been defeated already. Even before you begin."

"No, Mielo. We have both seen the worst of this world. We've seen what evil can do. There are things we have seen that no person should have to see. Sometimes, I just don't believe I will make it back to my city where the angels are, in Los Angeles," she said.

"Elena, you cannot let all this get to you. It can't break you. If you do, then Serena and Rafael, they will know it and they too will give up. All will be lost."

Elena silently broke down. Her face was crying but no noise came from her. This time Mielo held her tight in his arms. The commotion somehow woke Rafael who looked up to see if his mother was safe and then laid his head back down.

Mielo could feel Elena was changing and for the first time, he felt that she was starting to break—that she was losing all hope. Mielo had to make something happen. He had to go against his fears and move ahead with a desperate attempt to cross. He would not be able to wait much longer for help to come.

Elena held out her hand which held her own angel medallion.

"Mielo, I fight to live every day and just to live for my children. This medal of our lady is my only hope. My prayer is that someday we will all make it through and be back together at the city of the angels."

Mielo kissed Elena on the forehead and said, "I have promised my brother that I would see his family through and I am certain I will finish the job."

Elena's voice became less and less, weaker and weaker, until it was but a sleepy whisper. Mielo too had no more that he could say. The darkness had fallen upon Elena and there was nothing he could do about it. Now it was up to him. She may believe in this God she called Jesus Christ, but in truth he found it hard to pray. He remembered that he had said the same thing to Tio back at the mission on the day that his whole family was taken away from him by the river.

"You may believe in this Jesus, but I am too scared to believe in anything," were the words he told him.

Even though he did not know this God the way Tio and Elena did, he had learned at least this much. People need to be able to believe that things can happen. Maybe even things that are called miracles.

So he prayed. For the first time in his life, he prayed the way Tio had told him to do, only this time he really meant it. He touched the angel medallion as Elena slept and asked the Virgin to ask Tio and Elena's God to send some more angels and soon.

As the dark grew near, Mielo's prayers were cut off by the sound of gun fire coming from the camp just outside. He left the cave and moved out to where he could get a better view of the action. A Zeta coyote was using a hand gun to shoot people one at a time in an execution style. As Mielo moved in even closer, he could hear screaming and more gun fire.

33

Taken

Mielo saw all of it from a distance. He saw the shootings and now he spotted a helicopter going down in the ravine close to where he was hiding. The helicopter was green and had US words on it. Probably *La Migra*, he thought to himself. His first reaction was to run to help whoever was in the crashed helicopter but suddenly he stopped to think better of it.

If he went in to help, there was a good chance the Zetas would capture him. He could now hear the engine sputtering and an eerie high-pitched whining sound like it was ready to explode and erupt into flames.

He could now hear cartel soldiers off in the distance shooting wildly at the scene. That was when he saw a man and a lady officer who were both packing guns. They were both struggling to free the pilot from the airship. He went in closer. When they saw him, they both stopped pulling on the pilot and drew their weapons.

"I will help you! Don't shoot, I am American!" Mielo yelled in perfect English with both hands up high.

Mielo recognized the name sewn into the uniform of one of the officers. The name was Baca. He dropped his weapon down first, then the lady officer followed. They both went back to work on freeing the pilot.

"Can you help us? Get his legs free!" Baca said.

Mielo moved to the pilot's side and pushed his feet free from under the mangled instrument panel. Baca and the lady then pulled him out. Mielo then helped Baca drag the pilot away from the aircraft as more shots rang out.

The pursuing soldiers were much closer now. Bullets whistled over their heads. The lady officer fired back with her pistol. This must have surprised the Zetas because all of the sudden their shooting stopped.

"Do I know you?" Baca asked as Mielo helped him lift the pilot onto his back.

"I'm American. My name is Emielio Estrada."

"Do you need our help?" Suarez asked

"You cannot help me. I have a woman and two children with me."

"Are they illegal?" Baca asked.

"Yes. I cannot leave them."

"We have to go. But thank you for your help, Mr. Estrada. We need to take advantage of this pause in the gun fire as the best opportunity to run," Suarez said.

They both then stormed away with the pilot on Baca's back. Mielo traded one last look with Baca.

"Was Roberto your brother?" yelled Baca.

"Yes, Roberto Estrada! They killed him," Mielo yelled back to him while pointing at the soldiers shooting.

Suddenly, the shooting began again. Baca and the lady took off in the direction of the border. They were soon met by a US team who picked them up in a military style Hummer.

Things didn't go as well for Mielo. He ran fast and reached the cave without being captured or shot.

"What's wrong?" Elena shouted.

"Zeta! They're behind me. We have to go now. Grab Serena now, we have to go. No time!"

The Zeta soldiers had dogs that had tracked him to the cave. They turned the dogs loose on him and then beat him in front of Elena and the children.

They tied them all onto a long pole. The two children were tied between Mielo and Elena so that if either child didn't keep pace, Mielo and Elena would have to pick them up and carry the weight. Many times, Elena and Mielo would have to lift up the pole so the child wouldn't drag on the ground. They walked them all down to the Zeta compound at gunpoint.

Most of the Zeta compound belonged to Hector. Hector had set up his operations from there. There were about ten soldiers who had pledged their loyalty to him. Soon though, Hector would have to pay a price for crossing Z1, the boss. Defying Armando Vega was like a decree of war. It would not be long before Vega himself would come calling.

Hector had all this in mind when he arrived at the compound. He was now stealing the money from the child-trafficking business and had already spent most of it on arms. He had food, water, and plenty of arms. The compound also held crates of automatic rifles, grenades, missile launchers, and ammunition. In the end, if Hector wasn't coming out on top, he had decided to use the tunnel as his escape.

Once Mielo and Elena reached the compound, Serena and Rafael were taken away to be with the other children. Mielo and Elena were separated and locked up in rooms with no windows. Mielo was tied up and left on an desk chair. The room looked like someone's office. Other than the light that hung from the ceiling, there was no other light. In front of him on the desk was a bottle of tequila half-drunk and a pack of smokes. Mielo was alone for now, but he was pretty sure Hector had plans for him.

Within minutes, Hector entered the room with two of his soldiers like he had been in a hurry. He looked over Mielo's wounds. His face was bruised, lower lip swollen, and he had dog bite-marks on his lower leg that were still bleeding.

"They beat the shit out of you. That's good," Hector said.

Then he sat down across from him and leaned forward against the table. Taking a shot of tequila, he slammed the shot glass down on the desk while looking straight at Mielo.

"So now you are SOMOS?" he asked.

Mielo did not answer but instead asked him a question.

"Where is the Elena?"

"Safe and close, I will tell you more later. Now I have to ask you one more question. Are you SOMOS?"

"I am," he answered.

"Heroes to the *pinche* wetbacks. These *pollos*," he said.

"Why are you killing them, so many?" Mielo asked.

At first Hector dogged Mielo with his eyes. Then he paused and like when they were kids, he started his familiar one-sided grin slowly creeping across his mouth from left to right.

"You speak your mind even with your life on the line. If I tell you where she is, I will have to kill you," he said.

The other two soldiers in the room began to laugh out loud upon hearing the comment. Hector looked up and laughed along with them. Then he poured another shot, drank it, and lite up a smoke.

"They laugh because they know I will kill you anyway. The only reason you are still alive is because of your entertainment value. I am not sure how I will kill you yet. A leader in the *SOMOS HERMANOS* who just didn't make it across. Sad, very sad," he said shaking his head.

"But I must make you a big kill for all of them to see. Like your brother Roberto."

Mielo reacted to the comment by squirming in his chair. He then raised himself up and while still tied to the chair, spat across the room hitting Hector in the face.

"Roberto was ten times the *pinche* man you are today."

Hector wiped his face while continuing to show his grin.

"Besides I owe you. First for the fight we never finished at the Mission and then for the fight you blew up at *El Pollo Rancho*. Yes. That costs me *mui dinero*. You always fucked everything up for me. It's what you do, right *Essa*?"

"Tio Pedro," Mielo said.

Hector dropped his grin. The two locked eyes.

"Tio Pedro still prays for you," Mielo said hoping to get inside Hector's head.

"He is a *pinche* old man who needs to just fucking die. If I ever see him again, I will kill him first and then think about why. Not like you. I am being good to you by letting you talk to me before I kill you. You and your *pendejo* brother should have both been with me in the Zs."

Hector was pointing to himself while pounding on his chest.

"Then you would not be all fucked up like you are right now and almost dead. Besides *SOMOS* takes care of the poor. I have fucking money. Why would Tio Pedro pray for me? I am not poor."

Hector pulled out a wad of bills and threw it on the desk.

"You see? I don't have to buy shoes at the welfare store like you."

He then belted out a large laugh.

"Tio says there are many ways to be poor," Mielo answered, again trying to hit Hector's soft spot. Hector slowly took a swig from the tequila bottle and set it back down on the table. He could sense that Mielo was about to piss him off like crazy.

"There are those who have *mucho* money and many things, but they are still poor. Because they have no one who cares about them. You see, you may have all the money in the world, *Vato*, but when you die and you will soon die. . ."

Hector's face quickly flushed to a darker color.

"No one will know and no one will care except maybe Tio *Pedro*. That's because you are right. Tio *Pedro* does care about the poor. Even the ones who are poor in their heads."

Hector's face swelled in rage. He stood upright quickly and yelled to his men in Spanish.

"Hang him out with the dogs. The same ones that ate his brother for lunch. If they don't eat him to death, then we will smoke his ass and string him up for those *pinche SOMOS* to see."

He turned back at Mielo and said,

"I will make your death very slow and painful. Right now, we need to keep you alive to see if someone with money will pay for you and the bitch. But only for a day or maybe two."

Hector held up two fingers.

"You will be with my dogs in my secret yard. But you will not sleep like my dogs. You will have no food, no water. Then if you are still alive after two days, I will barbecue you on a stake and let those angry and starving dogs lick you clean to your bones."

Again, he broke into his evil grin.

"Just like brother Roberto."

Mielo looked back defiantly at Hector. He was waiting to see him break.

Mielo snapped off the words, *"Chinga tu madre,"* remembering from their childhood that the phrase would always set Hector off.

Mielo's words worked. They sent Hector into an uncontrollable rage.

"You want to know about the woman? We have sweet Elena. That makes two big trophies for me. Especially the woman, what a trophy! I have been saving myself for her. Ummm!"

"I caused all this trouble for you. The woman and the children are of no value to you. They were just passing with me to the north. Let them go," Mielo asked.

Hector now laughing again replied,

"I don't have time for this shit. To negotiate with *putos!* I do not have time to talk the fate of those who are already dead. Bring the woman to my bedroom now. I am very horny right now and need to be sexed up."

The next thing Mielo felt was the butt of a rifle against his face. Then he was covered with a cloth bag. They took him away somewhere down a short set of stairs. He could see nothing but could hear Elena fighting as they took her upstairs to Hector. Mielo was again helpless to do anything. The more he moved, the more he was hit and kicked by the soldiers.

Finally, he could see and hear no more. He could still feel and smell the evil in the room. Mielo never learned what happened to Elena that night. She never talked about it and when he asked, she never answered.

34

Dogs

Hector had ordered his soldiers to put Mielo out in the "dog pit." This was where all the dogs, mostly full grown Pit Bulls were held. They were usually kept in small cages, but tonight Hector had ordered his men to let them all out and they had not been fed that day.

Mielo was bound upright by leather straps to a tall and greased metal pole. It had foot pegs just high enough that the dogs could not reach and bite into Mielo's feet. The pole had been greased down and was very slippery. When Mielo would slip too far, he was able to keep the dogs away by kicking with his free leg. Once he was up there, he realized that if he lost his concentration for even one second and slipped, then he would be hanging by his hands to where the dogs could have their way with him from the waist down.

It was only a matter of time. Mielo was getting tired fast. Because the hand straps were leather, Mielo was able to work to stretch and loosen them enough to climb his way up the pole. Twice he slipped and was bitten on his kicking leg. He was eventually able to pull himself up and out of the bite range. His legs now bleeding, Mielo looked over to catch the soldiers watching him and laughing at his trouble. Mielo could tell that the dogs had been trained to attack and kill. They all were below him, snarling and leaping for most of the time. This seemed to further entertain the soldiers. They started to bet money on how long he would last up the pole and how fast he would die once he fell.

Mielo held himself on the pole for several more hours. Over time, the dogs seemed to become less interested and backed off. Finally, they went off to rest against a wall. Only then was Mielo able to drop and hang from his shoulders to rest his legs. Still, he could not close his eyes to sleep.

The dogs kept their eyes on him, waiting for his fall. They knew the routine. His joints ached, and were stiff and painful. He was thirsty and hungry, but his biggest problem continued to be his legs which were giving out on him. Even resting them off and on while hanging were not enough. He realized that soon he would fall to his death. He figured he only had a few more hours left. His only hope was that maybe Baca had seen him get captured and would come back to help him.

As delirium set in, Mielo's vision began to blur. His mind drifted off. He could smell the stench of what he thought was probably rotting garbage or maybe bodies just over the wall outside the dog pit. At times he thought he could hear what sounded like the children. If Serena and Rafael were in there, then at least they were still alive he thought. He then turned to thoughts of Elena and what could be happening to her. Those thoughts were more painful than what he was feeling in his own body. Darkness was beginning to cover everything.

35

No God

Elena had been held for many hours in what seemed to be Hector's bedroom. She had been bound to the posts of a large bed. The bindings around her wrists were painful, but the bed was soft and comfortable. Her mouth had been taped closed, but her eyes and nose were not covered.

The room had a desk with several stacks of old papers and photos around it. Elena could see the photos from a distance. It looked like some of the migrant children being held at the compound had been photographed for some reason.

"Soon you will be gone like the rest," came the words of Hector who was now standing at the doorway.

He walked over to Elena as though he was looking to be her friend. He reached up and quickly ripped the tape off of her mouth. Elena drew back from the pain of tape burning her skin as it came off.

"There we go. Now I can see those very sexy lips," he said.

He sat across from her in a swiveling chair.

"To this day, I do not understand how you could fall for that *puto* Roberto Estrada or his *pendejo* brother. All this time you could have had me," he said with his familiar grin.

"All this time, you could not see how I wanted you and now I will have to kill you. This is so sad. You know I took pictures of you?"

He reached over to pull his laptop computer out from a secret compartment in his desk. It was on and displaying nude pictures of her that his soldiers had taken when she first arrived at the compound.

It was done while she had been drugged and unconscious. The cartel was also very connected with the pornography business. When beautiful women were captured, they would take advantage of them by taking and then selling nude pictures. They would also make them work in films or straight up sell them as sex slaves in foreign countries.

Hector held the pictures up.

"I think these are my trophies. Yes, these are the trophies I will show to everyone. I think I will post them on my page!" he said.

"Can I see them closer?" she asked hoping she could learn more about what had happened.

"I cannot let you see. There is way too much *importante* for your eyes to see. Even if you will be dead before you could share it."

"Hector, what have you done to Mielo and my babies?"

Hector was holding Rafael and Serena at the compound with the intent of selling both off, so he straight up lied to Elena.

"The babies are gone. I let them go. We cannot have a nursery here and I did not want to waste bullets on them. So we released them out into the desert," he said.

"They are alive?"

"Last I saw. I don't know about now nor do I give a shit."

"What about Mielo?" She asked.

"He took the dogs for a walk," he answered, now laughing to himself.

Elena starred at the floor. She felt numb with worry but she tried to hide her fear from Hector.

"Hector, you have never been good to me or to anyone. How could it be that you would think I could choose you? When it is you who chose to be terrible to all of us and then you would laugh about it."

Hector stood still listening.

"You kill and beat people without any feeling. You have become an animal no better than the dogs you send to kill. While I find it too hard to forgive you, I think God will still forgive you. He will forgive you if you ask Him. If you walk away from all of this. This horror that you live in. He will forgive you," she said as she wept aloud.

All expression had left Hector's face. Like Elena had never seen before, she could tell by his face that he was thinking deeply in the moment. He then looked up to her, then to the sky, and then back to her. Then as he turned to walk out of the room, he spoke to her for the last time.

"I have no God."

36

Freeways

"You know Los Angeles is synonymous with the concept of the motor freeway," Jorden Helms said to Agent Suarez as they rode in their government town car sitting in the southbound lane on the Los Angeles 405 freeway. Traffic had slowed to a crawl.

"It looks to me like they got it all wrong. It has taken us over an hour to travel maybe ten miles?" Suarez replied checking her watch.

"Not really. You see it's part of the culture here. In fact, this is one of the only places in the world where the freeways are given an article when naming them. For example, we are on 'the' 405. We just transitioned off 'the' 210. If you asked someone in this city how to get to interstate 5 or if you tell someone to take 610 to 90 west. They will know right off the bat that you are not from So Cal," Helms said.

"And this is why you get paid the big bucks, right? To know these sorts of cultural nuances?" Suarez asked.

"Yes, this is what I do. I pay attention to the reasons why things are the way they are and I ask myself why? I think it was Yogi Berra who once said, *'Sometimes you can see a whole lot of things just by looking'*.

"For example, why do you think LA is one gigantic traffic jam? Poor planning? Too many cars? Not enough freeways? Well maybe that's the obvious reason, but the real reason is money, greed, and power."

"The root of all evil? Okay, you have me on the hook. Please continue to fascinate me, Deputy Helms."

"So here's a short history lesson. When LA was just a bunch of orange groves and the developers were figuring out how to steal water from the north, the car manufacturers in Detroit and Wall Street were also trying to figure out how they could benefit from the massive influx of people into the Los Angeles basin.

"So they bribed the city planners and the developers long before any thoughts of any form of mass transit got going. The result was a huge demand for a massive and modern freeway system. Concrete steel, on ramps, off ramps, etc.

"And of course, along with this came the demand for the automobile. At first, the automobile was king of Los Angeles. There were automobiles everywhere. With all their rubber tires, steel bodies, gas-guzzling engines and of course what LA was most famous for, the smog. And no one really cared about what all that stuff would do to the people down the road say sixty, seventy years later.

"Because as you know, they made their billions and of course they're all gone."

Helms points to the traffic outside the window.

"So this is what they left us to deal with."

"So it was all one big money grab?" Suarez asked.

"Why do I feel like I am supposed to read between the lines of your story?"

"Marty, I'm just saying sometimes we have to take a good look in order to really see what's really going on. Sometimes we need to look at everything, not just what we see in front of us. That's all I'm saying."

"Jordan, does this have anything to do with this morning's meeting?" Suarez asked as she sipped on her on paper cup of coffee.

Both Helms and Suarez had been scheduled to meet with Ricardo Morales, the Deputy Director of Mexican Consulate in Los Angeles. The purpose of the meeting was to discuss the situation at the border.

"Hold off for just a moment," Helms said as he interrupted the conversation. The window separating the driver came down.

"Yes, Frank," Helms said.

"Sir, the thing you asked me to remind you of, is on."

"Thanks, Frank," Helms replied as he turned the car's TV set off of mute to hear the national news of yesterday's incident.

CBS News has just learned and confirmed more killings at the US-Mexico border. The killing was near the California border and close to the Border Patrol offices in Campo, California. This is the second of two killings that have surfaced on the Mexican side of the border. The last one was two weeks ago in Texas. We have no estimates of the number of deaths this time, but at least one death is confirmed.

CBS has also learned that authorities have discovered a compound reportedly to be the northern base of operations for the Los Zetas Cartel. The report alleges the Zeta Cartel may be harboring minors and others for trafficking into the US.

Helms turned the TV down as his phone rang.

"Yes sir. Sir, we are about to go into a meeting with a *Senor* Ricardo Morales. I'm told he is the person who knows the most and is most connected to what is going on at that site.

"Yes, Agent Suarez is with me and she has a handle on the operations side. Yes sir, we have good intelligence. I am working with Agent Suarez and after this meeting, I am hopeful that we can get in there and sort this all out.

"No. I haven't heard anything about the position of their President or their military. It is on my agenda too. It's all pretty fresh news. Yes, I will call before I make any other moves. No, so far I have managed to avoid the press. But I don't see that going on much longer. Thank you sir, goodbye."

Looking over to Suarez, Helms hangs up the phone.

"This is going to be a media feeding frenzy if we don't stop it soon," he said.

"We need to go for the throat on this. Jordan, these cartel *banditos* are not working alone. They are too well-organized and strategic. With the amount of money they're making, there has to be some help coming from inside the country," Suarez said.

"I hear you, but you know I can't just go in and accuse the Mexican government of supporting these operation. Accuse them of working with the cartel? Of blatant killings of their own people? Of child trafficking? We just don't have enough intelligence to support those indictments," Helms said.

"Yes we do. I've seen it with my own eyes. So has Baca," Suarez replied.

Pulling into the consulate driveway and up to the doors, Helms looked directly at Suarez and said,

"Look, I intend to make a few points at this meeting that will in some ways insinuate their involvement. But I need to walk where we're not stepping on the flowers. I don't want to walk away from this meeting knowing there will be a price to pay later.

"Whatever we decide to do, we will need their cooperation at some level. We will need to give them room to decide when and where. This is not an FBI negotiation; it's a diplomatic discussion about how to solve a problem. That is how it will be handled. Are you on board?"

Shaking her head in the affirmative, Suarez asks,

"Your little story about the freeways earlier."

"Yes?" Helms said looking at her.

"You think it's the same? You know, the dog is being wagged? Just a different tail?"

Helms didn't answer. He just smiled as the FBI agent buzzed the consulate doorbell.

37

Embassy Meeting

An emergency meeting had been set for Helms by the US Ambassador. It had been initiated at the request of US authorities who were concerned about the bad press coverage.

They were assembled in a conference room at the Mexico Consulate in Los Angeles. Seated in the middle of a long and wide conference table was Deputy Helms. Beside him sat Agent Suarez and then standing by the door were two secret service agents. Seated opposite Helms, in front of draped US and Mexican flags, sat the Mexican ambassador to the US, Mr. Henry Fuentes. He had two staff assistants seated beside him.

Ambassador Fuentes began the discussion.

"Deputy Helms, it is good that you have come to us with this problem. I assure you that President Juarez is very much aware of this situation and has been briefed on the reported atrocities occurring at our border."

"Thank you and with all due respect Mr. Ambassador, only last month did we meet with Director Morales here in Los Angeles and quite frankly, his position was not responsive. We are now more certain that organized crime syndicates are involved in these crimes and they also appear to be well-funded and armed. Again to be quite frank, they appear to be operating freely and without any restrictions.

"So this visit is not intended to be as much diplomatic as it is a request for your country's assistance in dealing with this very serious border problem," Helms said.

The Ambassador's smile disappeared.

"Deputy Helms, we have not received such reports. Can you tell me more about this problem?" he said.

Standing up, Agent Suarez moved to the center of the conference table.

"Mr. Ambassador, sir, these were taken two nights ago by agents who were on business in your country."

She laid down four black and white photos of caches of weapons, and children bound and sitting in a circle. Then a shot of six bodies lying dead and then a face picture of Hector Alvarez.

"Mr. Ambassador, do you know this man? This is Hector Alvarez, a high ranking soldier in the Los Zeta Cartel."

Fuentes picked up the photos, looked closely and handed them to his assistant standing beside him. The assistant studied the photo then nodded his head up and down, and handed them back to the ambassador. The ambassador continued to study the pictures and then asked,

"The photos of the children. They are being held at the compound?"

"Yes, and the other bodies were killed execution style, This I witnessed myself."

"What business were your agents conducting?"

"As I previously stated, our meeting with Mr. Morales preceded this diplomatic trip. We had hoped to have more cooperation from him and there was a definite sense of urgency, so we acted on our own internal interests. As it is, we were restrained in taking any action to stop the killings," Helms added.

"We saw this from our airship. The Zetas fired shots at us which required our pilot to do an emergency hard landing. No one died but we witnessed much of this before we went down. We also saw a US citizen, a woman, and two more children taken by the Zeta men. Our pilot was seriously injured, but thanks to this man, the US citizen, we were able to get out of there alive."

"This is why our military reported a US helicopter down at the border. We received that intelligence last night. And the American press?" Fuentes asked.

"Yes. As you may have learned, this has become a major story which has piqued the interest of the US State Department and of course the President. I have spoken to Madame Secretary twice. She sends her best regards. However, both of them have serious concerns," Helms answered.

"Mr. Helms, can we speak in private?"

"Of course, Mr. Ambassador."

The room cleared.

"I am sure that you are aware that the information I am about to pass on to you is highly sensitive to my government, and it should be clear to you that I will deny ever having said it should you decide to source it."

"Yes, you have my assurance, Mr. Ambassador," Helms replied.

"We have removed Director Morales and in doing so, we have only recently become aware of the complete picture of what has been going on at the compound outside Campo.

"There is a connection between Morales and a Mr. Marco Ramirez whom I believe is in turn connected with the Zeta boss, Mr. Vega, and the man in your picture."

"His name is Hector Alvarez," Helms interjected.

Fuentes shook his head yes.

"Much money has passed between all of them and I know their activities have had a profound effect on our relations."

"Yes, particularly in the tourist community. It has practically ruined the markets. Most are too scared to travel," Helms said.

"And, this may only be the head of the dragon. We have learned that hundreds of the migrants from all over South America have been killed by the Zeta coyotes. They got away with it for a while. But now they capture and hold children. That puts them in the spotlight both here and in the US," Fuentes said.

"We have evidence that Mexican and US citizens, as well as children as young as eight are currently being held in stash rooms at the compound," Helms added. Fuentes looked away briefly, then responded.

"In some cases, our government has been deceived and resources have been used to assist in this effort."

Now looking down as he continued in a quiet voice.

"Mr. Helms, we are an honorable country and there are many who try to do the best for our citizens. We are ashamed of what has happened and embarrassed that it could happen under our noses without having the proper knowledge. Even more, to be tipped off by a neighboring country as to what is happening in our backyard is to say in your language, inexcusable."

"What is to be done?" Helms asked.

"I have received word less than an hour ago that our military is ready to move on the compound as early as this morning."

"On the compound?" Helms asked.

"Yes, on the compound and the surrounding area which brings me to an important point that I must make you aware. There is rumor of an illegal tunnel and crossings that have occurred through it over the last month. We know the entrance is inside the compound. But we do not know where it comes out. Somewhere just over the border. You should expect the Zetas and some of the captives who may know of it, to flee that way," Fuentes added.

"Will you need our assistance with the attack?" Helms asked.

"I will have our military leadership contact you. Since Agent Suarez has the working knowledge, I think it may be best for her to coordinate the mission. But Mr. Helms, I am certain that our government will want the operation to look as though we acted alone," Fuentes said.

"We can keep our end of it covert. Although, I can't control the press. They already have a whiff of what's going on. Understand I will need to share this with the top at the FBI and with our customs and immigration people. They will all need to approve the action."

"Yes, understood, but as I said before, discretion is important both for a successful military operation and the continued trust of our two countries."

Fuentes held out his hand to shake.

"Mr. Ambassador, give my best to your President."

"Thank you and again our apologies for this very sad development," said Fuentes.

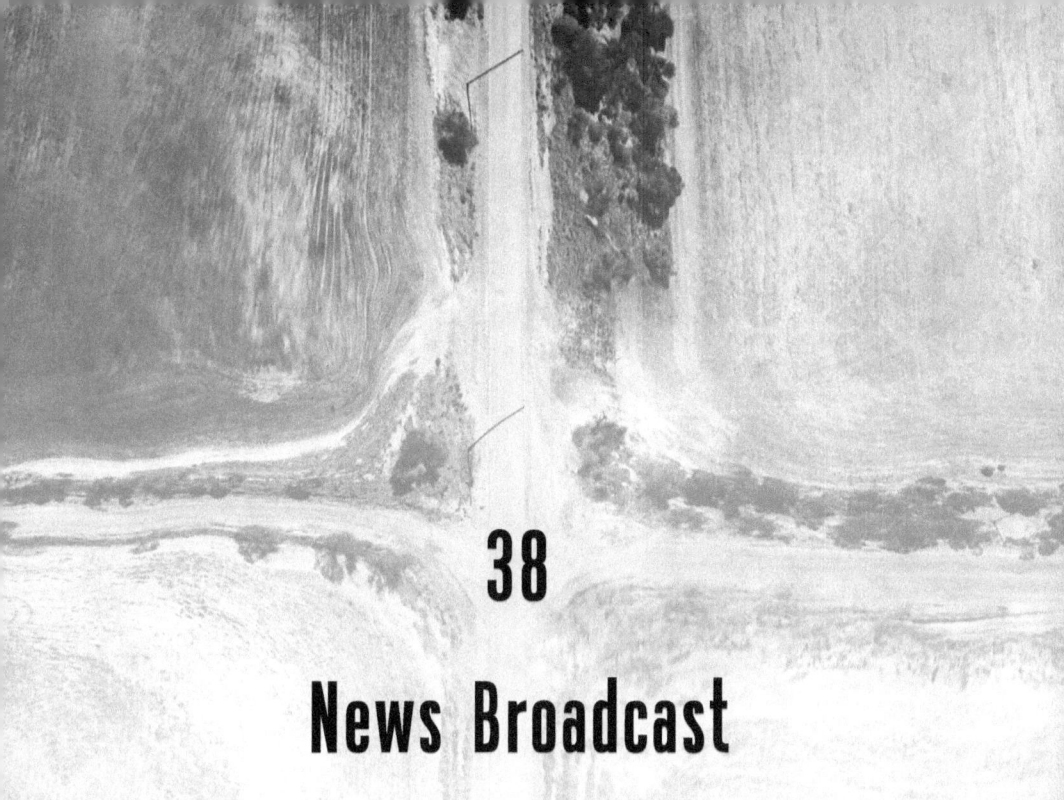

38

News Broadcast

Helms and Suarez returned to the Campo field office to prepare for the raid on the Zeta compound. Sitting in Captain Baca's chair, Helms was giving Baca and his men a briefing from the political perspective when he suddenly turned the TV mute signal off to hear the evening news.

In an apparent attempt to learn more about the recent killings and increase in child kidnappings in Mexico the FBI and Border Patrol officers out of the Campo field office conducted a covert surveillance on a cartel stronghold approximately two miles into the Mexican side of the border.

Helms suddenly turned the monitor off and said,

"How does this shit get out? It hasn't been twenty-four hours. I was afraid this was going to become a mess."

"What's the word, boss? Are we moving on this?" Suarez asked.

"Marty, they want you to lead this. Do whatever you and Baca need to do to make this thing go away. Then let me know so I can brief their people. They've offered whatever we need from their military."

"Really? I don't think we need fucking artillery. But it's nice of them to offer. We'll take it. Hopefully we won't need it. Most of this will be face-to-face, hand-to-hand police work. Let me get with my people and work some numbers we can be ready as early as this evening," Suarez said.

"That fast?" Helms asked.

"Fuck yes, No time to waste. We need to get the Estrada family out of there as soon as we can. The longer they are there, the more likely we find them dead when we finally breech the compound.

"He got caught because he helped us. The guy is dialed. He knew exactly what to do to help us and he didn't hesitate to do it. That's exactly the kind of people it feels good to risk your own life to rescue."

"Okay, then tonight it is. Get your troops in order. I'll meet you and Baca when we sit for your briefing at 1800 hours," Helms said.

Helms then took another call, and this time it was from the top. After a lengthy conversation, he hung up but continued to look at the phone and then at Captain Baca who said,

"You look like the game has changed."

"Who was that?" Suarez asked.

"It was a conference call with the state and the DOJ."

"Do they want us to stand down?" Suarez asked.

"No," Helms answered.

"Okay, then what are we doing with Alvarez, Ramirez, and Vega?" she asked.

Helms had no answer or reaction.

"What's wrong?" Suarez asked again.

"Mexico gets Alvarez. I think we have enough on Ramirez to make a move, but he won't be there tonight. But Z-1 and any other high level targets like Vega will require a federal indictment first," Helms said.

"Wait, are you saying that Alvarez and Vega could both walk away from this?" Baca asked.

"Sir, with all due respect to your position and authority, the state department handles things differently than we do. We are basically street cops and I have been given my mission. Both Alvarez and Vega are targets and if either one shows their faces, I intend to go after him," Baca said.

Helms interrupts forcefully,

"Marty, I understand your zeal, especially after what you have seen firsthand. But unfortunately the state department is mostly about relationships and what I am telling you is politics controls everything, even ICE," Helms replied.

Baca looked for Suarez to disagree, but she did not. She stood quietly. When Helms went back to taking a call, Suarez leaned over to Baca and said,

"That's not say though, that in the event that someone gets in our way they may inadvertently become collateral damage, Captain."

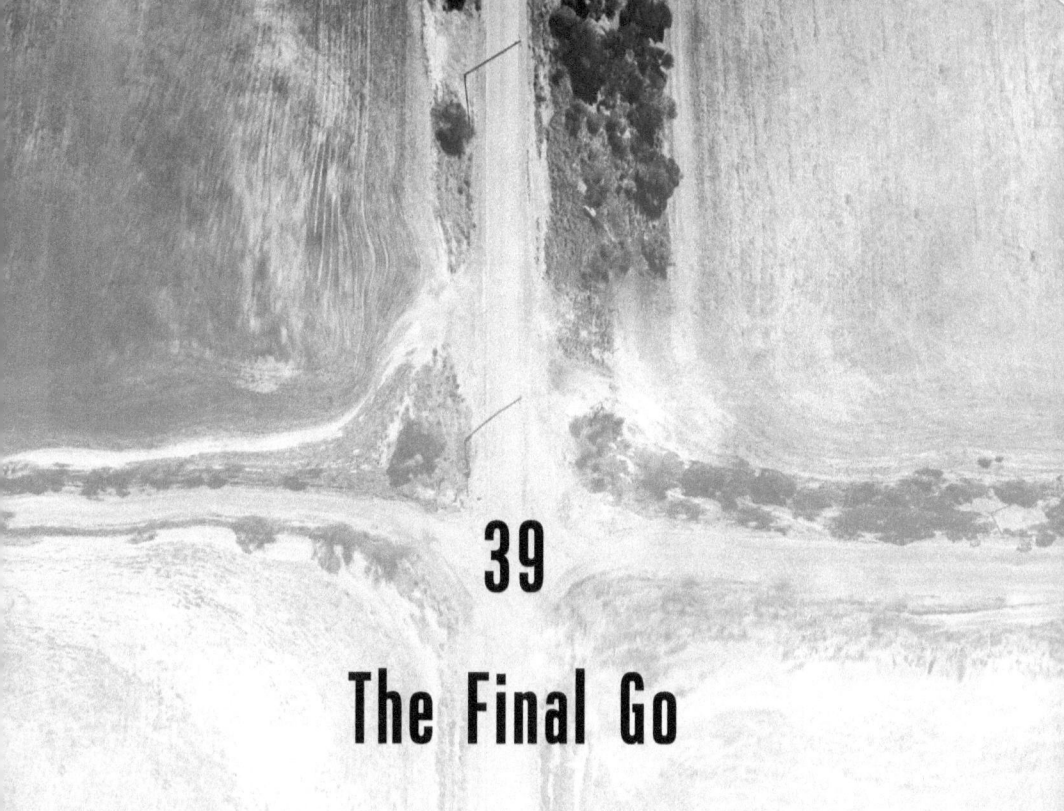

39

The Final Go

The command center for the assault on the Zeta compound was set up in the conference area of Captain Baca's office. Jordan Helms was on the phone to Washington, briefing the Secretary of State while Agent Suarez and Captain Baca along with several FBI and ICE agents waited for the final "go" from Helms.

"Within the next three to four hours I expect events to unfold. Yes, we have someone on the other end of this. I'm coordinating this with Agent Suarez. Yes, FBI Special Agent Marty Suarez. Yes I'll be sure to tell him."

Helms smiled as a tease to Suarez who threw a look to him for being referred to as a 'him'.

"No. Madam Secretary, please tell them thank you, but that is not necessary. Yes, but with all due respect, we won't need that type of asset. I believe we can solve this problem from our end without military being engaged.

"No, I don't believe that is necessary. I am confident with Agent Suarez and the local assets."

Helms looked at Suarez again.

"Yes, Captain Joe Baca. He will lead the US side. Highly competent, both of them. I will be in touch. Yes Mam and thank you."

40

Breaching The Zeta Compound

t was just before dawn when the teams reached their staging point about a mile in from the compound. There were two assault teams. Suarez was leading a team of six FBI agents. The remaining eight were from ICE led by Baca. They had all been briefed on "Operation Z" and were now prepared for the mission. Intel said that Alvarez was holding there and because he had crossed Z-1, an attack from within the Zetas on Alvarez was also possible. The entire compound was heavily guarded by the Alvarez's rogue soldiers and latest reports confirmed that the tunnel was now fully functional.

Suarez's team wore bodycams to fully document scenes, resources, ingress, and egress. Suarez and Baca met up just above a small ridge overlooking the compound. This was their final staging and their designated rally point.

"We're less than a click away. Just below that hill of brush. I don't think they have a clue what's about to descend upon them," Baca whispered.

Suarez was using binoculars and looking straight ahead. She did not answer Baca.

"What's wrong? That's a good thing right?" Baca asked.

"Yes, but do you see those supply trucks? Military grade. They have been well-supplied so don't be surprised to see heavy artillery lobbed at us. I guess I should have taken the Mexican army up on the offer for tanks. I'm used to handguns and semi-autos. Not looking forward to this heavy shit," she said.

"We may have underestimated their fire power, but we have been in this type of mess before and we know what to do. I was in Nam and the majority of my team has seen action in Iraq or Afghanistan," Baca replied.

"Joe, we'll stay with the same plan. Spread your team on the perimeter and on my go, open fire to distract them while we insert into the compound from the back. I don't see any other surprises. Let's move forward," Suarez ordered into her mic as she motioned back to her team.

"Remember, this is an intel gathering mission; the less we fire the better. Expect civilians and other hostages, avoid collateral."

She then turned back to Baca and said,

"We're on the go!"

Operation Z was underway with Suarez team heading to the rear entrance of the compound.

"Have you ever tried to stare down the devil?" asked Hector as the dawn of the morning drew near. He had been drinking for most of the night. He was preparing and expecting Z-1 to attack him and his rebel Zeta soldiers at any time.

Ziggy, his lieutenant, and the other soldiers were too worried about the stories coming back to them to answer his question. They had seen and heard enough of him. The word was that the *Federalies* were also planning to make an all-out assault on the compound. Alvarez was always drunk or high. They had all been given plenty of weapons and ammunition, but no plan. Alvarez had only one plan for the defense of the compound.

"Shoot at all of them and any of them. Shoot to kill."

That was the only thing he would say when they asked about a plan to attack or defend.

Alvarez began to answer his own question when an explosion suddenly ripped across the front porch of the compound shredding the front porch. The Mexican government had sent their own soldiers who had now begun to force their way into the grounds of the compound.

The explosion was a warning that they were fully armed and ready to destroy it all. Alvarez stood up and walked out onto the porch unloading a full magazine from his AK47. He spread his shots wildly across the front, randomly hitting several Mexican soldiers who dropped as he continued to move forward. Behind him, his men followed close with their guns at full blaze.

Above them, military helicopters swooped over, dropping gas grenades and providing backfire against the charge of the Mexican army who had now overtaken the perimeter of the compound.

Ziggy pulled Alvarez back down and into the compound, landing him behind a cement wall which provided a barricade from the ongoing shots. The explosion was also a signal to Mielo that the battle had begun.

"What the hell is going on?" asked Suarez over her radio.

"It's the Mexicans. Their military decided to show," Baca answered.

It was an unexpected development. Helms had not received any communication from the Mexican authorities. It was good that they were providing the distraction for Suarez's team. Now Baca's team would have to slow the assault by the Mexicans to protect Suarez's team which was ready to enter the compound.

Captain Baca's team held their position as he made contact with the Mexican military. The assault slowed as they waited on the status of the Suarez's team.

Shots could now be heard at the rear of the compound. This set off a barrage of automatic rounds from Zeta soldiers in random locations around the compound. Suarez's team had taken out a Zeta sniper who had been positioned in a tower. They were now engaging two Alvarez soldiers posted at the back entrance. Suarez's team had returned fire taking both soldiers out, one after the other.

Suarez and her team began their approach across the compound yard. The team slashed tires and dropped tablets into the fuel systems of the armored unit, trucks, and cars parked along the way.

At the entry door, they began to take an assault strike team position. Shots suddenly rang out from another sniper who was at the top of a large water tower. An FBI agent fell. He was hit in the shoulder and wounded. Moving forward, Suarez ordered the second sniper taken out. An agent immediately fired on the water tower. The Zeta sniper fell forward in a curling ball following his rifle to the ground. He laid motionless.

"Let's move. We're going in. Team Bravo remain and cover," Suarez ordered.

The team entered the compound through the rear entrance and down steps leading to a lower level. Simultaneously Baca and the military began an assault from the front and side of the compound. Surprisingly, no shots were fired back.

Baca's team continued to provide steady fire at the compound as a distraction for the FBI team now inside. Suarez moved her team forward down the main corridor. It was dark so the team activated their helmet lights and laser guides on their weapons. Suarez suddenly paused the team, raising her right hand. The team immediately squatted as they listened to the gunfire from just outside the compound.

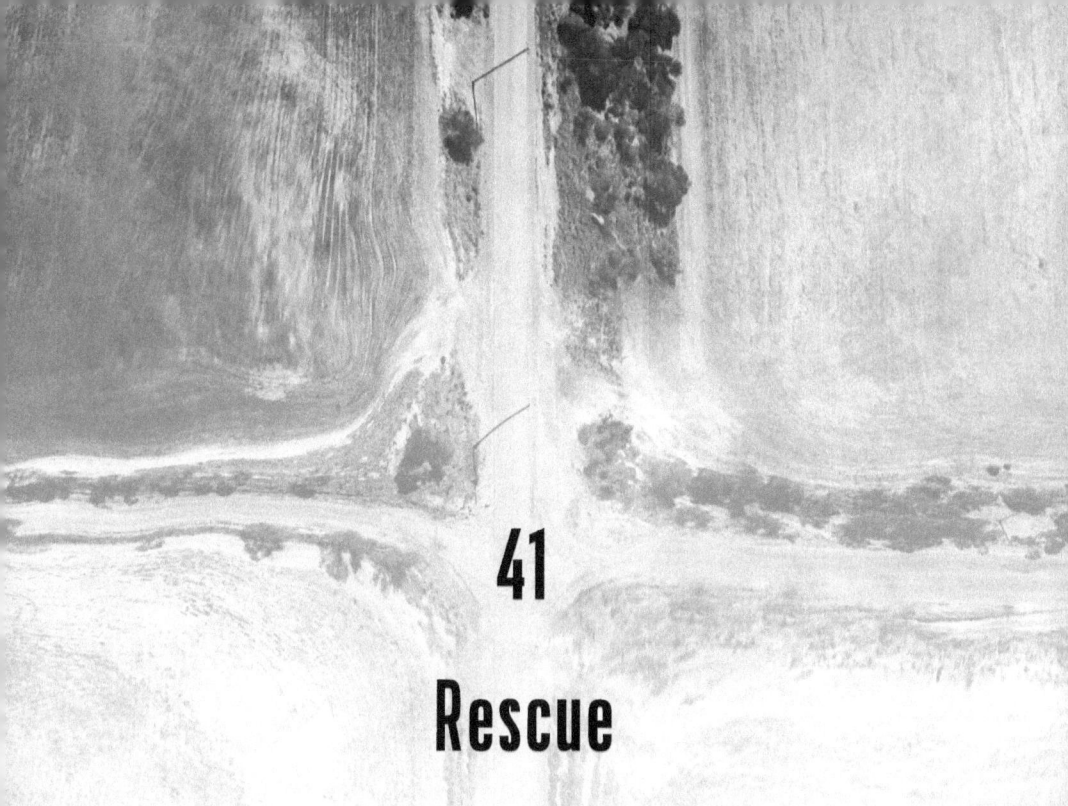

41

Rescue

"Proceed on my direction, expect something, anything, and remember, this place may have IADs, booby traps, just go slow," Suarez ordered.

As they advanced forward, the team suddenly reacted to ferocious barking on the other the side of the wall by pointing their weapons upon the wall.

"Hold your fire!" Suarez ordered.

She then held her hand up to signal she acknowledged the noise and she was moving forward to investigate. She turned a corner to find two guards. The first was immediately subdued with a single shot. The other ran to the end of the tunnel before being hit by another agent's fire.

The dogs were now barking more aggressively. Suarez proceeded into a dark room. Upon pushing a heavy metal door at the entrance open, a pack of large dogs charged her and the team full speed. Within seconds all of the dogs were downed by FBI team gunfire. Suarez then slowly moved in and did a check for weapons. She soon saw Mielo bound to the pole with tape over his mouth.

Still holding her weapon on him, Suarez recognized Mielo and ripped the tape from his mouth.

"Where is Hector Alvarez?" she asked.

"I haven't seen him for at least eight hours. I think he is here but I don't know where exactly."

"Get him down from there now," she ordered to her men.

Suarez shone her flashlight on Mielo's face to see several cuts and bruises.

"You are the American? You helped with the pilot after we went down last night." she said.

"Yes, we have met before. I was beaten and brought here after the crash. They weren't very happy that I helped you guys. I am being held with a lady. Her name is Elena and she is young with long black hair. I think they may be having their way with her," Mielo said.

Mielo was interrupted by another agent.

"Agent Suarez, we've found another one in the next room over."

"Can you get around on your own?" she asked Mielo.

"Yes. I am okay. Go and help her. She understands English."

"We have to leave you here. You can't come with us. But we will be back. I promise. I hope you understand," she said.

"Yes. I understand. Go! Help her! She is in trouble!" Mielo said.

Suarez made her move to the room that held Elena. The officers removed the gag and untied her. Suarez ordered her team to search and collect any visible intelligence.

"Get all the photos, thumb drives, any paperwork, or anything that looks like evidence."

"You are Elena?" Suarez asked.

"Yes," Elena answered weakly.

"I have two children. A boy and a girl. Please find them. Please find them for me," Elena pleaded.

"Do you know where they keep them?" Suarez asked.

"No. But I have heard them. Noises from down at the end of this hall. Behind a door."

Mielo was relieved when they brought Elena to him. Both were exhausted and Mielo was still bleeding. They embraced each other briefly.

"We're going to send you and the woman back with these two officers," Suarez said.

Elena moved to the desk to pull Hector's computer out of his hidden compartment.

The officers began to draw their weapons on her.

"Stop!" warned Suarez.

"What are you doing?" she asked Elena.

"There is *importante* stuff on this. I saw him putting stuff in it and he was very careful with it," she said.

"Alvarez?" Suarez asked.

"Yes. Hector hid his computer here," Elena said.

"OK, very slowly pull it out," Suarez said.

Elena pulled it out and handed it to Suarez. Suarez handed it to the officers who had several other backpacks full of similar material.

"That way," Elena said, pointing to where the noise was coming.

"Why? What is there?"

"That is where all the children are," Mielo answered.

"What do you mean?"

"Follow the noise. I don't know anymore," he answered again.

The team moved down the hall closer to a large locked iron gate covering a door.

"In here?" Suarez looked to Elena who nodded yes.

"Cut it," she said.

They placed a mini-torch onto the lock and soon the lock fell to the floor.

"You have cameras ready?" she asked her team just before she pushed the gate. The agents checked to confirm the cameras on their helmets were on.

"Here we go," Suarez shouted.

Pushing the gate aside, she then opened the door. There, in the room, sitting in a circle with their hands tied, were seven children ranging in age six to eleven. They were still and strangely quiet except for Serena who yelled for her mother. Elena ran to her. She held her and pulled the binds away from her wrists, freeing her. Then she turned and saw her son Rafael. Agents began to unbind the others when Suarez stopped them.

"We can't release them all yet. They will be in danger until we secure the whole building. As hard as it is to leave them tied up here, that is what we have to do for their own safety," she said.

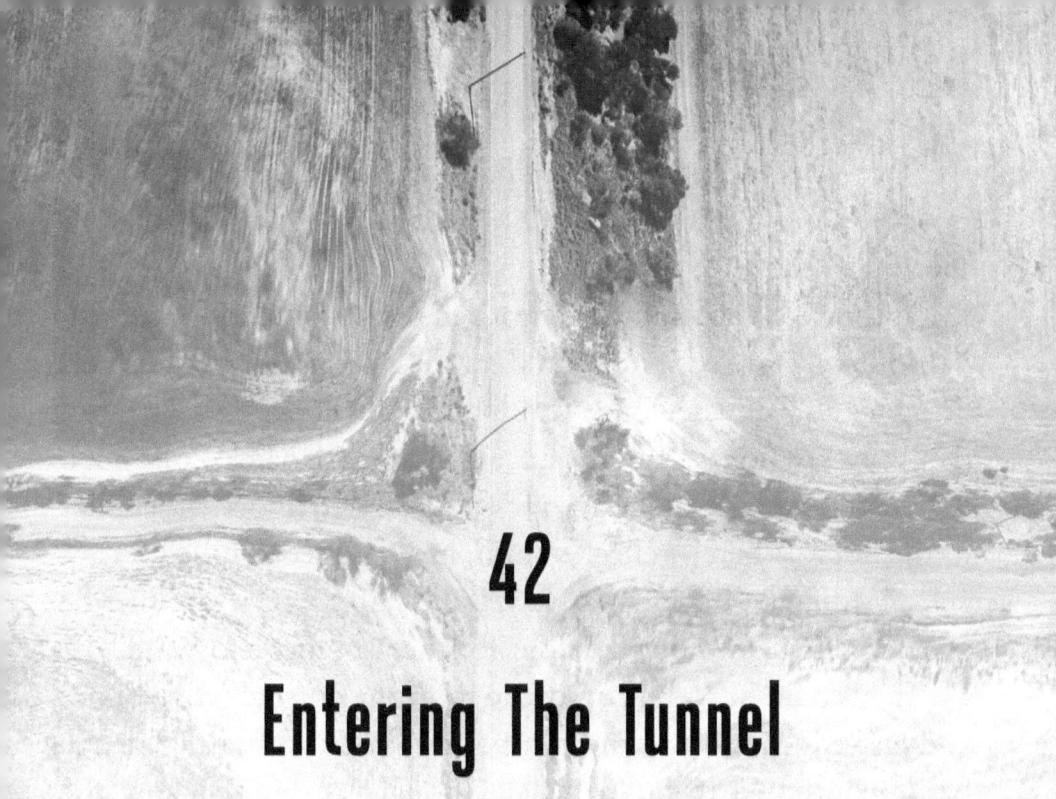

42

Entering The Tunnel

"We have to run," Mielo said "Me and the woman and the two children, we need to get to the tunnel. That is why we came here and that is what we need to do now. It is our only chance to survive. If we stay here, we will be killed."

Suarez took a few moments to absorb what Mielo was telling her.

"Are you sure? The tunnel could be very dangerous. If we discover other migrants, they may go that way as well. It could also be the escape route that Alvarez and the others take."

"We have to go," Mielo insisted.

Suarez again paused to think about how he had helped them the night before.

"Go," she said as she turned back to finish her mission.

Mielo and Elena quickly took Serena and Rafael and fled to the tunnel entrance.

As soon as Mielo and Elena reached the entrance to the tunnel, Mielo slowly looked in to see a Zeta soldier with his back to him firing his rifle down a long corridor. On the floor was a long rod that was used to keep the entrance door locked. Mielo continued forward and taking the heavy rod, he used it to knock the soldier to the floor. When he checked him, he could see that he was out and bleeding badly. He may have killed him, but it couldn't be avoided. He had to be taken out for them to move forward.

They could hear the gun battle from the outside grow louder and faster. The walls of the compound shook and rattled as the battle continued to build. Mielo thought to himself how the battle had been the perfect diversion to make it into the tunnel. He moved on, never really thinking much more about what he had done to the Zeta soldier, but he also didn't want Elena and the children to see what he had done.

"This way! Quiet! Follow with your head down. Don't look up or look at anything or anyone. Understand?" he said as he looked at Elena and then to the two children.

"Yes Mielo, they know and I have told them how to behave," Elena said.

"Okay, *Vamanos!* We must move on. Before there are too many. Follow me close!" Mielo said as he lifted Serena onto his back and Elena pulled Rafael along from behind.

Much of the compound had been damaged by the artillery shells. Many of Alvarez's men had already deserted or been killed by the attack. Even though they seemed to be overpowered, Alvarez and his most loyal men continued to resist.

Mielo reached a small ladder where at the bottom was a heavy door flattened to the ground. It was already open like it had recently been used. Mielo looked in to see dim lights that were on and that someone had gone in before him. He went in and looked for others but did not see anyone. He then helped the others down the ladder. They were now all in the tunnel.

Mielo slowly crept forward until he once again came face-to-face with another Zeta soldier. When he turned to look, Mielo noticed he was holding a shovel. He was sweating a lot like he had been working to prepare for Hector and his men to make a run. He dropped the shovel and ran to the ladder. He hurried up leaving the door to the entrance open. Mielo knew that this was the time to make his break.

"Let's go. Run fast," he said.

Elena picked up Serena and Mielo ran with Rafael forward and down a long draw of the tunnel. Soon the soldier returned and this time he was armed. He fired off shots, but they were already far enough away that he could not get careful aim. Mielo knew that if Hector was told he and Elena were on the run in the tunnel, he would soon be on their trail to kill all of them. It was then that the lights in the tunnel went out. Someone had cut the power.

Outside, shots could still be heard. Gasoline cans lay all about with flames bellowing into the sky. The front door slid open and out walked Alvarez onto the front porch. He again opened fire with a large automatic rifle, blindly firing in all directions. Two more men followed behind him. One had a rocket-propelled grenade launcher.

"Okay *putos*, so you want to fight with the king? Here we go. Let's see if you like this *Pistola gigante!* I want you to send it toward that crease where they are holding down. That is where they are hiding. Take a nice aim," Alvarez yelled.

"Boss man, the man and the girl, they are gone," said one of the guards who came running out from the compound.

"They have both escaped," he repeated.

"Fire!" yelled Alvarez ignoring the message.

The men fired the rocket at Baca's team where it exploded missing the target by fifty feet. No one was hit or hurt.

Alvarez and the remaining soldiers sat just to the side of the compound, close to the entrance.

"*Hombres*, when you walk with the devil, you die with the devil. I am not afraid to die. I know how to walk through bullets and live to tell the story," Alvarez yelled.

He then took a swig of wine out of a half-empty bottle and fired his pistol wildly at the Baca's men who were returning fire from the front.

"Boss man, it's bad. These are US Federalies," one of his soldiers said while trying to catch his breath.

"Most of our men, they are dead or run off. What do we do?" he asked shrugging his shoulders.

"Hold right here. Let no one near this area or into the compound. They will try to come here and rescue the pigs in the cells."

"We will die here, boss. They have too many. What should we do?"

Alvarez pulled two shotguns out of a long wooden box and handed one to them without answering.

Baca was in position and on his cell phone coordinating his assault in Spanish with the commander of the Mexican military entourage. Finishing his call, he called his team together.

"It's time to go in and get them. We will lead ingress. The FBI team has freed and secured the hostages. They are moving in from behind them. Let them move forward and attack and if they run, then they will run into us."

Baca's team then moved out toward the compound with weapons raised. When they crossed the porch, they drew shotgun fire from Alvarez and his men.

Suarez and her team came from behind Alvarez and opened fire. Alvarez returned fire, hitting Suarez in the neck. She returned fire with a three-shot burst which hit and dropped two of Alvarez's men. She then fired another three-shot burst into a broken wood beam holding part of the roofline. The eastern half of the compound roof then collapsed.

Hector emptied his shotgun in a fit. Then he reloaded and randomly fired off one round after the other just to intimidate and hold the Suarez's team pinned down. In the distance, military choppers were heard converging. Suarez checked her neck wound and realized it was small. She reloaded and pushed forward again with both teams converging on where Alvarez had taken his last shots. But Alvarez was nowhere to be seen.

"Chief Suarez, are you okay?" one of the agents asked.

"I was hit, but it's just a nick on the side of my neck."

She wiped her neck with her white sleeve and saw the blood. She winched slightly.

"Fuck! That stings. I'm okay, the bleeding has already started to clot. Let's proceed on. Fire at will," she said.

Across the gravel road, Baca's team opened up on the remaining Zeta members. Alvarez reemerged, now kneeling. He pumped shots directly at the Baca team. The team returned fire on Alvarez who ducked back. After drawing their fire, Alvarez rose back up again, this time with a grenade launcher. He fired into Baca's team. The impact was short and left of Baca. The shrapnel from the explosion hit an agent who fell to the ground. Fellow agents moved in to pull him back to cover.

"Fuck! Where did they get those?" Baca yelled.

Alvarez dropped the launcher and headed back toward the compound. The Mexican military soldiers joined in opening their fire on him as he dove through the door into the compound.

"Where the hell have they been? About fucking time they joined the party. Fucking Mexico! Move out!" Baca ordered.

As Suarez moved forward, she ran into a man, knocking him to the floor. The man quickly got back to his feet and came face-to-face with her. Then he took off running towards the tunnel. She realized that there were migrant hostages who had escaped and were now running freely.

"Drop down! Drop down!" she yells.

"Bajar! Bajar!" now signaling in Spanish and with her hands.

She squatted and fired two rounds at an armed cartel soldier who was shooting at the migrants. The soldier dropped. Then she swung around and fired again, killing another cartel soldier as he tried to return fire.

The crowd of escaping migrants started to clear and Suarez looked around for any sign of Alvarez. He was nowhere to been seen. He had somehow made it around her team and was now heading for the tunnel.

"Boss man! The tunnel is ready. But the man and the girl and kids went ahead of you," said the soldier at the entrance.

"What kids? You mean SOMOS? The prisoners that escaped?" Alvarez asked.

"*Si,* the prisoners that escaped. They went into the tunnel," he answered.

"And you did not kill them?" asked Alvarez as he pulled his revolver out and fired at the soldier. The soldier dropped against the compound wall and to the floor now motionless. Taking guns and ammunition from the man, Alvarez headed onward into the tunnel.

Suarez followed Alvarez until he entered the tunnel. She then entered and inspected the front end of the tunnel. She then climbed back out.

"It's been engineered and has lights. It goes to somewhere in the US. There is nothing we can do at this end. We need to let Captain Baca know about the other side," she said to her team.

She pulled her cell phone and dialed Baca.

"Yes Joe. It's over. We've cleared out everything. Scene is secured. Alvarez got away in the tunnel after the gun battle. He is armed and definitely dangerous. Advise your men not to negotiate with him. I repeat no negotiations! My advice is to shoot to kill!"

"Copy that," Baca said. Dropping his cell back in his satchel, he turned to Tatanni.

"Bad news. The FBI team discovered the alleged tunnel. It really does exist. They think it comes out in the US somewhere northwest of here. Marty thinks Alvarez went in."

Tatanni thinks about the tunnel and then says, "Tarlow. That warehouse in Tarlow!" now shaking his head in confirmation.

"What?" Baca asked.

"I didn't put it together at the briefing, but now that you say northwest and I think it through, we arrested some smugglers on the outside of a warehouse last week over in the Tarlow area.

"Turns out some of the smugglers were cartel and mostly Zeta. I bet they have that tunnel coming out in that warehouse in Tarlow. We couldn't get a warrant so we didn't get a chance to check inside," Tatanni said.

"That would make sense and it's only twenty minutes from here. Let's go!" said Baca.

Baca called to his senior officer.

"Turner, Tatanni and I have a priority mission and we have to go. Do you think you can hold this place?

"Yes sir. More manpower just arrived. Take six of my team with you. It will be tight, but I think we can get it done here," he said.

43

Face Off

Hector Alvarez forced his way into the crowded tunnel, killing and pummeling anyone or anything in his way. He was still drunk and high on cocaine. His hair was soaked with sweat that poured off his chin.

"*Puto* Estrada!" he yelled out. Mielo was far enough ahead of Hector that he could only hear his voice echo off the tunnel walls.

"When I catch you, I will beat you, all of you. I will have my way with Elena and make you watch! And then I will kill you like I should have done long ago."

Elena and Mielo struggled through the darkness of the tunnel. Now they could hear Hector's rants and it served as notice to them that their fates were in pursuit and close behind.

Alvarez turned the power back on so he could see. Then he began to shoot into the tunnel, firing and reloading his pistol at will. Mielo knew that having the power back was both good and bad. They could now see where they were going, but it was also another sign that the Hector was back in control of the tunnel.

He knew Hector had probably been told by the soldier guarding the entrance that they had entered into the tunnel. Hector would be on their tail for sure and he would be able to move much faster. Running with Serena and Rafael had slowed them down. Mielo could tell by how loud the shots were that Hector was closing in on him fast. It would not be long before he would catch up to all of them. They stopped to rest for only a few seconds when they heard more shots ring out followed by a scream. Hector was recklessly firing his gun and had hit someone behind them. Then they could hear Hector's voice cry out.

"I will kill anyone I see between us! The longer you run, the more people will die. Mielo, why did you take my girl?" he yelled out.

Elena turned to Mielo.

"We must go now, Mielo."

"No."

Mielo was sure they could not stay ahead of Hector all the way to the tunnel exit. He knew how much tunnel was left and did not want to take the chance to have them all killed.

"Listen Elena, I'll go and meet up with him. To slow him down. It is me he wants the most. Take the children, go on and do not look back. Save them and yourself."

"No, he will still come after us even with you gone and I don't know the way."

Mielo smiled while shaking his head no.

"Elena, we don't have time to talk about this. Trust me, just go straight ahead and you will know what to do when you get there. This will work. It is our only chance. The children need their mother more than their foolish uncle. Now go!"

Elena kissed him on the lips with her eyes streaming with tears. It was her way of letting him know she loved him and would do what he asked her to do.

"GO! And do not stop until you are out and free."

"God be with you, Mielo. We all love you. Goodbye, my dear friend."

Elena and Mielo turned in opposite directions and hurried on. Mielo occasionally would run into migrants trying to escape Mexico and Hector. They would back up for Mielo until it was wide enough for him to pass. Their faces were torn and filled with terror.

Mielo yelled out,

"Hector, I will meet you. At the opening. Then you can do what you want to me."

"I'm gonna fucking make you eat my *pistola*."

Mielo finally stumbled into a wider area of the tunnel. Hector was waiting, holding his pistol at his side. He gave his Maddog stare directly at Mielo. Mielo stood straight up in front of him. They had once again come face-to-face. Both stood dripping in sweat from the humidity of the tunnel. The poor lighting made it hard to see. Silence settled in as the tension between the two built.

"You are going the wrong way, *puto*. An unfortunate turn for you," Hector said.

Mielo threw his pistol to the ground.

"I have come to talk."

Some of Hector's men had now reached the opening where they could stop and watch the two square off. Hector raised his pistol and pointed it straight at Mielo and replied,

"I didn't follow you to talk. I followed you to kill."

He knew Mielo was unarmed. No one moved. It was as if their worlds had suddenly stood still. Just like at the Mission blacktop twenty plus years ago.

"First you steal from me. Taking my ball when we were little at the Mission. Then you steal the prize fight. Now Elena, a prize. I never got to open," Hector said with his evil grin.

Mielo just stared back.

"No. It's not the wrong way. It is what was meant to be all along. You are hunting me and now here I am," Mielo said

Hector broke into a weak laugh, a drunk sort of laugh.

"I have always liked you more than the others. You were never afraid of me like all of the others. You never showed fear. I like that. But now things have changed. You still think you can stare down the devil?"

Shaking his head and slowly opening up his grin to a familiar devious smile.

"You cannot stare down this devil," he said shaking his pistol at Mielo.

"It's not that I don't fear you. I fear you. But I have learned to stand still and face you. You have no power over me. Your power comes from the darkness. From the *cohete* you hold in your hand. Not from you.

"Your power comes from the threat of taking away things that belong to this world. Death is what you are about and death has no power over me. Because death is just a punk, like you, and it is what you will become in the end.

"When you die, that will be it. You're dead, you will just be a punk who died. I will go on. I will live again. But you will be no more than what you are right now. You will be death itself. You are death."

Suddenly Hector's smile was no more. No sick laughter came from his mouth. Mielo could see the end of his pistol was trembling as he tried to hold steady aim.

"I have lost my soul. The angels did not come for me like you and Elena. They have not touched me like they have you. They tricked me to enter my own evil soul and now I feel no sorrow. I feel nothing," Hector said

He pressed the pistol up to Mielo's temple and pulled back the trigger without letting it go. Mielo did not move. He stayed eye-to-eye with Hector. Hector's face had no expression. It was as if he had died. Then in a very short few seconds, he rested the trigger pin back. He then took two steps back and fired a shot into Mielo's left leg. Mielo dropped to the ground and while he still looked Hector in the eye, Hector fired another into his left arm. Mielo rolled to his side in pain.

Hector stood there still with his pistol now down beside him. A stream of smoke drifted off the barrel of his pistol. He continued to stare at Mielo in silence. Even his men had now run off. He was alone.

For the first time, it seemed that Hector Alvarez was afraid. He left Mielo bleeding on the ground. Slowly he staggered onward through the tunnel toward the US frontier. The migrants in the tunnel who had watched awkwardly now came out to help Mielo.

44

Shootout At Tarlow

Tarlow was a new development not far from Campo. It had several warehouses and a truck depot in the center. There were rail yards and truck terminals surrounding it. It was about ten miles southeast of where Interstate Five ran into the formal border between the US and Mexico.

When Baca rolled up with his team, black smoke was still bellowing in the distance from the scene of the raid at the Zeta compound. He spotted many migrants running across the open fields. He quickly set up a command post and then moved forward onto the suspected warehouse grounds.

The team forced entry into the large warehouse from where many of the migrants were coming. Once inside with weapons drawn, they encountered more migrants who were unarmed.

They quickly scattered through the warehouse. Baca went to his cell to call for more help. He soon found himself yelling to try and get above the noise inside the warehouse.

"We need a lot of help to get this under control. Yes, send them immediately. It's at the same warehouse where the bust was last week, at the big warehouse in Tarlow," Baca said as he ended his 911 call.

"Help is on its way. Looks like we got this one right, but we may have to pull back if this doesn't slow," he said to Officer Tatanni.

Within the tunnel, Elena found herself and the children twisted in with the others who had caught up to her. She pushed forward holding her children tightly. Frightened by all those around her, she leaned onto those in front of her. At last, she saw the light of the exit. She quickly lifted the children one by one up the ladder and then out to the floor inside the warehouse.

Baca and his team held their positions as they scanned the tunnel exit for anyone who looked cartel and especially for Alvarez.

A sudden explosion rocked the tunnel entrance. Fire erupted, then ruble and smoke. Shortly after, Alvarez stumbled out running through the flames. He had used a hand grenade to create his diversion as he emerged from the tunnel. Elena and the two children had come out just in time as the fire and smoke closed the opening of the tunnel. The tunnel was now choked off to all hope for the others behind. Many remained trapped. Looking back, Elena could now see that Hector was only a few steps behind her.

"That's him. That's Alvarez. Let's move on him," Baca said

They immediately pulled their rifles and moved in. Alvarez quickly realized that he had been seen by Baca and his men. He made an attempt to grab Elena but could not get close enough for a good grip. Instead of shooting to kill her, he instead fired off two shots at Baca and Tatanni, missing both times. He then turned and took off running into an adjacent unoccupied office. He barricaded himself against the steel wall inside. Baca and Tatanni followed him.

"That's it. Remember Marty said no negotiations," Baca said.

A steady flow of sirens could now be heard as more and more help arrived. Fire engines roared in. Unmarked FBI units also rolled into the parkway. Agents spilled out carrying shotguns. Several black and white patrol units had now set up traffic control at the main entrance to the park.

Baca looked through the office door hole to see the door on the opposite side of the office that Alvarez had entered lay open.

"Stay here and watch this door. He may try to get out when I go through the other side," Baca ordered.

Baca headed to the south side of the office where he could move in on Alvarez. Suddenly Baca discovered several migrants escaping out of the rolled up warehouse door. He called for a unit to cover the area, but just as he started to make the call he saw a familiar face with two young children in hand coming out. They were obviously on the run. Baca looked closer and longer. An awkward pause settled in as his eyes met up with Elena. He remembered the last time their eyes met. Elena froze for a moment, not knowing what Baca would do. Baca knew that Mielo had entered the tunnel with the woman and two children. He then recalled her crying face from the day of the raid at the Mission more than twenty years ago.

Nothing was said. Instead, Baca turned and continued his pursuit of Alvarez. Elena and the children moved on, cutting across a vacant lot toward the freeway.

Baca soon reached the other side of the office complex. He entered slowly and silently. Right off he spotted Alvarez holding still behind an office door. Baca slowly worked his way around to where Alvarez was holding. He then called on his cell to Tatanni.

"I'm going in. I have a clear angle. Be ready in ten."

Baca took a last look at his rifle. Taking a deep breath he counted off ten seconds.

He then ran full speed and body-slammed into the door. The door smashed full force into Alvarez. Alvarez tried to recover pushing back against heavy door, but Baca again body-slammed the door crushing Alvarez a second time. Baca then reached around to grab Alvarez by the arm. Pulling him from behind the door, he threw him across and into a large metal file cabinet. The cabinet fell on top of Alvarez pinning one of his legs. Alvarez's gun landed on the floor and out of his reach. Both Tatanni and Baca pointed their rifles directly at him.

"We really should have killed you back at the compound. Look at me! You sick fuck!" Baca yelled.

"How many people have you killed just today, Alvarez?" Tatanni yelled.

"I'm going to give you only one time to do what I say. Now put both hands on your head," Baca ordered.

"This is kind of like old times, huh? Baca?" Hector replied.

"You tell me only one time what to do and then I tell you to go fuck yourself."

"Oh ya. You're the spitter."

Alvarez doesn't look at Baca any more. Instead, his mouth begins his familiar slow left to right grin. In unison, he slowly reaches down into the side of his boot to pull a well-concealed knife.

"Stop! Are you going to give us a reason to kill you? Because it won't take much!" Tatanni yelled.

Hector ignored Tatanni's order and pulled the knife. As it cleared his boot, Tatanni was joined by Baca as they both unloaded their rifles into Hector. There was no doubt in either officer's mind that Alvarez was dead.

Beside his still body lay the knife. On the side was a carved-out Spanish word that read, "*Culebro*." Tatanni looked over to Baca who appeared shaken.

"No negotiations," he said.

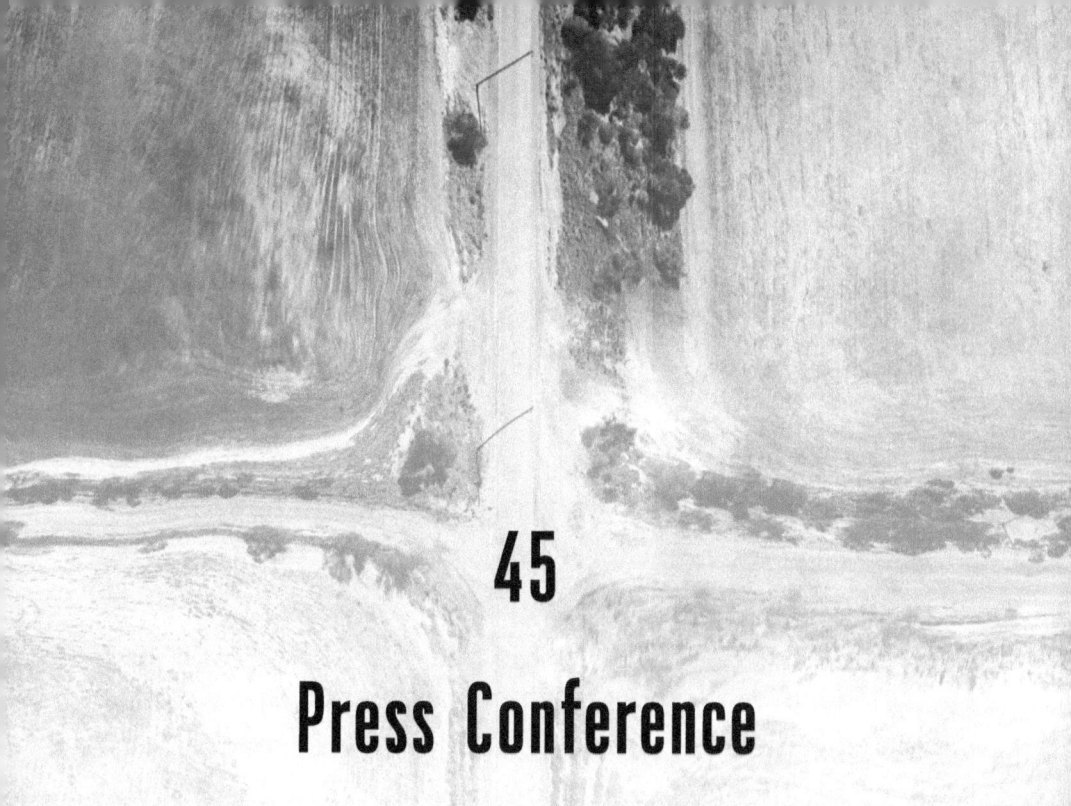

45

Press Conference

I t had been an extraordinary day and darkness was finally falling at the Border Patrol Headquarters in Campo when Suarez and her team returned. She met up with Baca and other authorities as the smoke from the gun battle at the Zeta compound still continued to smolder into the skies just across the border in Mexico.

There was still a lot to see and to speculate for the press. The scene was still fresh and the hostage children were still being processed. The casualty report had not been fully completed.

Suarez was ordered to report to Helms when she arrived back. When she caught up with him at the command post outside Baca's offices, he was at a podium and near the end of his news conference. She fell in beside Baca and Tatanni who had also just arrived back from Tarlow. All of them looked tired and worn.

Glances between them were exchanged as Helms answered his last few questions.

"So Mr. Helms, is it safe to say that this situation has been resolved?" the reporter asked.

"No. but I would say that there is no immediate danger. The threat to these people from this compound is no longer. But we have a lot more work to do with the Mexican government. Although, I am optimistic that we are on the right path."

Several reporters jockeyed to ask the next question. Helms picks another reporter as he glanced down at his wrist watch.

"This has to be my last one."

"Mr. Helms, in your judgment and based upon what has happened here today and over the last several weeks, can we assume that the involvement of the Mexican cartel reaches up into the higher levels of the government both in Mexico and in the US as well?"

"Well, right now, I would have to say that your premise is highly presumptuous. But it is true that this travesty reaches down to the lowest levels. It reaches the lowest levels of heinous crimes and it has been inflicted on some of the most defenseless victims, that being young children. And now I am sorry, but I have to move on," he said.

Suarez looked up at Baca and Tatanni.

"Spoken like a true politician," Baca said.

"It actually sounded close to the truth," Tatanni replied.

Baca looked at Suarez up and then down.

"You don't clean up very well," he said.

"We had to clean out our end of the tunnel. Did you know that the American was in there? The one who helped us with the pilot?"

"The kid from *SOMOS*? Emielio?" Baca asked.

"Yes. Not sure what happened. The story we got, sadly, was that he was shot. I tried to stop him and the girl and the two kids," she said.

Baca looked down and paused in thought as he realized the loss.

"Was it Alvarez? Did Alvarez kill him?" Tatanni asked.

"It happened inside the tunnel. It definitely sounds like his work. I sent a team back to get the body. So far they haven't found it. For what it's worth, I think *SOMOS* would want the body. He is a US citizen. I told my team getting his body out was a priority," Suarez said.

"I am sure the priest from LA will want to claim him and bring him back in the states," Baca said.

"No sign of the woman. I doubt she made it. They probably were lost too," Suarez said.

Baca remained noticeably silent but looked conspicuously at Tatanni. The awkward silence made Suarez suspicious.

"What?" she asked.

"We're not sure about where they are now. But the woman and two kids, we saw them come out the other end. We couldn't act. We were in pursuit of Alvarez," Baca said.

A long stare from Suarez set in.

"Dead? You got Alvarez?" she asked.

Baca and Tatanni both remained silent.

But Suarez knew the answer from their silence.

46

Somos Warrior

Mielo's wounds had been taken care of by the tunnel migrants who knew of Alvarez and had heard of Mielo. Alvarez had blown the exit into the US to where it could no longer be used to cross. So they moved Mielo onto a large blanket and dragged him back with them all the way to the compound. Afterwards, two Shepherds from *SOMOS* showed up. Since Mielo was legal, they took him to the California border crossing. When they arrived at the border station with him, the border authorities called for an ambulance. He remained at a San Diego hospital for almost a week while they treated his wounds.

When he was finally released, he had a cast on both his left arm and leg. Elena and her two children were also saved by the work of *SOMOS*. Elena managed to reach a gathering field where Tio Pedro himself picked her, Rafael, and Serena up and brought them back to the Mission in LA.

Two days after the Tarlow incident, Junior showed up at the Mission. Many of the SOMOS Shepherds were amazed that Junior had escaped and crossed the border on his own.

They all knew it was a tough time to cross because of all the press coverage around the killings and the droves of immigrants trying to cross into the US. Also at his age, he was a prime target for the cartels.

Tomas and Santino messed with him by calling him a "SOMOS WARRIOR."

They all knew it was in fun, but at the same time they really meant it. He definitely had their respect for what he had done and for what he could do on the other side of the border.

"Hey Warrior. Where have you been?" Tomas asked.

"I crossed the border yesterday, Ensenada."

"How? Where?"

"In my truck. I drove it here."

"No."

Tomas inspected Junior's ankles. They both had thick rubber bands around them. They were the same type that Mielo had described when he told them how Junior had stolen the old cattle truck. He had used rubber bands to attach newspapers to his feet, so that he could reach the foot pedals of the truck.

"Yes. You did," Tomas said, pointing to Junior's ankles.

"What about an ID?"

Junior pulled a US passport with the name Seth Martinez on it.

"I am Seth Martinez," he said.

He gave the passport to Tio. Tio looked it over. It was a remarkable resemblance between Junior and whoever Seth Martinez was.

"That would work," Tio said to Tomas and the others.

"The G-Men at the border station were too busy. So busy that they hardly looked at me," Junior said.

Tomas turned to Tio for a quick nod.

"I don't know how he gets away with that stuff."

"I can think of only a few people that he's been around most of his life," Tio teased.

Elena entered the room. She bolted straight to Junior. She held him and gave him a cheek kiss.

"This is not a party. It looks more like the men's club is meeting."

Both Junior and Tio moved to each side of her with their arms around her for a quick picture.

"I had a long talk with Fr. Santino." Tio said.

"Oh, so this is serious. You never use both of the title and name together unless it is serious. What's up?" she asked with a small chuckle.

"You know Father Santino is a lawyer and he says he can get you, Serena, Rafael, and Junior and all of you legal in just a few days." Tio said.

"Yes?"

"I have a plan and we have to do it right away. Mielo comes home tomorrow. You know I like to hear his confession. So I called him about this last night and he confessed that he was in love with you," Tio said, breaking into a short laugh.

"It was the first time I have ever been with him to where he was not able to say something. He just said to me: I will marry her. Anything to help make them legal. I will marry her even if it didn't allow her to become legal. That's all he could say. After that, complete silence. But if you love him Elena, we can get all of you legal."

The next day, Tio married them and found them a nice but small rental close to the Mission. Mielo agreed to continue to work for Tio on things related to *SOMOS* and Elena would learn how to teach "singing" to the choirs at the Mission school.

Even though things had settled and the three were once again home where they belonged, deep in his soul Tio Pedro still felt something was missing. He felt that something was still left undone. One of the four was still unaccounted. One more was left, only one more.

47

Resolution

After the incident in Campo, *SOMOS* had been of much more interest to the Los Angeles media. The Archbishop of Los Angeles and the Provincial of the Jesuits did not always like good press.

In general, good press that they controlled was preferred over good press caused by a group of rogue Jesuit priests. So they were still pretty nervous about Fr. Pedro's extracurricular activities.

"Do you know what one of the biggest problems in this country is today?" Tio quipped.

Fr. Dante sat back in frustration.

"The problem is twofold. One is there are too many lawyers in this country with not enough to do. And secondly, when they threaten these lawsuits, people like those in the church just cower down."

"I'm here to simply bring resolution to an ongoing problem here in the heart of the diocese. I am here to deliver a message from the Archbishop which has been endorsed by your Provincial. The message is to stop participating in this or. . .

"Or?" Fr. Pedro prompted.

"Or you may find yourself relocated to a much quieter and rural parish," Fr. Dante answered.

"I am seventy-six years old. Do you really think I care about your threats? I have lived with threats all my life. My entire life has been a threat."

"So I'm once again asking you and I am supposed to return this afternoon with your answer."

Tio took his glasses off and leaned into Fr. Dante.

"My answer is yes."

"Yes?" Fr. Dante asked.

"Yes. My answer is yes," Tio said shaking his head in agreement.

"There is your resolution. Now you have successfully completed your mission," smiled Tio.

"Very well then. My work is done here."

Fr. Dante stood, grabbed his coat and hat. He looked back at Tio one last time, smiled and left. Shutting the door behind him, Fr. Mario remained in the room with Tio.

"Will you stop?" Fr. Mario asked.

"No."

"What will you do?"

"I don't care what they think of me or where they send me. Yes, I took a vow of obedience. But it is obedience to my order and to the church and NOT to an Archbishop who is too busy to meet with me in person."

"Father David will most likely continue to ignore you until the Archbishop orders your compliance. Then he will have no choice. They will eventually shut you down."

"I know. Like I said, I'm into my late seventies. If they move me, it will be to an old priests' home where all of the inhabitants are rebels like me. Then we will take over the world."

"What of *SOMOS*?" Fr. Mario asked as he held back his laughter.

"Mielo is back. So is Santino and Tomas and Enos. All of them good Shepherds who know how to lead. They will not desert the mission of *SOMOS*. Hopefully never will the Jesuit order."

He placed his glasses back on.

"*SOMOS* will live on even without me. If it could not, then I have done a shitty job in my ministry of these people. *SOMOS* has grown to be much larger than me. And that in itself is enough proof that God is truly the leader of *SOMOS*. Not some old stubborn-ass Jesuit."

48
Calvary

Calvary was the mountain where they had crucified Jesus and it was also the name of the cemetery where Roberto had been buried. Fr. Pedro thought to himself that it would also be an appropriate final resting place for Hector. Maybe since Calvary was the place where Jesus had experienced intense physical and mental suffering, somehow the Lord might find mercy for the soul of Hector Alvarez.

Tio was pretty sure that Hector at some time in his short life, had also suffered intense physical and mental pain. He had been so badly damaged that no matter how hard Tio prayed, Hector was never able to find his way back. It would be very hard to forgive all that Hector had done, but Tio knew that even in all Hector's darkness, the Lord would never give up on him.

Calvary seemed a lonely cemetery. It was one of the places that could be seen when Roberto, Mielo, and Elena huddled as kids in the bell tower of the Mission. It looked lonely sitting all by itself at the top of those green rolling hills which faced west toward the downtown skyline of the city of Los Angeles.

It had been there a long time. Inside there were miles of small paths covered with ageless oaks that had stood witness to decades of human loss. The paths were flanked on both sides with grave markers of all sizes and shapes. They showed all of past lives that had been lived out.

It was clear that when the first part of the cemetery was filled, there were no rules. Graves were just dug in arbitrary spots and the tombs ranged from fancy mausoleums to just small flat rocks with barely enough room to put a name. Some markers had no names. Just words like BABY GIRL.

Today was a Sunday morning and the Estrada family had stopped at Roberto's gravesite to 'pray' their respects which is the way Tio would put it.

It was a place where Elena had come almost every day since returning from the south and it was the usual practice of the entire family to visit the site on Sundays after mass.

What was unusual that cold and gray morning was the sound of a single bell ringing from the tower at the Mission. It could easily be heard all the way to the cemetery.

Looking up and around, Elena could not see any services but she did spot Junior. He was on top of the hill beside where they were standing. He waved to her but he did not come down. He had already been to Roberto's grave that morning.

"I don't know," was Mielo's answer to Elena's question as to why the bell at the Mission was ringing. Elena was puzzled because she knew that Tio rarely allowed the bells to be rung. It had to be something very important.

Mielo stood tall with his family that morning at the gravesite. His leg wound had now recovered well but his shoulder was still in a sling. The white cast covering all the way to his hand stood out from behind the lapel of his dark suit. The whole family except Junior were there and dressed in their 'Mariachi suits' as Tio would tease when they were dressed up like that.

"You look very handsome," Elena said to Mielo. She pulled his open lapel back over most of his hand. It was Mielo who was about to tell Elena how beautiful she looked in her fresh dress. Mielo, his wife, and his two youngest children Rafael and Serena Estrada were all praying by the gravesite of their beloved Roberto.

Roberto's grave had been neatly tended to by Elena from the day they had returned from the south. Junior now mowed lawns for money and kept Roberto's grave perfectly manicured. It was blanketed with fresh flowers, Mexican candles, and rosary beads.

The tombstone was white with an angel gracing the top. The engraving read: *ROBERTO ESTRADA SR. Beloved Father, Brother, and Son. Rest in Peace.* Tio had insisted that the word 'Son' be engraved because he considered Roberto to be one of his sons.

Another thing that Tio would always say was "No one is fatherless. Like Jesus is our father and we are all sons of God." Even Hector would listen when he said stuff like that. It was these thoughts and words that suddenly struck Mielo's heart. It was about the ringing of the bell. He had realized that Tio had left to go south to get Hector's body and bring it back for burial.

Before leaving, he had asked Elena and Mielo if they would want to accompany him down and back. Elena agreed to go but

Mielo had been insistent that he would not go. Even though Hector had in the end spared his life, he admitted to Tio that he could not forgive him yet for all that he had done to Elena and his family. He admitted that the anger was still too fresh and he would not do anything that helped even the memory of Hector Alvarez.

After realizing that Mielo still needed her to be with him, Elena changed her mind and did not go south with Tio. Elena now stood watching Mielo's face which had suddenly changed.

"Mielo what?" she asked.

"The bell is ringing for Hector. Tio has brought him back and is burying him this morning," he answered.

"Then we must go, Mielo," Elena said, realizing that Tio was with Hector's body just on the other side of the hill.

"That is where Junior is. That is where he went. He must have seen Tio with the body. He followed him to the other side," Elena said.

"We must forgive. If we don't, then we will never heal our minds. We cannot give in to the evil. If it wins, we all lose. We must go to be with Tio now."

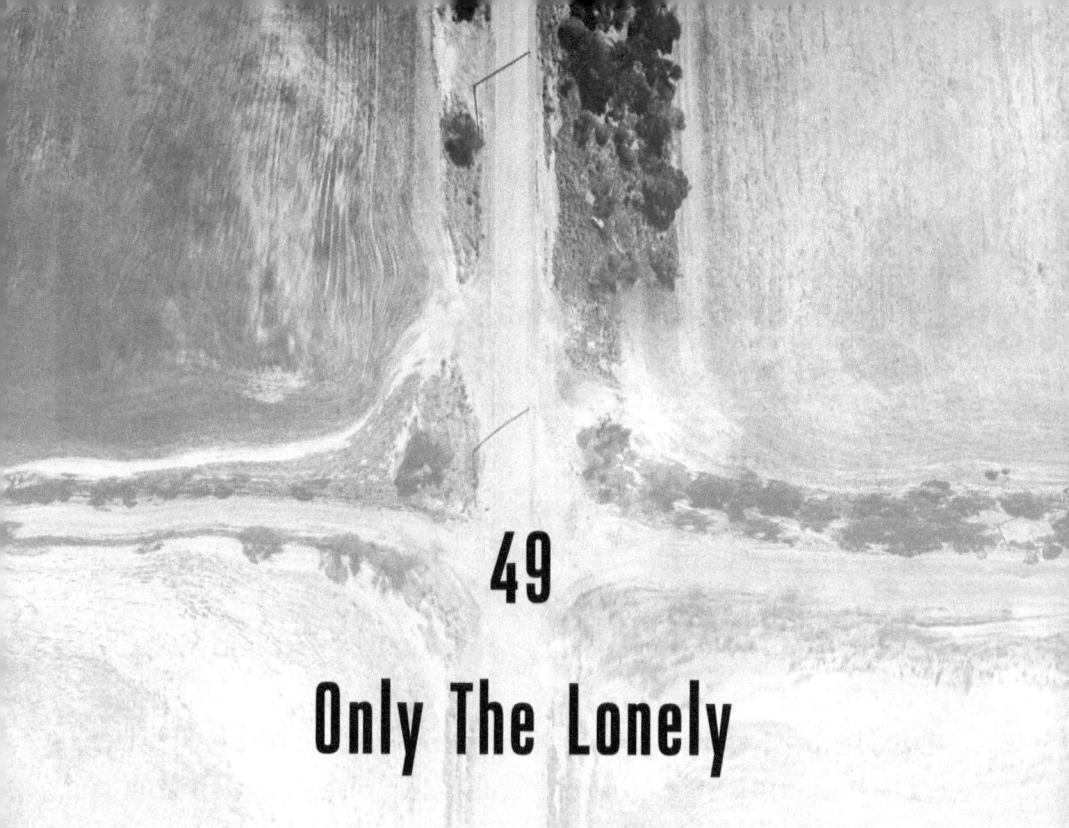

49

Only The Lonely

The wind was blowing Tio's dark purple vestments to where he had to press his elbows against them to hold them in place. He also held his Book of Rites in place before him. He looked around to see no one present to hear his words. Off and high up on the hill was someone, but he could not make him out. Other than that, Tio was only aware of the two young gravediggers who kept out of the sight while they quietly waited for him to finish.

That area of the cemetery was colder. There were less trees and the gravesite was exposed to the north where a storm seemed to be on the build. The sight of gray skies reminded Tio of the day he had met Hector. Hector had broken his heart that day and even today as he lay him to rest, he was still just as broken-hearted for the man.

Tio took his glasses off to clear them of the moisture. Then he held them in his hands while thinking of what to say. He could just say the prayers in the book and be done, but he had never served a funeral without a few kind words from someone.

The moment when Tio slipped his glasses back on, he saw and realized that Junior had been the distant silhouette he had seen earlier on the hill.

"I am here to help you, Tio," Junior said

It was true, thought Tio. He did need help. No one should go to their grave alone. Not even Hector.

"I don't have anyone to say some words. Do you want to?" Tio asked.

"I will say a prayer for him," came the voice of Elena.

Tio looked behind himself. To his surprise, he saw Elena and the rest of her family. Mielo like Junior could say nothing. Elena thought through it and stepped forward.

"Hector never wanted to be anywhere. Not even in the boat when we crossed the river that day. But I think sometimes he did want to be saved. The way we were all saved from the river that day.

"And like the officer who came to take us away. He knew we had all just lost our mothers and fathers. He had mercy on us and let us go with Tio. Because of that we were able to stay with Tio and we were saved again."

It began to rain lightly and the wind picked up. Tio took off his glasses and wiped them again.

"I think God will see what Hector had been through as a little boy and know how he got broken. And that he was broken really bad. So our prayer is that God shows his mercy. Because Tio teaches us that no one is beyond forgiveness and mercy. Even when they are dead. Amen."

As she made the sign of the cross and the silence took over, the words of his mother sunk deep into Junior's heart. He abruptly turned and walked away. He went back up toward the top of his hill.

50

Broken

"I think from now on I will call this spot, Junior's Hill," Mielo said as he walked up to find Junior seated on the freshly mowed grass. From that spot in the cemetery, they could see for miles. They could see the downtown skyline, the Mission bell tower, and most of the Heights. Mielo sat down beside Junior. He again tried to get him to talk about what he had been through. Tio said that he needed to talk about it. He told Mielo he was the best person to talk to him.

"The view is *primo* from here, but you are going to get soaked by the rain that's coming," Mielo said as he pointed to the west.

"The rain will not hurt me."

Junior began to trace imaginary figures on the grass with his finger.

"Mielo, why are some of these grave markers fucked up? Some are big and others just big enough for their name?" Junior asked.

Mielo thought it out for a few seconds.

"I don't really know why some people need to have a big ass grave marker. But the really small ones? I think maybe their name is all they had when they died," Mielo answered.

"Tio Mielo, am I broken too, like Hector was? What does that mean? When someone is broken."

"Tio says that sometimes people turn bad from stuff they go through. Then even when they know they are bad, they don't try to get better. Hector was busted so badly that he could never get fixed. That is what your mother was talking about."

"I've seen some really bad stuff that Hector did."

"Yes, you have seen some shit." Mielo answered.

"But you know, all the Shepherds call you the SOMOS Warrior. It may sound like they are joking with you but they're not. They call you that out of respect. You know what it means to be called a *SOMOS* Warrior?"

"No. Is it some kind of bullshit thing made up to make me feel better?"

Mielo cracked a partial smile at the thought of Junior calling him out for not being real with him. It was then that Mielo realized he was shooting too low with Junior. He saw that the kid was not only street smart, but smart like Tio. It was like he was talking to a little Tio.

"I guess it sounds like bullshit," Mielo said.

"You know Junior, I used to think all this God stuff that Tio preached was bullshit. That God was just Tio's God and none of the shit he talked about made any sense to me. But I will tell you one thing I have learned that is true.

It seems like when I try to be good, when I do the right things, then the whole world and maybe if for just a moment in time, seems like it is a better place. It seems like I made the whole world shift just by doing one little thing right. It's like being the one tiny grain of sand that tilts the scale in the right direction. It tilts it towards good and away from bad. So that's what I mean by making this world a better place only by one thing, and one person at a time.

I don't know if it is God. I don't know if the world is tilting towards God. I just know from in my gut when something is right and good. Junior I feel the same about you. I know that you are good. No, Junior you are not broken.

They call you SOMOS Warrior because you are someone who has been through the battle for the soul. You have been pushed all the way to the edge, but you still kept going.

You are still going and you have been through more shit than any of us. You may have been busted, but never broken. You have beat off the bad and made it through. That is what makes you a Warrior, a SOMOS Warrior, and that's no bullshit."

51

Beloved

"The Lord God is light, in whom no darkness lives." were the last words Father Pedro said over the gravesite of Hector Alvarez.

By the time Mielo and Junior had returned to the path along side of Hector's grave, no one was there. A small mound of dirt still stood out. It had been dressed on top with loose squares of grassy sod. There were no flowers or anything other than a small cross and marker that Fr. Pedro had left.

Mielo saw that a marker had been placed at the head of Hector's gravesite. The marker was not a cheap looking flat stone type with only a name, like the ones they had seen on so many other graves.

Both agreed that it had to be the doings of Tio or *SOMOS*. No one else would have taken the time or spent the money on Hector.

"What could Tio have put on the marker?" Junior asked.

"I don't know. Wicked? Evil? Broken?" Mielo quipped.

"Let's go see what it says," Junior said.

Reluctantly, Mielo agreed to pay one last visit to the grave. When they reached the marker, both read it in silence.

It read:

HECTOR ALVAREZ
BELOVED SON

The rain began to fall heavy. A white flash of light streaked across the western horizon lighting up a dark angry sky.

There was no more to say.

www.ingramcontent.com/pod-product-compliance
Lightning Source LLC
Chambersburg PA
CBHW050522110726
47899CB00005B/1556